The People's Church In Crisis

Harry L. Sheehy

The characters in this novel are fictitious, and any resemblance between them and any persons living or dead is purely coincidental.

ISBN: 0692576274
ISBN 13: 9780692576274

To my wife Carolyn,
for her unstinting support,
her insightful critique,
her editorial contributions.

PROLOGUE

February, 2040
Munich

Wilfried Drescher considered himself to be the luckiest man alive – lucky that he actually *was* alive! In the middle of a Sunday homily at St. Cantius, a Catholic Church in Munich, he collapsed with a heart attack, was rushed by ambulance to the Medical Center of the Ludwig Maximilian University of Munich and admitted to the Intensive Care Unit. Father Drescher was stabilized and on Tuesday was operated on for blocked coronary arteries. Four of them were bypassed, and he was in ICU, recuperating well. Drescher was indeed lucky, and had much to be thankful for.

The hospital chapel on the first floor was empty except for a young nun, dressed in the white habit all members of her congregation wore when on duty in the hospital. She knelt on the kneeler in the front pew, her lips pressed against her folded hands, and she prayed in a low, trembling voice.

"Lord, give me the strength to do your will, to fight evil, to destroy the powers of darkness, to strike back when the devil takes human form and leads your children astray."

The Voice had instructed her clearly:

"This is what you must do, Sophie – this is what you must do!"

She knew The Voice was right – it was always right.

Sister Sophie blessed herself, rose to her feet, and walked slowly to the back of the chapel and into the lobby. She was slim and on the tall side for a woman – just over six feet. Her carriage gave the appearance of dignity – a straight back, square shoulders, and a modulated gait. Her expression was blank, and her eyes seemed to be focused on something very far away. As she walked down the hall, she was oblivious to others who were also there.

The elevator took Sister Sophie to the floor where the ICU ward was located. She walked with a slow but deliberate stride into the ward entrance, and down the hall toward the room in which Father Drescher was recuperating. As she approached his room, she heard voices inside, most likely nurses giving him medication or taking his vital signs. Sister Sophie turned around and walked back to a visitors parlor. It was some 30 feet away, but from there she could see the door to Father Drescher's room.

In a few minutes, after seeing two nurses leave, she went back and quietly entered the room. Father Drescher was asleep. Attached to his right arm was an IV tube for medication drips, and sticking out of his chest was a tube for drainage.

She reached into her pocket and produced a small black case which she opened on the bedside stand. In it were two vials, a hypodermic syringe and two injection needles. She attached the smaller needle, filled the syringe from a vial containing a strong sedative, and injected it into one of the ports on his IV tube. Father Drescher's breathing became steady and deep – the sedative was working.

Next she attached the larger needle to the syringe, filled the syringe from the other vial, and injected its contents into his heart through the surgical area that had been closed with sutures.

Quickly, Sister Sophie placed the vials, hypodermic syringe and needles back into the case, slipped it into her pocket, and left the room in her normal modulated pace.

She returned to the first pew in the chapel on the first floor where she had been before, knelt down and blessed herself.

"Thank you, my Lord, for the strength to carry out your divine mission, and the wisdom to do it so successfully. I feel blessed that I had the opportunity to rid the world of at least one evil spirit."

Chapter 1

August, 2047
Chicago

"It can't be as bad as all that, Fred. Maybe Patel is disappointed because his horse didn't win the race. The College of Cardinals surely wouldn't have made a terrible mistake in their choice for the new pope."

Fred looked out the window for a minute as he rubbed his chin, then turned his gaze to Scotty. "Cardinal Patel ended the conversation by declaring the church was in mortal danger!"

***

Fred Whitaker hadn't yet recovered from the traumatic event at the Vatican that prompted his early return in May to his suburban Evanston home – the murder of Pope Francis Xavier on the very day Fred, the first layman elevated to cardinal in several hundred years, was due to review with the holy father the results of his Voice of the Laity opinion survey of Chicago Catholics.

Several weeks before, Chicago's Cardinal Archbishop Albert Rooney had also been killed – shortly before Fred was scheduled to discuss with him his survey findings, and how they should be presented to Francis Xavier. The shock of that tragedy still weighed heavily on him.

Could this all have been avoided if I had not accepted the high honor bestowed by the pope, as well as the assignment to find out what Chicago Catholics really thought about their church?

***

Fred didn't make this appointment with Scotty today to discuss the problems facing the Catholic Church, although the conversation morphed in that direction. It had been three years since he retired to spend more time with his family, only to have his plans rendered null and void by Francis Xavier's persuasive summons.

Now he was at loose ends. A relaxed retirement was out of the question. He wanted his old job back.

This wasn't impulsive on his part, or a rebound. Fred explored the issue thoroughly with his family – his wife Elaine, and his sons: the outspoken teenager Chris, and Bob, just back from an admissions interview at the Stanford University School of Medicine.

Elaine fully understood, and encouraged him. "Fred, go discuss this with Scotty," she insisted. "You two understand each other. He may have some insights to share."

"And don't forget, no matter how terrible things have turned out, Divine Providence is playing a role here," she reminded him. "There's more for us to do, but as yet we don't know what that is."

Then Chris chimed in:

"Dad, you had a vision of what you could do for the church, and it was pretty spectacular. You did what you said you would do, and you did it well. You made a big difference – no one could have done it better. And you got the whole family involved in this thing. You made a positive difference in my life – in Mom's life and Bob's too, I think. Lots of terrible things happened, but you did the right thing. I'm proud of you!"

***

"Fred, you are very much missed at K&E. You are 'of counsel' now, but that's not the same thing as being a full-time partner.

Your services are needed. Many of your former clients would be overjoyed if you were back on board. And, needless to say, Rachel Fischer would be ecstatic to have her old boss back on the team, and would insist she be assigned as your executive assistant once again."

Joseph "Scotty" Campbell, managing partner at Kirkland & Ellis, had the looks, demeanor and carriage that radiated class, importance, and authority. Handsome, white hair, a full white mustache, six feet three inches tall, a trim figure and immaculately dressed, he was right out of "central-casting" for the head of one of the most prestigious law firms in the country. Almost as tall and equally trim and fit with graying brown hair, Fred's presence commanded attention and respect, but without the dramatic statement of Scotty's.

"Give this some serious thought. We need you, and I think you need us."

Fred's furrowed brow showed he was in deep thought as he pursed his lips and nodded his head several times.

"I've actually been thinking about this, Scotty. And I'm pleased to hear I'd be welcomed back on the team. I'll work hard – you know that. However, there's something else lurking in the shadows for me, and I don't know what it is. This survey of the laity I did for Francis Xavier changed me. It opened my eyes to what the church might look like, and somehow I think I will have a role in making this happen, even though things ended so badly. I don't know how long my tenure at K&E will be this time."

"I don't think that's a problem, Fred. Nothing is forever. Just like before, you'll make yourself invaluable to the firm again, right from the get-go – you don't need a learning curve to get you up to speed. You can't sit around twiddling your thumbs, Fred – you need to do something productive.

"Let me add, for the time being, it would be prudent for you to maintain the security detail that protects your house and family. Of course, the Vatican won't be willing to foot the bill any more, but K&E will, at least for the foreseeable future.

"In short, Fred, this would be good for us, and good for you. And who knows? If you get another gig going with Rome, I just might stick my nose into it again!"

Scotty, like many converts to Catholicism, was quite committed to the church, devout in his religious practices, and considered it a privilege to be involved with an innovative mission like the challenge Pope Francis Xavier gave Fred. In his heart, he hoped something like this would materialize again.

Scotty Campbell had a meeting with Cardinal Patel after the funeral for the murdered Cardinal Rooney, so he knew Patel and was favorably impressed by him. He took any assessment by Sanjay Patel quite seriously.

"You say Patel claims the church is in mortal danger. So you're telling me there's no chance the new pope will resurrect your Voice of the Laity project?"

Fred shook his head. "Not even one in a million, Scotty, according to Patel. After Antonio Ruggieri was elected Pope Pius XIII three days ago, I phoned Cardinal Patel to get his fix on the new supreme pontiff. As you know, upon the death of Francis Xavier, Patel had to resign his office as secretary of state. He told me not only was there no chance Pius XIII would reappoint him to this position, but even if he did, he could not possibly accept it. 'Why is that?' I asked him. He didn't really answer my question, but said this was not a good day for the church."

CHAPTER 2

Early 21st Century
Rome

Human evil never materializes out of a clear blue sky. It comes with a history, a back-story. A cauldron of its ingredients will simmer over time, producing a foul and rancid stew.

For all intents and purposes, Antonio Ruggieri and Dieter Kaufmann might as well have been joined at the hip. They entered the Pontifical Lateran University as young seminarians during the second decade of the 21st century, on the same day of the same month of the same year. Other than the fact that one was a tall, blond and fair-skinned Bavarian, and the other a short, black-haired and swarthy southern Italian, to hear them talk, one would think they were carbon copies of each other.

Ruggieri and Kaufmann were conservative – not just conservative, ultraconservative – far-right of their classmates in how they viewed the practices of the Roman Catholic Church.

The two of them longed for the era when the faithful didn't question clerical authority, and did exactly what they were told. For some people, such a longing could reflect a deep-abiding piety, a conviction the road to salvation was straighter and smoother when the faithful followed unambiguous instructions without question. This is not what motivated Antonio and Dieter.

"Too many priests water down our religion, turn it into mush – it makes me sick!" Ruggieri would harangue, spitting out his words at Kaufmann. "They think it's their job to give 'feel good' therapy to the worthless multitudes, the morally weak who want the church to do things their way. That's not what the church was like in the past – we need to get back to that. You and I are destined to play a decisive role, to be in control, to reestablish orthodoxy and discipline, Dieter. That's our destiny – that's what we're supposed to do – that's what we're going to do."

***

Antonio Ruggieri came from a middle-class family in Cosenza, a city in the region of Calabria. His father had worked hard as a factory owner to achieve what he had. He taught his children the importance of out-competing their opponents, that winning was not just the best thing – it was the only thing.

"The world is full of losers, Antonio. I've never been one, and you must never be one, either. The other guy may be out to get you, but you've got to get him first!"

His father's attitude of equivocating morally impelled him to cooperate with dons of the local Mafia family – to supply them with equipment they needed without it being traced, and they, in turn, helped him further his manufacturing business at the expense of his competitors.

Antonio had no desire for a career in business, but he had his father's ambition, intelligence and enough moral ambiguity to put achievement before ethics. He envisioned a life in the clergy as his road to power and success, and focused on that goal from the time he was a freshman in high school.

"The Catholic Church no longer has the strong authority it exercised for many centuries," he would tell his father. "I plan to be instrumental in bringing that back. I will be successful and rise in the organization – maybe all the way to the top!"

Over 1,000 kilometers to the north, in a different country and a different culture, Dieter Kaufmann grew up in a household that inculcated in him the same ethical relativism and the drive to achieve at all costs. His father, a Munich banker, was driven to create all the wealth he could, no matter how his actions affected those around him. Embezzlement was not out of the question, and he was arrested for it on two occasions, but never convicted. He was Dieter's role-model.

When Antonio and Dieter met at the Pontifical Lateran University, they soon discovered they were singing from the same sheet of music. Their years at the Pontifical Lateran University were the beginning of a symbiotic relationship that would contribute to their advancement in the church. They both were determined to achieve power, and were committed to helping each other do it.

"We need to protect and support each other, Dieter. We are destined to bring strong leadership back into the halls of the Vatican. You and I are going to do this, and we can't let anyone or anything stand in our way!"

After their ordinations, they briefly served their dioceses as parish priests. Then Ruggieri became a professor at the Gregorian University, and Kaufmann's political skills resulted in his elevation to monsignor and the head of Catholic Charities in Bavaria. Before long, both were appointed to minor but not insignificant positions in the Roman Curia, a launching pad from which Ruggieri ascended to prefect of the Congregation for the Doctrine of the Faith, was ordained a bishop and archbishop, and finally elevated to cardinal. Kaufmann, with the help of Ruggieri's powerful influence, was able to engineer his elevation to auxiliary bishop at his home Archdiocese of Munich and Freising, and ultimately to cardinal archbishop.

Over the years, Ruggieri and Kaufmann watched out for each other, always rendering assistance when needed, clearly aware that the rise to power for each of them was inextricably intertwined with the other's advancement. Ruggieri was the senior partner in this relationship – more wily and conniving, more aggressive and considerably quicker on his feet.

However, in 2040, Kaufmann would play a key role in Ruggieri's reappointment to his prefectural position in the Curia after the election of Pope Paul VII – a role that hinged on the crazy behavior of Kaufmann's emotionally unstable and mentally ill niece.

Chapter 3

June, 2022
Mittenwald, Bavaria

To most people who knew her, including her parents, Sophie Mueller defied description. At times she was sweet and pliable. At other times, she was headstrong, shook her long blond curls defiantly, was arrogant, and threw temper-tantrums.

She lived in a dream-world with make-believe friends who were more real to her than the other children her age she knew – children with whom she did not get along at all. Sophie's looks were very plain, and her sensitivity about this bordered on the paranoid. She was tall for her age, quite strong, and would attempt to dominate anyone who crossed her, especially boys. Sophie was not a fun person to be around.

Sophie was pious, knelt by her bed and said her prayers every evening, and attended Mass not only on Sundays but sometimes during the week. She was considerably brighter than most 10-year olds, continually questioning everything and impatient with anyone who could not provide her with answers.

If you asked six different people "What is Sophie Mueller like?" you would probably get six different answers.

She did "weird" things, her classmates would say. She was always mumbling to herself (actually, she was talking with her imaginary friends). Sometimes she wore socks that didn't match. Someone would say something not particularly funny, or maybe even sad, but Sophie would laugh uproariously.

One time, she and some other girls were walking down the street, and she asked them, "How many second story windows do you think there are on this block?" They looked at her in amazement. "There are 32," she told them, "and 36 in the next block."

"You counted them?" they asked her incredulously.

"Of course," she replied. "Don't you know that's important?"

***

Mittenwald is a small town at the foot of the Bavarian Alps. It has a rich history of violin-making which dates back to the 17th century, and before that, being situated on the main trade route between Augsburg and Verona, was a center of commerce. In modern times, Mittenwald has depended on the tourist trade, especially winter sports enthusiasts. As owner of a sporting goods store, Sophie's father, Gebhard Mueller, served outdoor devotees by selling skiing equipment in the winter, and hiking and camping gear in the summer.

"Sophie, where do you think you're going so early in the morning? You haven't even had your breakfast yet," her mother Eva inquired as Sophie headed out the kitchen door which opened onto a large meadow bordered by a grove of evergreens about 200 yards beyond. This was the third time she had done this, and again at 6:30 a.m. She took with her a satchel with unknown contents.

"*Mutter,*" Sophie replied, her face expressionless and her eyes focused somewhere in the distance, "it is God's will that I learn as much nature as I can. Early morning is the best time. You mustn't come between me and God's will."

She went to the edge of the woods where there were two small animal traps she had removed from her father's store without telling him. In one was a small rodent, probably a rat, and the other held a rabbit. Sophie knelt and said a prayer.

She reached into her satchel, removed a pair of heavy-duty work gloves, and one-by-one removed the animals from their traps, putting them each into separate thick-gauge plastic bags with holes so they could breathe. Then she put the bags into her satchel and re-baited the traps, one with a carrot, and the other with small pieces of meat.

In little over an hour, Sophie returned home.

"What do you have in your satchel?" her mother insisted on knowing.

"*Mutter*, look at the nature God has given me!"

Her mother was horrified. "Where did you get those?" she demanded.

Sophie began one of her temper tantrums. "God wants me to have these – that's all you need to know." She shouted at her mother, "That's *all* I'm going to tell you!"

Sophie stomped out of the kitchen, opened the basement door, and slammed it behind her.

There was a workbench in the basement her father used when he built cabinets and repaired furniture. She spread a plastic tarpaulin over the surface and placed a wooden board on it. Putting on her heavy-duty gloves again, she removed each animal from its bag, and nailed it to the board through its limbs.

Over the next two hours, with a knife, a razor blade, and a pair of tweezers, she meticulously dissected the animals. She apparently was trying to learn something from the dissection, but nevertheless she took no notes on her activities – Sophie had an almost photographic memory. After she was through, she cleaned up the board and tarpaulin, and disposed of the carcasses in the outside garbage can.

Beyond a doubt, Sophie Mueller marched to a different drummer. Where she might be marching to was troubling to everyone.

Chapter 4

May, 2024

Eva Mueller found it extraordinarily challenging to be the mother of her only child Sophie. Eva was painfully shy, exceptionally introverted and not at all sure of herself. The demands of supervising the life and activities of her unusually headstrong child seemed to be considerably beyond her capabilities.

"Eva," Gebhard would lecture her, "you are much too lenient with Sophie! You have to draw the line – let her know who's in charge. She is running roughshod over you!"

Gebhard Mueller was no shining example of a parent either. He left the raising of their daughter entirely up to Eva. He was totally engrossed in his work which occupied about 12 hours of his day, and expected peace and quiet, and a well-ordered household when he came home in the evening. His criticism of Eva's parenting could equally apply to him.

As the child grew from infancy to pre-teens, the abnormality of their youngster became glaringly apparent, though they were not able to admit it to themselves. They never even considered a medical diagnosis – to have a sub-normal child would be a disgrace, a black mark on the family escutcheon. Surely they thought, she would grow out of it. However, that wasn't happening.

"My brother, the auxiliary bishop, has talked about a Catholic girls boarding school," Eva told Gebhard one evening after Sophie had gone to bed. "It's been years since Munich has hosted one. No one has wanted to send their daughters to a girls only gymnasium – too much like entering a convent – but Dieter disagreed. He felt there was a need for such a school.

"These days, many parents are afraid for the morals of their daughters as they enter puberty. He and a group of his associates presented the issue to the Sisters of Mary Magdalene and they agreed to take on the challenge, establish a high school – a boarding school for girls. It opens this fall."

"If your brother is for this, I am against it," Gebhard bellowed with no ambiguity, waving his hands above his head. "Dieter Kaufmann is always up to something! This man is devious, Eva. We've talked about this before, and I think that, reluctantly, you agree with me. I'll tell you this – when I shake his hand, I count my fingers afterwards!"

"He's ambitious, Gebhard. He wouldn't have gotten as far as he has in the church if he weren't. He's the archbishop's right-hand man, you know. You shouldn't be so hard on him."

Eva had difficulties in conversations like this with Gebhard. She was always tentative – almost apologetic – as she attempted to express her opinions and feelings. As a result, she often failed to make her point, no matter how valid it might be.

"Our archbishop, Cardinal Metzger, fully supports this school," Eva added, "and is on the board of directors. Many civic leaders are behind it. We should look at it."

In spite of her uncertain manner of expression, Gebhard began to take Eva's suggestion seriously, especially when she named the other board members – all prominent citizens of Munich. Although Gebhard had taken virtually no responsibility in raising Sophie, he was terribly disturbed by the way she was turning out. Something had to be done.

"Things are out of control, Eva. Our Sophie is now 12 years old. We need to look at our options. We need to talk to your brother about this. You check with him – see what you can find out about this school. It just may be the nuns there can straighten Sophie out!"

This was "wishful-thinking" on Gebhard's part.

CHAPTER 5

Once seminarians at the Pontifical Lateran University completed their studies and were ready for ordination to the priesthood, they saw themselves on the threshold of a life of devotion and service to the church and its faithful. Ruggieri and Kaufmann, however, totally lacked any such idealistic motivation.

"We have something our classmates lack, Dieter – clear-cut objectives, a strategy for how we will achieve them, and a 'roadmap' that will tell us where we are at each step along the way. Blind luck is not going to determine our future. We will create our own luck; we will control our own destinies!"

And controlling their destinies they did most effectively, thanks mainly to the machinations of Antonio Ruggieri. He was adept at making the right connections, and taking full advantage of them.

One of Ruggieri's childhood friends, Paolo Andreano, was an up-and-coming lawyer in Rome, and like Antonio, had close family ties to the Mafia. After Ruggieri identified members of the church's hierarchy who could be instrumental in influencing his and Dieter's career moves, he would ask Paolo to dig up all the dirt about them he could find – things they were hiding which, if known, could damage their reputations and careers. Ruggieri would use this information to "gently" persuade these individuals to use their influence in his and Dieter's behalf.

This strategy worked quite well. By 2024, Ruggieri had a significant position in the Congregation for the Doctrine of the Faith, was ordained a bishop, and was considered a likely candidate to be the congregation's next prefect. Earlier that year, Kaufmann was ordained as an auxiliary bishop for the Archdiocese of Munich and Freising.

With his heavy responsibilities in Munich, and the unrelenting demands of the autocratic cardinal archbishop to whom he reported, the last thing Dieter welcomed was a call from his sister in Mittenwald, requesting an appointment to talk about family problems.

Chapter 6

On the Tuesday morning after her discussion with Gebhard about Sophie's problems, Eva left Mittenwald in the family car for the 105 kilometer drive to Munich to meet with her brother, Bishop Kaufmann. She traveled alone, since Gebhard made work his excuse for not accompanying her.

"Eva, you know the season is at it's busiest right now. I can't leave Hans alone in the store for an entire day. You must handle this issue by yourself. After all, matters concerning Sophie are primarily your responsibility!"

The truth was Gebhard would have preferred to walk over broken glass barefoot than engage his brother-in-law in a conversation about anything. Dieter Kaufmann, he felt with justification, was pompous, very much wrapped up in himself, and quite Machiavellian. Just as he believed that supervising and disciplining Sophie was Eva's responsibility, so were any dealings with her brother.

In Munich, Eva drove to the Palais Holnstein, the archbishop's residence where her brother had his office. Bishop Kaufmann greeted her warmly.

"*Kleine Schwester*! How good it is to see you! It has been a long time – much too long!"

Eva gave him a big hug. "I have missed you, *älterer Bruder!* We talk on the phone now and then, but it's no substitute for seeing you face-to-face – in person! I know how busy you are with your work for the archbishop, and I am pleased you could make time for me today."

Dieter Kaufmann rarely had time for any relatives, not even his younger sister. The fact that her husband was Gebhard Mueller didn't help – his dislike for him was almost on a par with Gebhard's aversion to Dieter. Kaufmann could sense Gebhard Mueller's disapproval, and from Kaufmann's point-of-view, anyone who didn't approve of him might as well not exist.

Dieter Kaufmann was a handsome man, 47 years of age, silver-white hair, five feet eleven inches tall, high cheekbones, a trim, athletic figure. He smiled readily, but it was a crooked smile, and seemed as if it were pasted on his face, rather than an expression of how he really felt.

"You spoke to me on the phone about concerns you have regarding your Sophie," Bishop Kaufmann said, initiating the conversation as they sat down on the sofa in his office.

"Yes, Dieter," Eva replied, her voice trembling slightly with emotion, partly due to her concern for her daughter, and partly her fear that her brother might not be willing to be of any help. "Gebhard and I are at our wit's end! As you know, *mein Bruder,* Sophie has been a handful ever since she could walk and talk. It has only gotten worse. She does strange things, says strange things. We thought she would grow out of it, but that isn't happening." Eva buried her face in her hands as she began to sob.

Dieter Kaufmann was not one to react to a woman's tears, even his own sister's. He sat quietly until she regained control of herself.

"You told me some time ago you were instrumental in getting the Sisters of Mary Magdalene to establish a boarding school for girls. Gebhard and I thought the nuns would have a good influence on Sophie, and she is now ready for her first year in high school. Can you intervene for us to make sure they accept her? We are desperate!"

Bishop Kaufmann stood, and walked over to the window, standing there for a minute or two with his hands clasped behind his back. He had little interest in this family, much less the child. On the other hand, he wanted his family members to recognize he was an extremely important, powerful and influential man.

He turned around and looked at Eva with a studied expression of sympathy. "Sister Eugenia is the principal of the Queen of Heaven Academy, *mein Schwester.* I will talk to her today. You should call her later this week and arrange for little Sophie to be enrolled this fall. I am sure the influence of these good nuns will inspire the child and help her grow into a normal and healthy adult."

Dieter Kaufmann didn't know how wrong he was.

Chapter 7

2024 – 2028
Queen of Heaven Academy
Munich

> *"You are chosen, Sophie – you are chosen. You will do great things. Listen to what I have to say!"*

The Voice was speaking to her again. She heard it clearly, distinctly. The message was unambiguous. She always knew she was different than others, that she had a role to fulfill, totally out of the ordinary, and more noteworthy than any other mortal. She knew this as far back as she could remember; but now, The Voice was confirming this in no uncertain terms, and speaking to her on a regular basis. She told no one at the Academy about this – who would believe her?

***

Her first year at Queen of Heaven had been disastrous – for her and for everyone around her. Like her life in Mittenwald, she couldn't get along with her classmates. And like her life with her parents, she chafed under authority. Her classmates made fun of her. She wouldn't follow the directions of the nuns, and they continually had to discipline her. She was put on probation more than once. The school was used to handling difficult girls, but the principal, Sister Eugenia, seriously considered admitting defeat and expelling her.

She considered this action as a last resort, since Bishop Kaufmann had personally requested his niece Sophie be admitted to the school.

But then, in her second year, Sophie began hearing The Voice for the first time.

> *"Sophie, you will do important things, extraordinary things. Focus on that! Your teachers and your classmates aren't as smart as you. Leave them alone – do not fight with them anymore. Don't waste your energy. Use them, don't abuse them."*

"Who *are* you?" Sophie demanded to know, time and time again. The Voice would not respond to her question. It would only repeat what it had just said.

> *"You will do important things, extraordinary things."*

Sophie still had her imaginary friends that no one else but she could see. They were real to her, they always had been real. They were her "roommates" – none of the other girls were willing to room with her, and that was fine with Sophie.

She would ask her imaginary friends who The Voice was. They simply answered:

"Do what The Voice tells you, Sophie. Do not ignore it."

Sophie was sure The Voice was God, or at least an angel of God. The Voice would speak to her every few days, and she took its dictates quite seriously.

Once she began hearing The Voice, a change took place in Sophie's behavior. Before she was insubordinate and argumentative with her teachers. Now she bit her lip, and followed their instructions, even when she was convinced they were dead wrong. The Voice told her to do this. Her imaginary friends told her that she must pay attention to The Voice.

Things also improved in her relationships with her classmates, although they were still far from perfect. Where she had been consistently confrontational with them, she was now more accepting and patient, and focused on what they could do for her. *"Use them, don't abuse them,"* The Voice had told her. They continued to sometimes make fun of her, but she tried to ignore that. Her imaginary friends were her trustworthy companions – her real friends. They mattered to her, not her classmates.

Sister Eugenia, as well as the nuns who taught her, marveled at this stark change that manifested itself over a period of weeks. She no longer felt Sophie was a candidate for dismissal. Relieved and somewhat amazed that she had changed, Sister Eugenia was especially thankful she didn't have to explain to Sophie's uncle, Bishop Kaufmann, why his niece was no longer welcome at the academy.

Still, it was obvious to anyone who had frequent contact with Sophie that she was far removed from the norm. She didn't participate in competitive sports with her classmates. She had no time or interest in the "girl talk" so common with most teenage girls. She still spoke with her imaginary friends as she walked through the halls, but many of her classmates assumed she was on her cell phone.

And bright? Her extraordinary intelligence was so great, especially in the physical sciences, it effectively intimidated the other students.

Sophie spent as much time as possible in the chemistry lab conducting experiments more typical of university graduate students. She was especially interested in experimenting with chemicals she compounded herself, which she hoped would temporarily or permanently paralyze, but not destroy, the muscles of experimental animals – a morbid interest that probably was an outgrowth of her animal dissections in Mittenwald.

Liabilities aside, her exceptional gifts, and the scientific awards she accumulated during high school, brought her to the attention of the provincial for the Sisters of Mary Magdalene.

The provincial's interest set Sophie on a life-changing trajectory – one that would prove tragic not only for Sophie, but for many others as well.

CHAPTER 8

August, 2030
Vatican City

Since Giovanni Ganganelli was elected pope in 1769 and assumed the name Clement XIV, no pope had taken that name until Mexican Cardinal Diego Quesada, prefect of the Congregation for the Doctrine of the Faith, was elected after the July death of Benedict XVII, and became Pope Clement XV. Like the previous Clement, Quesada was a Franciscan, but unlike Clement XIV who suppressed the Society of Jesus, Clement XV showed considerable respect for the Jesuits.

As prefect, Quesada valued Antonio Ruggieri's contributions. He thought this young bishop was smart, took on the more difficult tasks and got the job done. At times, the prefect needed to propagate some discipline or new policy in a diocese or archdiocese where the presiding bishop objected and was uncooperative, or even obstinate. Quesada would then send Antonio there as his personal representative, and within a few days, the otherwise recalcitrant prelate was brought into compliance. Prefect Quesada assessed Bishop Ruggieri as having exceptional political skills.

Antonio's political abilities were indeed good, but the key to his success was usually his well-honed skillfulness in identifying his target's weak spots and exploiting them, often with the help of his attorney friend Paolo Andreano and sometimes even Mafia operatives. Although his strategy was out-and-out blackmail, because he orchestrated it so subtly and deviously, no one could accuse him – much less prove – he used blackmail, not even the victim.

These actions were part of the Ruggieri-Kaufmann "roadmap" – their master plan, devised back in the seminary, to ensure their successful advancement in the church's hierarchy. Antonio fashioned for himself a flawless track-record at the Congregation for the Doctrine of the Faith, and had the absolute confidence of Prefect Quesada. In Munich, Dieter's efforts were similarly focused, and his superior, Cardinal Metzger, archbishop of Munich and Freising, trusted him to get the job done, and considered him to be totally dependable.

Whenever a pope dies, all principal curial officials resign, and – more often than not – are reappointed by the next pope. Since the next pope after the death of Benedict XVII was Clement XV, former prefect of the Congregation for the Doctrine of the Faith, a replacement was needed for that position and Antonio's strategy and hard work paid off. Clement appointed him the new prefect, and shortly afterward, elevated him to archbishop and then cardinal.

Later that year, Cardinal Metzger of Munich passed away. Since Ruggieri had the pope's ear, Dieter Kaufmann became the new archbishop of Munich and Freising, and within a year, he, too, became a cardinal.

Things could hardly be going better for Antonio and Dieter.

Chapter 9

2028 -2034
Bavaria

Life as a Sister of Mary Magdalene seemed perfectly suited to Sophie – now Sister Sophie. At their house of formation convent in Augsburg, the sisters spent most of their time in silence, speaking to others only when necessary. This was fine with Sister Sophie.

Among religious congregations in the Catholic Church, the Sisters of Mary Magdalene were an anomaly. Their main mission was administering to the needs of others as health professionals – physicians, therapists, nurse practitioners, and researchers in the health sciences. Operating their Queen of Heaven Academy for girls in Munich was an unusual activity for the congregation.

Before her graduation from the academy, the provincial had recruited Sophie to join the congregation. Sophie's reputation as a gifted young scientist was by now common knowledge. She seemed destined for advanced studies in biochemistry, and she had a reputation for piety. The Sisters of Mary Magdalene wanted her. The Voice told her a life of service in this congregation was her mission. Her imaginary friends encouraged her. She didn't give her decision a second thought.

After her period of formation in Augsburg, she was enrolled in the Ludwig Maximilian University of Munich, and shared an apartment with two other nuns who were also students there. Living in close proximity to Sister Sophie was difficult for anyone, but these two sisters accepted this eccentric woman as the "cross" God wanted them to bear, at least while they were at the university.

After receiving her BS, Sister Sophie continued at LMU for her MS, and then her PhD. As part of her PhD program, she was required to do a two-year internship. She applied to several labs in Bavaria, Austria and Switzerland, and was offered a position at almost all of them. She chose The Swiss Alpine Laboratory in Bern, Switzerland because of its outstanding reputation.

Swiss Alpine felt it was their good fortune to entice such a talented biochemist to do her internship with their firm. Ultimately, their decision had unintended catastrophic consequences.

CHAPTER 10

The Sisters of Mary Magdalene had no house or hospital service in Bern, so the first challenge for the congregation, and for Sister Sophie, was where she would stay. Though she was considered an asset to the Sisters of Mary Magdalene, they were realistic enough to worry about Sister Sophie fending for herself in a strange city without putting herself, and perhaps others, in danger. She was a volatile human being.

Although their daughter was no longer the direct responsibility of the Mueller family, her religious superior's concern was strong enough to prompt her to ask the Muellers for their assistance in finding a suitable place for Sister Sophie to stay in Bern.

"I am terribly concerned about Sophie moving to Bern, and being by herself," Eva revealed to Gebhard in her usual tentative manner, eyes searching the room as if there was a secret answer hiding somewhere, waiting to be found.

"She's a grown woman," Gebhard responded gruffly. "Besides, it's the responsibility of her religious order to see she is taken care of and protected. She is no longer a dependent of ours. Are we going to intervene every time some new challenge swims into her life?"

"She's still a fragile girl, hardly a full-grown woman," Eva retorted in a pleading tone of voice. "We had hoped the boarding school might work some magic with her, but it didn't turn out that way. She's not normal, Gebhard – you know that! We can't just throw her to the wolves."

Gebhard Mueller had a hard time accepting that, in spite of their best efforts, Sophie had not matured and become a normal member of society. It caused him shame. Over the years, he and Eva had tried to hide this fact from others. Everyone knew about the "strange Mueller girl" and whispered behind Eva and Gebhard's back. The Muellers knew this talk was going on.

Eva racked her brain for a way to convince Gebhard they must in some way intervene and ensure suitable living arrangements for Sophie in Bern.

"People talk about our strange daughter, *mein Mann*," Eva reminded him. "Sometimes they think she is different because we have done something wrong. What will they say if Sophie has an unfortunate incident in Bern that could have been prevented if only you and I had made the proper living arrangements for her?"

Gebhard drummed the table at which he was sitting with his fingers. He said nothing for a minute or two, clearly lost in thought.

"You're right – we can't leave ourselves open to that accusation, *mein Frau*," he acknowledged reluctantly. "I don't like to face this reality, but we must accept the fact that, *occasionally*, we may need to step in and assist our daughter, even though she is now the responsibility of the Sisters of Mary Magdalene.

"I have a friend in Bern, you know – Otto Richter – who has a large sporting goods store there. I see him at trade shows now and then, even last July actually. Otto tells me he has an apartment for rent above the store. This might be ideal for Sophie. I could explain the situation to Otto, and find out if the apartment is available for rent, and if he would take responsibility for looking in on Sophie occasionally."

Gebhard phoned his friend Otto and, to his surprise, Otto knew about Sophie. "I have a niece who is also a member of that religious congregation, Gebhard. She has told me about your daughter, that she is – what should I say – 'different.' Let me talk to my niece first."

Otto phoned back later. "I have spoken to young Gertrude, my niece. She told me to go ahead, that she will tell us how her sister nuns handle Sister Sophie. An unusual woman, she tells me, but she says hardly dangerous. Sister Sophie can have our apartment, and my wife and I will keep track of her. Gertrude says she will tell Sister Sophie about the arrangement, and how nice it will be!"

Eva and Gebhard breathed a sigh of relief.

"You were right, Eva," Gebhard admitted. "Sophie will be in good hands with Otto and his wife. We need to do something nice for them someday."

CHAPTER 11

July, 2034
Vatican City

The Conclave to elect a new pope lasted eight days – irrefutable evidence there was no clear front-runner for the office. When Cardinal Augustine McIntyre, archbishop of Sydney, Australia was finally elected, he chose the name of Leo XIV. As is customary, one of his first duties was to appoint prefects of curial congregations, all of whom had resigned upon the death of the previous pope, Clement XV. Like many of his predecessors, he reappointed the former incumbents to continue on with their assignments at the Curia – with one exception.

During his tenure as archbishop of Sydney, McIntyre had several disputes with Cardinal Ruggieri. True, the Congregation for the Doctrine of the Faith wielded considerable authority when it came to assuring the orthodoxy of priests, theologians and teachers of religion in the church's dioceses and archdioceses throughout the world. But prior to Ruggieri, the prefect usually consulted with local bishops before taking disciplinary action. Not Antonio Ruggieri. And in the process, he went toe-to-toe with the strong-willed McIntyre a number of times, and on issues the archbishop of Sydney was convinced the prefect of the Congregation for the Doctrine of the Faith was grossly overreaching. There was no way the new pope was going to award such a key position to a man he didn't trust.

"This is outrageous!" Ruggieri yelled at Kaufmann, who was still in Rome after the pope's installation. "This man has no right to deny me the position I perform so well!" Ruggieri pounded his fist on his desk several times, his neck turned red, his dark eyes bulged. The visage he presented was about as frightening as finding oneself directly in the path of a tornado.

The "man," of course, had the "right." He was pope, and curial prefects served at his pleasure. But nobody, not even a pope, was supposed to tell Antonio Ruggieri what to do.

"He has appointed me to an inconsequential position on the Pontifical Biblical Commission. This is an unforgivable insult! And who did he give 'Doctrine of the Faith' to? Christian Bauer, of all people!"

"That man doesn't have the backbone you do, Antonio. When he was bishop of a small Bavarian diocese, he couldn't provide the discipline required of a church leader. I was glad to see him transferred to a minor position in the Curia. But now this! What can the pope be thinking?"

"You and I are a team," Ruggieri reminded him. "I am destined to someday control the church, and you are going to help me do that. This pope has put up a road block – a road block that's totally unacceptable!

"We must think, Dieter. No problem is insurmountable. Bauer must be removed. What can we do to make sure he fails and I get my old position back?"

Chapter 12

August 2034
Bern

Sophie settled comfortably into her new living quarters with amazing alacrity, as if she had lived there all her life. No one was living with her, for which she was grateful. The Richters were pleasant and non-intrusive, offering to help her in any way they could to acclimatize herself to life in Bern.

Actually, she wasn't living alone. She had her friends, visible only to her, with whom she had shared most of her life. She would have felt lost without them. Their presence supported her; their attentive concern gave her comfort; their advice always helped her through difficult times. She was never lonely.

And The Voice – every few days she clearly heard The Voice. She was sure this was God speaking to her, guiding her, preparing her for an important mission in life.

"You will do important things, Sophie. Do not lose your focus. Listen to me!"

Bern is a sophisticated city with a rich heritage, dating back to pre-medieval times. A number of fine museums, showcasing history, art and science, enliven the cultural life of Switzerland's capital. Theater, festivals, and sporting events are sources of entertainment for both those living there and the city's many visitors. However, these opportunities were totally wasted on Sophie.

Her routine never varied, even on Sundays. Every morning she attended Mass at a nearby church, and then had coffee and a sweet roll. Afterward, she walked a kilometer's distance to The Swiss Alpine Laboratory where she worked until late afternoon. On her way back to her apartment, she would stop to pick up some groceries. After supper, she sometimes watched television, but usually read – lives of the saints, or scientific texts and journals devoted to her research areas.

***

Her internship couldn't be better, Sophie thought. The Swiss Alpine Laboratory was engaged in pure research, not targeted for specific commercial purposes. When they developed something that had a practical value, the lab licensed it to a manufacturer who was able to exploit it. Sophie, as it turned out, was given free reign to follow her interests wherever they took her.

During her lab work in high school, and continuing while working on her BS, MS and PhD, Sophie maintained her interest – actually her fixation – on developing compounds that would paralyze muscles.

Americans used substances such as midazolam, hydromorphone, potassium chloride and vecuronium when they put a criminal to death by lethal injection. Sophie was determined to develop something new – something that would paralyze a muscle permanently, cause no pain, leave no trace, and have no effect on the chemistry of the muscle.

She took the current compounds, broke them down into their component parts, and combined them with other chemicals that Indians in the Brazilian rainforests, she learned from scientific literature, used on their poison darts. After much trial and error, she managed to produce a substance she called Serum-C, and her animal experiments verified it did exactly what she intended.

Expressing herself, orally or in writing, was very difficult for Sophie, but in spite of this, she produced a detailed description of the productive results she had in developing Serum-C, and presented these results to her division supervisor.

"Sister Sophie, I have read your report thoroughly," Dr. Eric Schmidt informed her at the meeting he called to discuss her results. "This paper is truly a *tour de force,* one of the best I have seen in my division. Take me to your lab and let me see for myself the condition of the animals on which you experimented."

Sophie showed him the rats, rabbits and dogs she used in her experiments with various muscles subjected to Serum-C. She also showed him slides of paralyzed muscles from sacrificed animals which confirmed no microscopic evidence of anything abnormal appeared in the paralyzed specimens. Afterward, they returned to the director's office.

"Sit down, Sister Sophie," Schmidt requested, as he also sat down at his desk, leaning back in his swivel chair. "This work you have done is most significant and creative. You are to be commended for your truly amazing results. However, Serum-C presents a substantial ethical problem.

"There are, as you know, muscle paralyzers on the market, have been for some time. The main difference between them and your innovation is they can be traced in the body, whereas yours can't. That's dangerous. Serum-C could provide an open door for criminals to use for nefarious purposes without leaving any kind of trace. We can't have that!"

Sophie couldn't handle anyone questioning the importance of her work, or even disagreeing with her. She interjected, her voice rising, her hands shaking, her face flush.

"Dr. Schmidt, this drug is going to have an important use in the future! I don't know what that is, but my companions tell me so, and The Voice tells me I have a mission . . ."

"Your *companions*?" Dr. Schmidt interrupted, in total amazement, "And *the voice*? Sister Sophie, what in the world are you talking about?"

Everyone at The Swiss Alpine Laboratory knew Sister Sophie was a very strange woman who had no friends. She appeared to be the stereotype of a complete loner, never socializing with staff members, rarely talking to anyone. What she was saying made absolutely no sense.

Was Sister Sophie hallucinating, Schmidt wondered.

Sophie's mental and emotional problems were indeed severe, but she was extremely intelligent. She realized Dr. Schmidt's "challenge" had precipitated her sputtering out her inner secrets. She had let her guard down.

"Just a figure of speech, Dr. Schmidt. I was excited – that's all. Please disregard what I said. I just know that inventions or breakthroughs that don't appear important at the time, often prove to be valuable later on."

"Sister Sophie, I want you to destroy any Serum-C you still have, as well as your copy of this report and any of your notes containing the formula. I view this discovery of yours tantamount to the creation of a lethal lab-developed bacteria. Serum-C must be eliminated before it gets into the general population and wrecks havoc on humanity!"

Sophie bit her lower lip, got up and left Dr. Schmidt's office. She had made a terrible mistake in the heat of emotional stress and anxiety to let anything slip about her companions and The Voice. She had never done this before, and hoped she had back-tracked successfully.

Back in her lab, her friends were waiting for her, and told her to keep some vials of Serum-C. "You will need them," they admonished her. And again she heard The Voice.

"Nothing is going to stop you, Sophie. Your mission is noble. You will succeed. Nothing will stop you. You will succeed."

Dr. Schmidt picked up her report and read it again.

This formula clearly has value. It may be a humane way of killing animals in a slaughter house. It can stop the heart immediately, leave no residue, and keep the meat from being poisoned, but we must keep it out of the wrong hands – criminals, terrorists, crazy people. Crazy people, like Sister Sophie!

Swiss Alpine's policy was to share credit for new breakthroughs, as well as their economic returns, with the scientist who made the discovery, even if the scientist was an intern. The company believed not to do so would be stealing intellectual property.

But not from a crazy person, like Sister Sophie – she'll never know.

CHAPTER 13

August, 2034
Vatican City

When Antonio Ruggieri held a grudge, he never let go of it. He was vindictive to the extreme. He didn't care for Augustine McIntyre when he was cardinal archbishop of Sydney, and even less now that he is Pope Leo XIV. This man had the audacity to appoint Christian Bauer as prefect of the Congregation for the Doctrine of the Faith instead of reappointing Ruggieri to the job that was rightfully his. Antonio was obsessed with his hatred for Leo XIV.

On top of it all, Bauer is a "weak sister," he fumed, *who doesn't have my drive and intestinal fortitude to make the hard decisions, and see them carried out. This blatant affront is an intolerable thorn in my side, and I am determined to see it removed.*

Neither he nor Dieter could come up with a plan of action to correct the situation.

"Have you talked to Paolo Andreano about this," Dieter asked Antonio in a phone conversation. Amazingly, Ruggieri had overlooked bringing attorney Andreano into the equation, a gross oversight for someone determined to leave no stone unturned.

"Not yet, but that of course was part of my plan," Antonio quickly responded, never one to admit he had overlooked anything.

***

Paolo paced the length of Antonio's office with his hands clasped behind his back, his eyes focused on the floor two or three steps ahead of him. "There's little you can do about this in the short run," Andreano told him, stating the obvious. "There's no court of appeal when the pope has made a decision. He's both first and final arbiter, but you of course know that.

"What you have to do, Antonio, is to lay the groundwork for undermining Bauer in the long run, and establish yourself as the right man – the only man – to take his place.

"I'll have my operatives dig into his background, examine his past. No one is perfect – we're bound to find something."

"For the first time since Bauer was appointed, Paolo, I am beginning to see a distant beam of light in the darkness. This man has to have an Achilles' heel. We need to find it, and exploit it, to blackmail him, to force him to resign."

Andreano's men found nothing – absolutely nothing. No skeletons in Bauer's closet. It became clear more drastic action was needed.

CHAPTER 14

July, 2036
Munich

Sophie completed her two-year internship at Swiss Alpine, and returned to the Ludwig Maximilian University of Munich to finish her remaining coursework and write her dissertation.

Upon receiving her PhD, the Sisters of Mary Magdalene put her in charge of a division at the laboratory for the Medical Center of the Ludwig Maximilian University of Munich, a lab facility that serviced not only this hospital, but met the laboratory needs of many smaller clinics and medical facilities throughout Munich.

Although Sophie's people skills were notoriously poor, interpersonal communications were not an important part of her new position. Specimens arrived at the lab to be analyzed, and there were exact procedures and timetables to follow for every request. The technical staff at the lab knew what was expected of them, and, as long as they did what they were required to do, they had very little contact with Sister Sophie. Only when they didn't follow the prescribed procedures did Sophie get involved. Since everyone was aware how strange she was, they did everything in their power to keep their contacts with her to a minimum.

Sophie enjoyed her work. Most of the analysis was pretty routine, so she usually delegated those requests to other staff members. But she kept the more complex and interesting cases – the real challenges – for herself. On a regular basis, however, her mind would return to the vials of Serum-C she had stashed away in her apartment's refrigerator.

Her invisible friends had told her: "Keep the serum – you will need it."

"Need it for what?" she would ask them.

They would only repeat, "Keep the serum!"

CHAPTER 15

February, 2040
Vatican City

Pope Leo XIV's death was not unexpected. He had been diagnosed with liver cancer, and although most cancers were curable by this time, the strain infecting Leo was not. Several months before he died, he had part of his liver removed in the hope of eliminating all his cancer cells. However, in recent weeks, the cancer had not only returned but had metastasized. His case was terminal.

Ruggieri's single-minded determination to get his assignment back as prefect of the Congregation for the Doctrine of the Faith never abated. He was fixated on discrediting or even eliminating Bauer as a competitor. Paolo had arranged, through Mafia connections loyal to the Ruggieri and Andreano families in Cosenza, to have the position of evening doorman at Bauer's apartment filled by a Mafia operative who would act on Ruggieri's behalf, if necessary. The election of Pope Leo XIV's successor, Pope Paul VII, was presenting the opening Ruggieri was looking for.

"Dieter, I have some good news," Ruggieri informed Kaufmann by phone, shortly after Kaufmann returned to Munich following Paul VII's election. "Although the pope has reappointed Leo XIV's curial officials, he is delaying the selection of the prefect of the

Congregation for the Doctrine of the Faith. He has announced that it will go to either Bauer again, or to me."

"This opportunity sounds too good to be true, Antonio!" Kaufmann replied. "Do you know when he will make his decision?"

"He has set a deadline for three weeks from today. We can't let Bauer get that job back! Both you and I have too much to lose if I don't get the appointment! We need to think, Dieter – we need to think. Get back to me right away with your thoughts."

CHAPTER 16

February, 2040
Munich

One day, when Sophie was thinking about her vials of Serum-C, she heard The Voice say:

> *"Go to the man of God for guidance, Sophie. He will tell you what to do."*

Was this the sign she was waiting for? A man of God will let her know what her mission is, what she is to do with Serum-C? But what "man of God" is this? She thought about this long and hard, and then it dawned on her.

Of course! There is a man I know – truly a man of God. Why did I not think of him before?

She had not seen her uncle, Dieter Kaufmann, now cardinal archbishop of Munich and Freising, since she had taken her religious vows nine years before. She knew of no one who more accurately fit the description as a "man of God" than her uncle.

She phoned the Palais Holnstein, the archbishop's residence, and asked to speak to the archbishop. Not surprisingly, the receptionist told her he was not available. Sophie told the receptionist that Cardinal Kaufmann was her uncle, and could she leave a message?

The receptionist responded, "Just a moment, Sister Sophie." Within a minute, Uncle Dieter was on the phone.

Cardinal Kaufmann had no desire to speak to Sophie Mueller, or any member of her family for that matter. However it had been 16 years since his sister had asked him to intervene and facilitate Sophie's enrollment at the Queen of Heaven Academy. The family was not being a nuisance, and he didn't want it said he refused to talk to his own niece. It was well-known in Munich's religious community that she was strange, and that in itself might present a minor crisis if he refused.

"It's good to hear from you after all these years, *mein Nichte.* What can I do for you?"

"*Mein Onkel,* I have something extremely important to share with you. I invented a drug at the laboratory in Bern. They tried to take it away from me. The Voice tells me it is important, and I must tell you about it." Other than her slip with Dr. Schmidt at Swiss Alpine, she had never mentioned anything to anyone about The Voice. But she must tell her uncle, the man of God, so he appreciates the importance of what she would relate to him.

"The *voice,* did you say, Sophie? What kind of voice? What are you talking about?"

"I must see you, *mein Onkel.*"

Kaufmann was now genuinely concerned. Not only was his niece very strange, but now she was hearing voices. She might be seriously deranged, and do or say things that could embarrass the Kaufmann family, especially himself. He must evaluate her and if needs be, recommend to the Sisters of Mary Magdalene that Sister Sophie be institutionalized. He told his niece to come see him the next day.

CHAPTER 17

Sophie showed up at the appointed time. Cardinal Kaufmann greeted her in his parlor. "Tell me about everything, Sophie – the serum you developed, your problems with The Swiss Alpine Laboratory, the voice you hear – everything!"

For the next hour, Sophie described her relationship with her invisible friends, the only real friends she ever had; The Voice she began to hear at the Academy and the positive guidance it had given her; her conviction that this was indeed The Voice of God. Dieter Kaufmann listened, almost in disbelief – "almost," that is, since what he was hearing helped explained a lot about this weird woman. Beyond a doubt she was schizophrenic and had been her entire life. But she was also a pious woman who firmly believed she was doing God's work. And she was convinced Dieter Kaufmann was anointed as the man of God who would give her direction, tell her what she needed to do with Serum-C.

Sophie may have been a pious woman, but Dieter was hardly a pious man, much less a man of God. He was a manipulator who believed the end justifies the means. And the end – the driving objective motivating his actions – was to turn heaven and earth to have Antonio Ruggieri elected pope, and in the process, further his own ascent up the hierarchical ladder of the Catholic Church.

Ruggieri had phoned him earlier in the day about a problem that could affect, either positively or adversely, Ruggieri's career, and by extension, Kaufmann's. Dieter also had a local problem, and it suddenly dawned on him that Sophie's lethal Serum-C might ultimately play a role in dealing with both.

"Sophie, you are a wise and holy woman to listen to the promptings of The Voice. It is truly God speaking to you, encouraging you to contribute to His kingdom on Earth," he told her as he rose from his chair, went over to where she was sitting, and gently placed his hand on her shoulder. "I am indeed the man of God the Lord spoke to you about, *mein Nichte,* and together we can advance the Divine Plan."

Sophie's face lit up in a broad smile, and she heaved a sigh of relief as if the weight of the world had been taken off her shoulders.

"I have two vials of the serum, *lieber Onkel.* The Voice directed me to seek your instructions on how they should be used."

The opportunity Sophie was presenting seemed almost too good to be true. Three years before, Father Wilfried Drescher, a Dominican priest, had been assigned to the Dominican monastery in Munich. He was an effective and fiery preacher, a reform-minded cleric with a large following, a man who took positions opposed to his own – much too often for Kaufmann's comfort and peace of mind. If Drescher had been an archdiocesan priest under Kaufmann's complete authority, he would have transferred him to some obscure outpost of the archdiocese and given him a position with very little exposure. But Drescher was not an archdiocesan priest. He was a member of a religious order over which the cardinal had limited control. Kaufmann would do anything to get rid of him – anything.

Father Drescher was recuperating from heart surgery at the Medical Center of the Ludwig Maximilian University of Munich, where Sophie had her laboratory. Kaufmann's conniving mind spotted a totally unexpected gift that Sophie was dropping into his lap – the opportunity to test the serum on a human being for future use by Ruggieri, and, at the same time, the elimination of a thorn in his side.

"Sophie, there is an evil spirit, in the guise of a man – a priest no less – who is recovering from surgery in your hospital. It is the will of God that this incarnation of the devil be removed before he does any more damage. That's why The Voice sent you to me – to eliminate him once and for all. No one must know what you are doing. You must also be prepared to do this again in the future, if it's necessary. You must act right away. And you need to give me the other vial."

"God's will be done," Sophie replied solemnly, taking in a ragged breath.

A day later, Sophie phoned Kaufmann. "I have done God's will as you directed, *Onkel* Dieter. The evil spirit is dead, and the hospital records show he died of heart failure."

CHAPTER 18

February, 2040
Rome

"My niece is a chemist. She says it leaves no residual traces – it breaks down immediately after the heart is paralyzed. However, you need to use a large needle to get it through the chest. People who examine the body will be able to see the hole in the chest."

Two days after Antonio Ruggieri informed Dieter Kaufmann about the unexpected possibility of his being reappointed head of the Congregation for the Doctrine of the Faith, Kaufmann phoned Ruggieri about Serum-C, its successful use by his niece, and the fact there was a vial left.

"Come to Rome right away," Antonio responded with considerable enthusiasm, "and bring the vial with you."

***

Kaufmann came to Ruggieri's residence a day later with the vial.

"I have spoken to a physician friend, Dr. Amaro," Ruggieri told him. "He is totally trustworthy. We grew up together in Cosenza, and his father was an operative in the Mafia. He assures me someone will eventually find a way to identify Serum-C. Sooner or later, The Swiss Alpine Laboratory will license it, and authorities will be able to trace it to its source, to the lab where your niece worked."

Ruggieri tapped his pen several times on his desk as he thought about what he would say next. "There's also the problem of the large needle hole. If we need to use this substance more than once and not have it discovered early on, we must find a way to mask the fact that it was injected. Amaro suggests a gun shot to the heart after the injection will preclude an autopsy and delay any attempt to trace Serum-C. And we don't have to be concerned about the accuracy of the gun shot – the victim will already be dead!"

Chapter 19

Ruggieri, Kaufmann and a third cardinal joined Bauer for a before-dinner drink at Bauer's residence two days later, and then the four of them went out for dinner. During the evening, they found out Bauer's schedule for the next day. He was to be at the Vatican, briefing Pope Paul VII on Congregation for the Doctrine of the Faith issues.

"Dieter, this is our opportunity!" Ruggieri informed Kaufmann, when they were alone at the end of evening. "When Christian is away tomorrow, I'll have my secretary, Father Bivona, deliver a gift-wrapped bottle of Christian's favorite sherry – the kind we finished off tonight – to the doorman on duty at his place. The doorman will leave it on Bauer's desk, so when he returns at the end of the day, he will think it's a gift from us. The sherry will be laced with a strong sedative, which will put him to sleep before the night doorman, who works for me, comes up to inject him with Serum-C. Fortunately, I had previously arranged to have a Mafia operative on duty as night doorman at Christian's apartment, and my foresight is now going to pay off!"

"How do you know he will have some sherry when he returns in the evening?" Kaufmann asked him.

"He told us he always has a glass before his supper. He will be thankful that we were so thoughtful as to replace the bottle we emptied last night."

Exactly as Ruggieri had planned, Bauer found the bottle when he returned in the evening, and then had a glass of sherry before he prepared dinner. Shortly afterwards, the night doorman, after knocking and getting no response, let himself into Bauer's place. With rubber gloves on, he injected Serum-C into the heart of the unconscious Bauer, who was sitting on the sofa in his study with a book in his lap. The doorman disposed of the remaining sherry in the kitchen sink, placed a silencer on his pistol, and shot Bauer in the heart at the site of the injection. He then rummaged through his desk, scattered papers on the floor and left – all in less than 10 minutes.

***

The Carabinieri's investigation of the crime was unproductive. There had been a number of break-ins in the neighborhood in recent weeks, and they assumed this must be part of the same pattern. True, no valuables were taken, but the murderer had gone through Bauer's desk looking for something, and, of course, shot the cardinal dead.

Dieter Kaufmann had returned to Munich early on the day of the murder, and was subsequently informed this native of Munich was slain. Since Bauer had no family to take responsibility for his body, the authorities asked Kaufmann what should be done with the corpse.

"His remains must be returned to Munich as soon as possible," Kaufmann instructed, "so we can inter him in a crypt at our cathedral."

Certain Vatican officials were uncomfortable about the speed with which this case was being handled, and suggested an autopsy be performed.

"Absolutely not!" Kaufmann insisted. "The Carabinieri has determined how he died. Besides, an autopsy would desecrate the body."

Despite the urgings of some senior Vatican administrators who questioned the true cause of Bauer's death, Kaufmann would not budge from his position. A number expressed amazement that the Munich archbishop asserted an autopsy would "desecrate" a body – a strange and unusual position to take.

Antonio Ruggieri was elated.

No one in this affair has been implicated. The less than professional handling of the investigation is more than I could have hoped for! Even the night doorman was given nothing more than a perfunctory interview – had he seen anyone who shouldn't be there, did he hear anything. His answers, of course, were "no."

But his joy knew no bounds a week later when the pope reappointed him to his old position as prefect of the Congregation for the Doctrine of the Faith.

There was no question in Ruggieri's mind that most people, if they ever found out, would be shocked by his unethical and immoral – even criminal – actions. However, he was convinced the rules didn't apply to him. For his entire life, the maxim "the end justifies the means" had served him well. He occasionally had some qualms that disturbed his conscience, but, at times like that, he would remind himself this is not a perfect world and compromises must be made by the more gifted to achieve progress. Then he would reflect on a saying attributed to Vladimir Lenin: "To make an omelet, you must break a few eggs."

CHAPTER 20

August, 2047
Chicago

Fred was settling in at Kirkland & Ellis again. He was even given his old office back. Rachel Fischer was now his executive assistant, just as before, and nothing could have delighted her more!

"Mr. Whitaker, I can hardly believe I am working for you again. This is better than a dream come true! Never in my wildest imagination could I have guessed . . . you're the best boss I've ever had. I hope this isn't just temporary. This is permanent, isn't it?"

"I'm on board for the long haul, Rachel. It's great to be back, especially since I know we'll be working together again. You're still studying for your certification as a paralegal, aren't you? How's it going?"

"I'll finish my course work by the end of the year," she replied with excitement. "I can hardly wait!"

"I'm sure I'll be able to utilize your new expertise, Rachel. Having this arrow in your quiver will really serve you well."

Rachel prepared an announcement of Fred's return for all K&E's Midwest clients, and Fred made a list of certain former clients he would contact personally to inform them he was back as a partner in the firm. A number of his past clients invited him to meetings, either at their offices or at lunch. In the midst of all this planning, Fred received a phone call from Cardinal Sanjay Patel.

"Mr. Whitaker, I phoned your home and discovered you were with the law firm again. This is good news, since I need to see both you and Mr. Campbell in the next few days."

Fred was astounded. "You want us to come to Rome, Your Eminence?"

"Not at all," he replied. "I've been asked to attend the U.S. Conference of Catholic Bishops meeting in Washington, D.C. in eight days to discuss the status of Catholicism in the subcontinent and Southeast Asia, and its relations with the U.S Catholic Church. I am again archbishop of Bombay, my former assignment. My replacement when I joined Francis Xavier as secretary of state recently passed away. I have been reappointed.

"After my presentation to the USCCB, I want to meet the two of you in Chicago. This meeting must be very confidential. No one must know we are getting together. Can we do this?"

"I'm sure we can, Cardinal. Let me get Mr. Campbell on the phone."

Fred and Scotty agreed to meet with the cardinal, even though Patel would not divulge any specifics about why he needed to see them.

"All I can tell you, gentlemen, is this meeting involves matters of a most urgent nature. It has to do with the very survival of the Catholic Church!"

Chapter 21

A meeting in 10 days was set up with Sanjay Patel. Fred and Scotty blocked out the time, but did not tell any of the staff with whom they were meeting. Further, they decided not to meet with him at K&E's offices. Instead, they reserved a conference room at the Union League Club.

Sanjay Patel arrived at the appointed time in the club lobby, and was warmly greeted by Fred and Scotty. After finding their meeting room, pouring themselves some coffee from a carafe on a side table, and sharing a few cordial pleasantries, Patel got down to the matter at hand.

"I hardly know where to start, gentlemen. We – the entire Catholic Church – has experienced a trauma unprecedented in church history. It is not an overstatement to say it's a crisis of biblical proportions, and it's not over yet."

He paused for at least a minute, his nut-brown brow furrowed, his otherwise trim physique considerably thinner than the last time Fred and Scotty saw him earlier in the year. Sanjay Patel looked wane and tired. His stress level was high, and very evident.

He sipped his coffee and continued. "The ordeal for you, Mr. Whitaker, has been especially brutal. The threats to your life and your family's, the murder of your archbishop, Cardinal Rooney, and then the pope before you could discuss your findings with him – I wish we could say this dreadful chapter of church history is entirely closed. I don't believe it is."

Scotty asked him: "Have the Carabinieri made any headway in solving Francis Xavier's murder?"

"No, they haven't," Patel responded with a large sigh. "Further, the Vatican is giving very little cooperation to the Carabinieri in reconstructing the last few hours prior to the pope's death – what he did, what his schedule was, who saw him.

"Especially troubling is the fact that two people who might have information, are clearly not sharing it – Camerlengo Cardinal Mario Lusardi, and the former prefect of the Congregation for the Doctrine of the Faith."

Fred gasped: "The former prefect – Cardinal Antonio Ruggieri – now Pope Pius XIII?"

Patel didn't say a word. He just nodded slowly.

Scotty jumped into the conversation again. "Cardinal Patel, are you implying the man who is now our pope had something to do with the death of Francis Xavier, or at least, knows who was involved? That's shocking!"

"I am making no accusations, Mr. Campbell. The fact is that Ruggieri, before his election, and Lusardi, his camerlengo, had effectively stonewalled the Italian authorities. With so many cardinals not trusting Antonio Ruggieri in the first place, this lack of cooperation only solidified their negative opinions of the man, and increased their suspicions."

"This hardly seems possible," Fred uttered in total amazement. "If so many cardinals had reservations about Ruggieri, why in heaven's name did the College of Cardinals elect him to be the supreme pontiff of the Catholic Church?"

"A number of factors came into play," Patel responded as he sat back in his chair and folded his hands under his chin. "Francis Xavier was an accomplished leader and very much a progressive. Expectations for his papacy were high.

"However, with his murder, following on the heels of the murder of Chicago's Cardinal Albert Rooney, also a progressive, a wave of acute fear engulfed much of the church's hierarchy – could there be a conspiracy afoot?

"The College of Cardinals was hesitant to take a chance with another liberal pope. The choice for pope this time had to be someone with a proven track record of espousing conservative values."

"Cardinal Patel," Fred interjected, "that still doesn't quite answer the question of why Antonio Ruggieri was elected. There's no lack of conservative cardinals to choose from. Why did the College of Cardinals elect a man whom many did not trust and respect?"

"This was a convoluted process, Mr. Whitaker. Over the years, Antonio Ruggieri saw the priesthood as a means to exercise power and control."

Scotty broke into Patel's narrative. "I've seen parish priests in Chicago who are excessively ego-driven. They alienate both their parishioners and their bishops. And they don't go anywhere. How did Cardinal Ruggieri pull off his advancements?"

"Cardinal Ruggieri always did his job very competently, and made it a point to ingratiate himself with the powers-that-be," Patel continued. "Further, Ruggieri had developed a dossier on many cardinals – facts about them they would not want the rest of the world to know.

"When Pope Francis Xavier was assassinated, Ruggieri saw his opportunity. He had a small cadre of supporters, a group of prelates who owed their positions to him. Ruggieri had pulled the right strings for them, and he could always count on their votes in Conclaves.

"But he needed many more votes to achieve his plan. When the cardinals gathered in Rome for the Conclave, he met with many privately – those for whom he had developed dossiers. In effect, he blackmailed them! He ensured himself he would get their vote."

Fred and Scotty looked at each other in total amazement. Fred spoke.

"This sounds preposterous, Cardinal Patel! How could that happen?"

"Even cardinals have skeletons in their closet, Mr. Whitaker – some cardinals but certainly not most. They may date back decades, but they are there. Ruggieri had informants. He knew everything about everybody!"

Fred gave a large sigh of utter frustration, got up and began pacing the room with his hands in his pockets. About a half a minute later he stopped abruptly, put the palms of his hands on the conference table opposite Scotty and Patel, leaned forward, and shifted his eyes back and forth between these two men.

"Damn it! This can't be the end game! A visionary pope makes me the first lay cardinal in centuries; my mission is successful; I win the support of my archbishop; then the archbishop and pope are murdered; the murders are unsolved; and a questionable pope now leads the church. This positively can't be the end game! Is there nothing we can do?"

"I think there is something we can do," Patel responded with a tone of conviction. "That's why I came to Chicago to see you. I believe we can make a difference, but it will take considerable courage."

***

"Several prominent European laymen have expressed to me their outrage over the unsolved murder of Francis Xavier. They can't believe law enforcement has come up empty-handed, with no viable leads to follow. They want to know what they can do to help, if anything – perhaps bring their influence to bear on the authorities to intensify the investigation."

Fred interrupted Patel. "I must tell you I've had some well-connected Chicagoans – friends of Albert Rooney – come to me with the same frustrations. Not only are they infuriated his murderer hasn't been caught, or even identified, but they're deeply disturbed that my mission – Francis Xavier's mission – to give a voice to the laity was brought to such an abrupt end. They are convinced that Cardinal Rooney's murder and Francis Xavier's assassination are all part of a plot. They want to take action, but feel stymied. They don't know what, if anything, they can do."

Sanjay Patel folded his arms, nodded, and – surprisingly – began to smile. "These prominent leaders in their fields are not alone, I am sure. For every one of them who has come to us, there must be tens of thousands – hundreds of thousands – of Catholics throughout the world who had high hopes for Francis Xavier's plans and now feel totally disenfranchised.

"I've been giving this serious thought, gentlemen. What would you think about us conducting our own investigation?"

CHAPTER 22

Sanjay Patel opened his briefcase and removed a folder.

"Here are the names and the contact information for ten people who are not only anxious to see a full-scale private investigation mounted, but would be willing to make a substantial financial contribution to ensure its success. They are businessmen, lawyers and even a prominent politician. One of them owns a private investigation agency, and says headway can be made if no one knows such an inquiry is in progress. Then the guilty parties are more likely to be caught off-guard.

"These individuals are so concerned about the future of the Catholic Church, and Christianity in general, that they are willing to make a strong commitment – and take considerable personal risk – to solve this blatant threat to the church."

"I assume," Scotty commented with a somewhat incredulous expression on his face, "you think Fred and I should also be interested in getting personally involved in such a risky business."

"More than that," Patel responded. "I would like your firm to take charge of this clandestine effort – if you are interested, if you think it can be done, if you believe you have the expertise. Regrettably, I can't be directly involved in such an enterprise. My profile is too high. There's no way I could keep the Vatican from finding out what I was up to. And, as I think I've already made clear, Pius XIII must never find out about this.

"No one I know is aware I am meeting with you today, except Cardinal Stefano Paganelli. He is the senior cardinal bishop, a man I trust without reservation, and I know he is equally distressed about the turn of events at the Vatican. He is low-key – not on anyone's radar – and is not identified with me. You'll remember our meeting with him the day before Francis Xavier's murder, Mr. Whitaker. At some point, he may be of help to you. I will keep him abreast of what's going on."

Fred and Scotty stared at each other for what seemed like an eternity. Not a word was spoken, but much non-verbal communication was going on.

Scotty spoke. "To answer one of your questions, Cardinal Patel, we do have some expertise in conducting a covert investigation. The White House asked us to oversee a secret investigation four years ago – one they didn't want any federal investigative agency to be aware of for very unique national security reasons. Fred was involved in this operation. We learned a lot about this kind of assignment, and we were successful."

Patel's gut feeling told him he was rendering his audience benevolent – firing Campbell and Whitaker's imaginations, and at some level, their sense of duty. He warmed up to this realization as he continued his argument:

"If you did this successfully, gentlemen, you will go down in history as linchpins in the progress of the modern church, practically propelling it into the 22nd century. Your contributions would play major, if not indispensable, roles in the lives of hundreds of millions of Christians throughout the world for countless centuries. How often do we have a chance to radically impact the course of history in a positive way?"

"Cardinal," Fred responded, "you make your case in a powerful way. The only thing you left out is that Scotty and I would probably be candidates for sainthood!"

All three of them laughed.

"I would vote for that, Mr. Whitaker," Patel added with a broad smile. "I think people have been canonized for a lot less!

"I can hardly expect a snap decision from you – there's too much at stake, I am sure. I fly back to Mumbai late tomorrow afternoon, with a stop in Rome to report on my meeting with the USCCB. I will leave you now, but I'd like to come back to see you tomorrow morning. If the two of you would discuss this issue after I leave, and reach closure on your course of action, then tomorrow we can discuss how to proceed from here, how to maintain confidentiality, and how to help ensure a successful course of action.

"This doesn't give you much time I know, but there are people who are anxious to get going, so I think we must strike while the iron's hot. The sooner we act, the more likely we'll be successful."

Scotty replied, "Please meet us back here in the lobby at 9:30 a.m. tomorrow. Given the urgency of your request to see us, I reserved a room in the Union League Club for two days, just in case."

Chapter 23

When Sanjay Patel arrived at the Union League Club the next morning, the three of them went to the same room they had the day before. A waiter brought them a pot of coffee and a platter of mini-Danish pastries. He put them on a side table with a hot plate for the coffee.

Scotty initiated the conversation. "Fred and I talked for about two hours after you left yesterday, Cardinal. We feel this venture is risky – extremely risky. Under normal circumstances, we would have turned it down without a second thought. But these are not normal times, to say the least. These aren't just plain unsolved murders. We're talking about the pope and our Chicago cardinal archbishop.

"It seems there may be a conspiracy going on at the very highest levels of the church. Such an ungodly scheme threatens the church's very structure and could adversely impact Christians and non-Christians throughout the world for many decades to come. We see this as a serious crisis, and we find it extremely frightening."

Fred broke in. "This is uncharted territory. We lack any benchmarks we can rely on – any precedent we can use as a guide."

"What we're trying to say, Cardinal," Scotty continued, "is that we can hardly say 'no' to you. The stakes are too high. The challenge is too great to pass up. The consequences of just accepting the status quo are unthinkable. We wouldn't have sought out a task like this – not in a blue moon – but it's here, staring us in the face.

We're not turning away. It's got to be done by someone, and we're going to take it on."

Sanjay Patel rose from his seat, reached across the conference table, and shook each man's hand.

"I can find no words to express my relief, gentlemen," he uttered appreciatively. "You've given me a real sense of hope, that whatever evil is threatening the church will finally be brought to an end. I'm confident now we will overcome it!"

***

Patel's list of concerned parties who wanted to help consisted of three Dutch businessmen, two prominent Frenchmen, three German businessmen, a German politician, an Italian lawyer in Rome and an Indian factory owner in Mumbai.

Fred had been contacted by three people: a lawyer he knew from the beginning of his career, an entrepreneur, and a banker. Scotty also had contacts with individuals who were concerned and wanted to help: the owner of a sports team, and the executive director of a major not-for-profit foundation.

This group of personalities comprised an impressive list of movers and shakers from three continents. They were all troubled enough by the events of the past few months that they were willing to stick their necks out and go on record as wanting to do something about it. However, their wanting to do something and their actually signing up to do it were two entirely different things.

"We need to find out how serious these folks are," observed Scotty. "The passion of the moment can impel them to throw their hats in the ring, but more sober consideration later may dampen their ardor for serious risk-taking."

"When I return to Mumbai," responded Patel, "I will contact the people on my list and query them. They need to know we are talking about a significant contribution of time and financial support."

"We'll do the same with our list," added Fred. "Beyond a doubt, a number of them will have second thoughts about personal involvement. As soon as we've firmed up our participants, and you've done the same, Scotty and I will set up a secret meeting so we can get to know each other, establish a plan of attack, and get financial commitments. We're going to need lots of dough!"

"Lots of dough?" Sanjay Patel repeated with a confused expression on his face.

"That's American slang," Scotty volunteered with a big grin. "Fred is saying that to do this successfully, we need to have major financial commitments – we'll need lots and lots of money!"

But Scotty told himself: *More than money, we'll need lots and lots of intestinal fortitude!*

CHAPTER 24

A week later, Cardinal Patel phoned Fred. "Mr. Whitaker, I've finally contacted the 11 individuals I spoke about, and explained fully what would be required if they wanted to be involved. I made it clear that there was no turning back once we got started. Six of them pledged their time and financial support to this endeavor."

"That's excellent, Cardinal. We also called the five names on our list, and three of them want to move ahead with this. We'll be in touch with all nine of them right away to set up a planning session in the near future. We'll be sure to keep you abreast of our progress."

Patel gave Fred the names and contact information for the five Europeans and one Indian who consented to be involved in this mission: Bram Vandelinder, a Dutch banker; Sebastian Gehrmann, a German cargo ship fleet owner; Theodor Keitz, majority owner and CEO of a Frankfurt-based manufacturing conglomerate; Philippe Saint-Martin, a Parisian philanthropist; Paolo Andreano, a prominent lawyer in Rome; and Raj Magar, a venture capitalist in Mumbai.

To this list, Fred added Ben Partelow, a Chicago corporate attorney; Brett Higgins, owner of the security firm that had protected the Whitaker family for the past two years; and Marsha McGuire, executive director of Rotary International and beneficiary of a sizable family fortune.

Before ending his call, Patel added, "I don't think you should be calling me in Mumbai, Mr. Whitaker. There's too great a chance my line may be tapped. I'm calling you now on a phone that's in someone's else's name. I think it's better that I always call you."

"We have an office in Mumbai, Cardinal Patel," Fred responded. "When we need to talk to you, we'll have our resident partner get in touch with you. He'll tell you that your 'nephew' wants to talk to you. Then you can call us. How does that sound?"

"That sounds fine," Patel agreed. "We'll do it that way."

After the call, Fred walked down to Scotty's office, and informed him the team was finalized. "What will we call it, Scotty?"

"How about the 'Working Group?'" he responded.

"Very funny, Scotty," Fred replied with a touch of sarcasm in his voice. "Quite creative!"

"I'm being serious, Fred. This team, as well as our project, has to be completely invisible. 'Working Group' is about as pedestrian a name as you could imagine. If the wrong person heard the name, they wouldn't think anything of it."

The Working Group was now born.

The next order of business was to put together a meeting of these nine individuals, plus Scotty and Fred. Since they were located on three different continents, this was no small task.

With winter not far off, Fred and Scotty had been toying with the idea of a ski vacation with their families at Snowmass in the Colorado Rockies. They had done this before, but not since 2043.

Scotty had a client, Frank Altman, a Texas oil man – a wildcatter – who had a vacation home about three miles northwest of Snowmass Village and had let them use it when he wasn't there. His home had eight bedrooms, a guest house with five additional bedrooms, and a large cavernous living room that would be ideal for meetings.

"Altman's place would be great for such a large group, Fred. It's no mountain cabin – it's a mansion!

"With luck, the 'cabin' will be free for a week this winter. Let me get in touch with Frank, tell him we have a really important client meeting coming up, and see if the house is available anytime between January and March."

Availability turned out to be no problem. Altman had fallen off his motorcycle on a sharp curve recently and broken his right leg in two places. A skiing vacation this year was out, and he told Scotty the house was available anytime he wanted it.

It took three weeks to contact all the people in the Working Group, reconfirm their commitment to the project, and find an open week in their busy schedules to attend this critical first meeting. All of them realized how crucial it was to maintain absolute secrecy.

The agreed-upon cover story was a work meeting and ski vacation with business associates. Three of the members – Keitz, Saint-Martin and Higgins – didn't know how to ski, but they thought it would be fun to take some lessons and finally learn. Scotty said he would arrange that.

Everything was set for the last week in January. Everyone was looking forward to the meeting – everyone including the one participant who had signed on with the sole intention of doing all he could to destroy the Working Group's mission.

CHAPTER 25

Latter Half of 2047
Vatican City

It's been said that clothes make the man. Whether this is true or not, clothes, along with other trappings, give some indication of what sort of man now occupied the Chair of Peter.

In the early 21st century, Pope Francis wore an unadorned simple white cassock with a plain white mozzetta or short cape covering his shoulders. Instead of an ornate gold pectoral cross often worn by a pope, he wore a common iron pectoral cross from his years as an Argentinean bishop. He lived in the Domus Sanctae Marthae, the Vatican guest house, rather than the papal apartments at the Apostolic Palace, and drove a 1983 Renault sedan. Subsequent popes also kept their dress simple, although they moved back to the elaborate papal apartments.

With the June, 2047 election of Pope Pius XIII, a dramatic change of style was ushered in. The red mozzetta was reintroduced – satin in the summer, velvet with ermine trim in the winter. The highly crafted gold pectoral cross was back. Pius XIII not only lived in the papal apartments, but had them lavishly redecorated. Most significant of all was the return of the triple tiara he sported at his inauguration, a regal headdress not worn since Pope Paul VI's installation in 1963. This symbol, more than any other, announced to the world a new day had dawned in the church of Rome. Progressive initiatives were over; leadership would be dictatorial and authoritarian; and failure to follow the Vatican's strict rules and regulations would not be tolerated.

The model for those serving as the pope's advisors also changed dramatically. Every pope has had advisors, and has consulted with them based on their expertise in the issues at hand. Cardinal Ruggieri, as prefect of the Congregation for the Doctrine of the Faith, had developed a closely-knit cabal of seven advisors – more like co-conspirators – who were indebted to him for the positions they held and collaborated with him on his schemes. As Pope Pius XIII, the seven now served as his "kitchen cabinet" - influential churchmen he knew he could depend on without any fear of their violating his confidence.

Now he was counting on their support as he engineered a complete make-over of the Catholic Church.

CHAPTER 26

January, 2048
Colorado

Scotty chartered a 10-passenger turboprop to fly the Working Group from Denver to the Aspen-Pitkin County Airport, not far from where they were staying at Snowmass. Not everyone could get to Denver at the same time, so they agreed to assemble at the Courtyard by Marriott Denver Airport Hotel, arriving over a 48-hour period. The hotel, like most Courtyards by Marriott, was nicely done and comfortable, but not where the rich and famous stay, helping the group keep a low profile.

They boarded their charter flight after all 11 had arrived. The day was cold but clear both in Denver and at Snowmass, with fair weather clouds in between. With only 10 passenger seats, Fred sat next to the pilot in the so-called co-pilot seat, an experience he was looking forward to.

The pilot was gregarious, and explained to Fred everything he was doing, which Fred found fascinating.

"See those clouds below?" the pilot asked Fred. "We can't see a thing, but I have the plane on two beacons – old-fashioned triangulation technology – that tell me exactly where we are. Below us now are the ski slopes of Vail."

All of a sudden, there was a break in the clouds, and skiers could be seen schussing down the mountain below. "See," the pilot said with an ear-to-ear grin, "I told you I know where I'm going!"

Fred laughed, enjoying the banter, and definitely relieved that the pilot, with his 20th century navigational system, knew where he was going.

When they arrived at the airport, a van with ample room for all was waiting for them. The van and driver would be at their service for the entire week. They drove several miles north on Highway 82 to Bush Creek Road, then southwest until they reached the side road leading to Frank Altman's vacation home.

After everyone was settled into their rooms and freshened up, they congregated in the spacious living room for socializing and cocktails. Afterwards, they boarded the van for the drive down Highway 82 to Aspen for the first of many dinners they would enjoy at one of the town's fine restaurants.

The next day they began the routine they would follow for the entire week: breakfast at the house, prepared by Altman's live-in cook and property manager, Jill Blankenship; a three-hour strategy meeting (the first day's meeting began with a short prayer, suggested by Fred); lunch prepared by Jill; skiing on the Snowmass ski slopes until 4:00 p.m.; back to the house to freshen up; cocktails in the living room; and finally dinner in Snowmass or Aspen. Their last evening was a celebratory banquet at Aspen's finest restaurant.

CHAPTER 27

A number of issues were on the agenda for their meetings that week: what work needs to be done, and who will do it; who will co-ordinate this project; what is their timetable; what do they need to do to ensure secrecy; how will they communicate with each other; and last, but definitely not least, how much seed money will they need, what is the maximum amount they will spend, and who will be responsible for the dispersal of these funds.

It was assumed by everyone that Fred Whitaker and Scotty Campbell would run the show. After all, Cardinal Patel had tapped them to organize the affair.

"Fred and I have discussed this thoroughly," Scotty informed them. "Fred will be the man in the field, doing the leg-work, making sure our strategy stays on track. His cover will be that our firm is doing legal work for one of you."

"That should be me," volunteered Theodor Keitz. "Danube Industries is a very big conglomerate, one of the biggest in Germany. One of our companies is always in need of legal work. Besides, we have used Kirkland & Ellis in the past, so your involvement with us wouldn't be unprecedented."

"That sounds good," Scotty responded. "Regarding my role," he continued, "I will serve as overall coordinator. I'll make sure everyone is pulling in the same direction, problems are quickly and successfully solved, and funds are available when we need them. While I do this, I'll continue to manage Kirkland & Ellis.

"It's important that the funds we accumulate stay out of the U.S. – too great a chance it appears like money-laundering if they're kept here. Bram Vandelinder, you own a bank in Amsterdam, and other financial firms. You're the logical person to handle the money."

Bram agreed. "I'd be glad to, Scotty."

"We'll set it up so no funds can be distributed without the secure electronic signature of two of us. Marsha McGuire, that should be you and me. You've managed large sums of money, and I'm a veteran trustee. We've worked together before, and very well. With our signatures verified by Bram, moneys can be distributed. That should establish sufficient fiduciary control."

Ben Partelow, an experienced international lawyer, volunteered to help Fred and Scotty with any legal issues that needed untangling. Sebastian Gehrmann informed the group he had agents in a number of European ports, and they could prove to be valuable sources of information.

Theodor Keitz said one of Danube Industries' companies was a detective agency, and could handle investigative work in Europe. Brett Higgins offered his agency for the Chicago investigation into the death of Cardinal Albert Rooney. He also said his agents would continue to protect the Whitaker family *pro bono.* Saint-Martin, Andreano and Magar, although they had no specific assignments, made it clear they were available for any tasks that materialized for which they were capable.

The remaining task – the pivotal one which would make the rest possible – was funding the scheme.

After some debate and discussion, they decided each member's initial contribution would be five million dollars, or a total of 45 million. (Fred and Scotty were not expected to be contributors, though both said they would give something.) Since the group members had "signed up" for this operation unconditionally, they also committed to further possible assessments, perhaps another five million each, if additional funds were needed for the mission.

They agreed that any of them who ran up expenses for this venture – employee salaries, supplies, travel, etc. – would not contribute those goods and services, but would be reimbursed for them out of the fund in order to maintain transparency and make it possible to monitor costs.

"That includes the protection you give the Whitaker family," Scotty advised Brett Higgins. "The nature of this project demands you continue providing them with security services for the foreseeable future, and you need to be reimbursed."

They ended their series of strategy sessions as they had begun them – with a prayer for the successful completion of their mission.

There was one problem – apparently a small problem. Paolo Andreano said it would be a few weeks before he had sufficient capital available to contribute to the funding. He had an obligation that stood in the way, a temporary matter he assured them. Once it was cleared up, he would transfer the money to the trustee, Bram Vandelinder. The group members all acknowledged this as being acceptable.

What no one could have possibly guessed at the time was that money was the least of their problems with Paolo Andreano. In fact, he would be instrumental in efforts to bring their mission to the brink of failure.

CHAPTER 28

February, 2048
Vatican City

Shortly after his election the previous summer, Pius XIII convened his "gang of seven" to celebrate his ascendancy to the papacy and acknowledge their successful efforts on his behalf. They all knew the days of laissez-faire were over.

Now Pius XIII needed to bring them together again to plan a strategy to reverse the many ill-conceived reforms of his predecessors. Attending this get-together were Cardinals Flavio Scarpelli, prefect of the Congregation for Divine Worship and the Discipline of the Sacraments; Francois Basse, prefect of the Congregation for the Evangelization of Peoples; Angelo Molinaro, prefect of the Congregation for Bishops; Dieter Kaufmann, former archbishop of Munich and Freising, and now secretary of state; Vittorio Tornebene, archbishop of Milan; Antonin Zoromski, former archbishop of Krakow and now prefect of the Congregation for the Doctrine of the Faith; and Umberto Sciara, archbishop of Naples.

Before the meeting, the group received their marching orders: analyze the most flagrant ways the church has deviated from orthodoxy since the Second Vatican Council, and propose actions – short-range and long-range – to rein in the reformers and correct the damage already done.

The meeting was productive. They branded for replacement those bishops and archbishops who were too accepting of lay initiatives that deviated from the ancient practices of holy mother church. They identified for removal prominent theology professors who had been too creative in their handling of time-tested church doctrine, especially in the field of moral theology. Finally, they ferreted out the names of well-known politicians who claimed to be Catholic, but who tolerated – and sometimes even sponsored – government acts and laws antithetical to the church.

In the midst of their meeting, Father Gustavo Bivona, Ruggieri's former secretary and his administrative aide since he became pope, entered the papal library.

"Father Bivona, how dare you interrupt our meeting! I gave you explicit instructions we were not to be interrupted."

"An emergency phone call, Your Holiness! I apologize, but the caller says its information you must have before your meeting is over."

Pius XIII excused himself and went to his den to take the call.

"Your Holiness, this is Paolo Andreano. I have just returned from a meeting in the United States. You and your advisors need to know what transpired, and what the implications are. It's not good news!"

CHAPTER 29

February, 2048
Chicago

Elaine threw her arms around him and gave him a big kiss. "It's good to have you home, Fred. I can hardly wait to hear about how things went at Snowmass!"

Chris left his room on the second floor and ran down the stairs to give his dad a warm welcome. Goldie, their Labrador retriever, jumped up on Fred, whining with excitement. Everyone wanted to hear about the meeting.

They understood that whatever Fred communicated to them about sensitive matters must go no further. As he explained the intricate "plot" the Working Group devised during their week-long retreat at Frank Altman's vacation house, Elaine fidgeted in her seat, her lips tight, her fingers nervously drumming on her thighs.

"Something's clearly the matter, Elaine," Fred observed. "What have I said that's disturbed you?"

Her brow was knitted as she looked up at the ceiling, attempting to find the words she wanted say. Elaine's eyes then settled on Fred and she gave a deep sigh sitting back in her chair and folding her hands in her lap.

"Maybe my ego's offended, maybe I'm a little jealous," she admitted to Fred, now with a faint smile on her face. "I'm embarrassed to say this, but I kind of feel hurt. When you met with Pope Francis

Xavier and took on the Voice of the Laity mission, I was with you. I contributed to your plans, helped analyze your surveys and shared your excitement as the project came together. My life was placed in mortal danger, just like yours.

"Now you've taken on a major assignment to bring the murderers of Cardinal Rooney and Pope Francis Xavier to justice and rid the church of elements threatening its vitality and the well-being of God's children for centuries to come.

"I feel I've been left out, Fred. I had a role before. I see no place for me now. I don't want to be just a placid bystander – I want to contribute."

Fred was stunned, and speechless! Sanjay Patel's unanticipated and unsettling information about the church's crisis and his unprecedented proposal of how to deal with it, had totally preoccupied Fred's consciousness.

"Elaine, you know I couldn't have completed the work for Francis Xavier without your unstinting support and active participation. I'm afraid I've been so preoccupied with the challenge Cardinal Patel threw at Scotty and me that I've been a bit myopic. Or maybe I had blinders on.

"I'm definitely going to need you, sweetheart. The size of this undertaking is overwhelming, mindboggling! I'll be honest with you – I'm not sure if we can pull this off. We've taken on a herculean task, an endeavor with hurdles that so far have stymied the FBI, the Chicago Police Department and the Carabinieri. It seems practically inconceivable that a small band like our Working Group has the foolhardy temerity to even think it could succeed where some of the best investigative organizations in the world have failed. Add to that – we suspect these murders are part of a scheme that may go all the way to the top of church leadership. And did I forget to say this will probably be extremely dangerous? You wonder if I need you? I certainly do! But I don't want to put you in danger."

***

"It's almost five o'clock, Elaine. Care to join me in a before dinner drink?" Fred went into the kitchen, and returned with two bourbons and soda. Chris got himself a can of soda pop from the refrigerator. Elaine sipped her drink, and looked intensely at Fred.

"After the hazards we faced with your assignment from Pope Francis Xavier, I think we both know what danger is like. As a matter of fact, we think it still lurks – look at all the security agents we still have on our property! Being in danger hardly sounds like a problem any more – it's more like the norm around here. The issue is what my role will be. You clearly need all the help you can get!"

Chris sat quietly, listening to this exchange between his mother and father. Finally he spoke up. "Dad, you're not forgetting, are you, I was also pretty involved in your opinion survey project for the pope? You've got another big job now, and I'd like to be part of it. I'm sure Bob would, too, but probably can't since he's about to start med school at Stanford."

The room was now silent. Fred looked at Elaine whose lips were twisted in a smirk. And Chris, whose arms were folded across his chest, had an expression of mild frustration on his face.

Fred got up and threw his arms above his head with some frustration of his own. "Listen, you guys. Neither of you will be on the outside, looking in. I don't have the specifics yet, but there's more work to be done in Chicago than we can even imagine at this moment. Much more than was dumped into our laps by Francis Xavier two years ago.

"I'm not sure how we're going to get from Point A to Point B because I'm not sure where Point B is. We've faced danger before, but the new dangers will be potentially greater by several degrees of magnitude." He fixed his gaze on Elaine. "This worries me, for your safety and Chris's safety – not to mention my safety. We've got to be extremely careful; we can't say anything to anybody. Is this something you are willing to do? Is it something you can do?"

Elaine and Chris looked at each other – Elaine with an expression of grim determination, and Chris with the wide-eyed excitement of someone about to embark on a thrilling adventure.

Elaine spoke up. "Fred, I don't see this as a new project, a new assignment. To me, the task you've accepted from Cardinal Patel is really a continuation of the work you began for Pope Francis Xavier, not something new. Call it 'Phase Two.'

"In 'Phase One,' you accepted the appointment from Francis Xavier as the first lay cardinal in hundreds of years, a major event in the history of the church. You were given the mission of determining what were the hopes, dreams, and aspirations of Chicago's laity, as well as their concerns and issues with the church.

"The 'powers of darkness,' so to speak, did everything possible to defeat your mission, even killing church leaders. Now starts 'Phase Two' of your mission – to find out who the evil-doers are and bring them to justice.

"Remember when you received your assignment from Francis Xavier? Remember you asked me if I was on board for this challenge? I said 'sign me up!' That hasn't changed, Fred. I'm with you all the way."

Chris listened to his mother with highly focused attention. The visage of excitement no longer shined forth from his face. He slumped a bit as she went on.

Finally, when she was finished, he raised his hand as if he were in a class at school and wanted to be recognized by his teacher. His dad looked at him and nodded.

"I can't say it as well as Mom did, but I agree with everything she said. As that old saying goes, 'it ain't over 'til it's over,' and it's not over, Dad. You were awesome in the job you did for the pope, but the bad guys made sure you never got to present your report to the pope and the College of Cardinals. It looks like your job – our job – isn't over.

"I learned a lot in 'Phase One.' I know how to take responsibility and to finish what I started. I'm good at thinking problems through. I hope you don't think I'm bragging, Dad, but you need me. I can help you finish the job."

Fred wasn't sure whether it was a blessing or a curse having his wife and son involved as operators. On the one hand, a high level of professional expertise was needed, more than he could possibly expect from his family, no matter how hard they worked, or how much he trusted them. On the other hand, they would attract little attention, seeming unlikely participants in a clandestine investigation. Further, they could perform tasks and garner data in a casual and informal way that would be extremely difficult for professionals to do without attracting attention.

"Scotty and I have a lot of work to do before we're ready to roll with this thing. In the meantime, give thought to what each of you might contribute to this effort. Consider every idea that comes into your head, even if it seems farfetched. You could be on to something and not even know it. Just remember – nothing about this is to be leaked to anyone, not relatives, not best friends, no one. I can honestly say that to do so could put someone's life in danger, perhaps your own!"

CHAPTER 30

Autumn, 2047
Atlanta

Richard Ciorra had misgivings about assuming the presidency of the United States Conference of Catholic Bishops. Who wouldn't? The Catholic Church in America – like the universal church – was in crisis and had been for most of the century. As archbishop of the Archdiocese of Atlanta, he had faced many challenges: financial problems, dwindling church membership, a lack of priests, a continuing clerical sex abuse problem, and more. He wasn't alone. Bishops throughout the country experienced the same dilemmas but with solutions constantly alluding them. He felt accepting the mantle of USCCB president at this time was tantamount to taking the problems he already faced in Atlanta and multiplying them by approximately 200 dioceses and archdioceses in the country.

To top it off, he would have to speak for the American church at the Vatican, a responsibility that gave him a very uneasy feeling. Things had changed in Rome, and it wasn't for the better. Antonio Ruggieri, the dictatorial and doctrinaire prefect of the Congregation for the Doctrine of the Faith, was now supreme pontiff, and made it clear he intended to give very little autonomy to local churches throughout the world.

This is going to exacerbate problems that are already intractable. People who currently have difficulty with the church will decide it's not worth hanging on any longer!

The latest directive from Rome troubled him greatly – not only him but the majority of USCCB members. Pope Pius XIII had appointed Chicago's auxiliary bishop Thomas Costello as archbishop for that archdiocese, the position the murdered Cardinal Albert Rooney had held.

Shortly after the Holy See announced Costello's appointment, David McLaughlin, cardinal archbishop of New York, vented his frustration and anger to Archbishop Ciorra in a phone call.

"This is preposterous, Richard – totally beyond the pale! It is inconceivable Pius XIII would do anything this insane! To appoint Tom Costello to head the church in Chicago. *Tom Costello*!"

Archbishop Ciorra quickly interjected: "Can you think of any bishop in the USCCB – can you name even one – who has been more ineffective, more useless as a committee member, less incisive in his analysis of issues before us, than this auxiliary bishop of Chicago? I can't think of one!"

"Never in my years serving the church," McLaughlin practically shouted, "have I witnessed an auxiliary bishop made archbishop of an archdiocese without first heading up a smaller diocese for a period of time. And to be appointed Chicago's archbishop – a prelate that usually gets a red hat shortly afterwards – with no previous experience, defies imagination! And unlike his predecessors, the pope didn't even ask for any input from American bishops!

"I phoned Cardinal Stefano Paganelli at the Vatican before I phoned you. He tells me, in his experience, popes always seek the counsel of prominent curial officials and other prelates before appointing a bishop to become head of a diocese or archdiocese. In this case – involving one of the most important archdioceses in the country – the pope spoke to no one whom Paganelli is aware of. This is most distressing."

"Not only that, David," Ciorra added, "but this man is reactionary, an archconservative. He will not only poison the Archdiocese of Chicago, but adversely affect Catholicism throughout the United States."

Chapter 31

Autumn, 2047
Orange County

News of Costello's appointment had a totally different impact on Martin Ramsey, administrator of the Office of Evangelization in Southern California's Diocese of Orange, recently promoted from monsignor to auxiliary bishop. Ramsey was overjoyed! He felt it couldn't get any better than this! As founder of the ultraconservative Ecclesia Vera Society, Ramsey was delighted that the head of its Chicago cell – someone whom he was sure had played a role in the demise of Cardinal Albert Rooney – was now the leader of the Chicago archdiocese.

Of course, he couldn't be absolutely sure what role Costello played in the cardinal's death, since, when he created the Ecclesia Vera Society to purify the American Catholic Church, he wrote rules mandating that no cell should know specifically what another cell was doing. There could then be no shared guilt if one cell got in trouble with the law. What the cells did share, though, was the same goal of purging American Catholicism of even the hint of progressiveness.

The mission of the Chicago cell was to emasculate the Voice of the Laity project, with which Pope Francis Xavier had charged lay Cardinal Fred Whitaker. The murder of Albert Rooney, who supported this project, went a long way toward accomplishing that mission, but Ramsey couldn't be sure Costello was involved in the killing. However, he did put two and two together.

With Antonio Ruggieri – my mentor since I studied for the priesthood in Rome – now the pope, and Tom Costello heading the key Chicago archdiocese, Ecclesia Vera is bound to see success in the United States! Ultimately, with the pope's leadership, the universal church will return to the purity it once enjoyed!

Nothing better could underscore the new leadership style or the new environment Pope Pius XIII was establishing than the Apostolic letter he sent to all bishops shortly after his election. In it, he condemned Francis Xavier's attempt to provide the laity with a stronger say in the policies and governance of Catholicism. He made it unequivocally clear such an innovation was antithetical to the best interests of God's people, and contrary to Christ's intention when he gave the keys of the kingdom to St. Peter.

Never had Martin Ramsey been so optimistic about achieving the Ecclesia Vera's objectives. He had plans, big plans, projects the society could undertake – must undertake – to end Catholic liberalism in the United States. The plans were ambitious, aggressive and even dangerous, but never had the climate been so favorable for moving ahead.

CHAPTER 32

March, 2048
Chicago

Fred and Scotty got together for the first of several meetings. They had an agenda overloaded with challenges:

- *To whom in the K&E office, and elsewhere in Chicago, would they communicate the nature of this project?*
- *What were their priorities, and how would they achieve them?*
- *What specific roles would the Working Group's members play, and how would they get started?*
- *Who outside the Working Group needs to be involved and how can confidentiality be ensured?*
- *What sort of timetable needs to be established, and how will they oversee it effectively?*
- *What threats do they face, and how can they mitigate the danger?*
- *As managing partner of K&E, how does Scotty keep his hand on the tiller without exposing the new responsibility he has assumed?*

"Scotty, Elaine knows what we're up to. There's no way I can keep such a secret from her. Our marriage is founded on an unshakable mutual trust, and to my knowledge we've never let each other down. Even my son Chris – only 15 now – knows about the project. He is trustworthy beyond any question. During my mission for the pope, he grew up quickly, and my confidence in him is without reservation.

"Both of them are itching to be involved. I can't say 'no' to them. They were invaluable during my work for Francis Xavier, and I'm sure they will be again. They can do things that you or I couldn't do without drawing unwelcome attention."

Scotty approved. Fred was greatly relieved, since he had already told his wife and son there would be a place for them.

"In smoking out the Chicago perpetrators, they'll be lots to do," Scotty agreed. "I have a feeling they'll find things that otherwise might be overlooked. Now, what do you think about our own staff?"

"I can't visualize proceeding without the cooperation of our executive assistants" Fred responded. "I have unqualified confidence in Rachel. During the analysis of the opinion survey, she was indispensable in the effort. She has a fine analytical mind and solved problems that stymied the rest of us. As you know, she's now a paralegal, which will make her even more valuable."

"My feelings are the same about Barbara, Fred. We've worked together for years. She's never let me down."

They called Rachel Fischer and Barbara Nagle into Scotty's office for an afternoon meeting, explaining the project fully, including the dynamics leading up to the decision to attack these problems and how crucial it was to maintain complete secrecy. Fred and Scotty were also completely candid about the potential dangers facing anyone working on the project.

"Think this through, consider whether you can make such a commitment, and get back to us," Fred requested as the meeting drew to a close.

"I don't need to think it through," Rachel volunteered as soon as Fred finished speaking. "I'm on board all the way. When I worked with you and your family on the opinion survey analysis, Mr. Whitaker, I developed a keen sense of how the lives of so many people would be favorably affected by what we were doing. Cardinal Rooney and Pope Francis Xavier were murdered, and all of our hard work seemed for naught. To me, this new effort seems to be a continuation of our project. Now we're going to make things right, bring justice, and finally give the people what they need."

Fred displayed a broad smile, and nodded. "I knew I could count on you, Rachel. You've just added to my sense of confidence about the project."

Barbara spoke up. "Rachel, you told me a lot about what you were doing with the Whitakers. I found it fascinating, and extremely important. I love the work I do for Mr. Campbell, and he knows that," she declared with a big smile in Scotty's direction, "but I must admit I felt a little jealous about what you were doing. Now Mr. Campbell is asking me to be a player in a crucial drama to see justice is done and Mr. Whitaker's mission resurrected – a drama fraught with danger and hard work. I can't say 'no.' I don't need to sleep on this. My decision is made."

Scotty stood up, put his hands on his hips, and announced with untypical enthusiasm in his voice. "You know, there's that secret bar hidden behind the mahogany paneling at the end of the office I usually open only for important clients. This afternoon I'm making an exception. It's almost five o'clock – let's seal this significant working relationship we've just hammered out with a drink together!"

CHAPTER 33

Fred and Scotty filled the next three days with many hours of intense planning. After consulting with Theodor Keitz at Danube Industries in Frankfurt, they decided Fred would leave for Germany in a few days to meet with Theodor and Adolf Klein, the head of Danube's detective agency, Apollo Protection and Security.

Scotty was to remain behind the scenes in Chicago, coordinating activities and making sure the plan stayed on track and was moving in the right direction. Elaine would work closely with Brett Higgins, the owner of the Great Lakes Security firm who was overseeing the Chicago portion of the investigation. Brett would determine what avenues Elaine could pursue more effectively than his own agents, many of whom Elaine knew well because of the months of protection the Whitakers had received from Great Lakes.

The plan for Chris's role could best be described as *ad hoc*. His main job was to do his high school work, and his services would only be used on occasion as needed.

***

At the end of the last session, after plans were finalized, and all members of the Working Group were phoned and briefed on the game plan, Fred returned home and filled Elaine in on the final arrangements.

"I'm leaving for Frankfurt in nine days, sweetheart. Before I go, I want to take care of any loose ends – anything that can't wait for me to return after a two-week hiatus. Think about any repair jobs I've forgotten about – now's the time I should do them."

"At the moment I can't think of anything," Elaine replied. "However, I guarantee you as soon as your plane takes off, all sorts of things will come to mind!"

Chris was disappointed the plan didn't include a defined assignment for him, but his father assured him he would have a role to play.

"When we were analyzing the opinion survey data, Chris, you were invaluable. You could see certain issues that alluded the rest of us. I'm quite sure this will happen again. Also, there will be situations where we need answers, and a security detective's involvement would be all too obvious. That's where you might come in, sort like a stealth bomber. You could get answers but remain practically invisible."

Fred's assurance made Chris feel better – gave him some peace of mind that he wasn't going to be on the outside looking in.

As Fred's departure date approached, he felt a sense of confidence. So much careful planning had gone into this, so much strong commitment from people who could make things happen. It wasn't going to be easy, he realized, but they were ready. Fred radiated optimistic self-assurance. One way or another, he was sure, this scheme was going to work.

Little did he know that, even before he boarded the plane for Frankfurt, the plan was being radically compromised.

Chapter 34

March, 2048
Vatican City

Paolo Andreano had never been to Cardinal Mario Lusardi's office before. Lusardi's suite, located on the floor below the papal apartments, had a dark mottled marble floor which was partially covered with exquisite oriental rugs that blended so well they could have easily been custom-woven for the setting. Two walls were mahogany-paneled, a third one fitted with a large mahogany floor-to ceiling bookcase, extending corner-to-corner. It was replete with ancient books and manuscripts, which probably should have been conserved in humidity and temperature controlled library stacks, and contemporary volumes on a wide range of fiction and non-fiction themes. In the center of the room, in front of a large window overlooking St. Peter's Square, was the camerlengo's highly-polished desk, a beautiful leather inset with decorated margins of gold inlay adorning the top surface.

Paolo thought his meeting with Lusardi went well. Although he hadn't expected the invitation, he really wasn't surprised. His phone conversation with the pope a few days before was brief but to the point. He didn't know all the details yet, but Paolo was sure Pius XIII was experiencing fully the impact of what transpired at the Working Group's Snowmass meeting two weeks ago. The pope's grim tone of voice led Paolo to believe the former Cardinal Ruggieri was now determined to take appropriate action.

So a call from the camerlengo appeared to be the next logical step. The pope needed to follow up, but he couldn't afford the possible exposure of meeting personally with Andreano, nor could he ask his secretary of state Dieter Kaufmann to do so for the same reason. It had to be a confidant of his, but one less likely to draw unwelcome scrutiny if noticed by others. Lusardi's involvement made sense, and came as no surprise to Paolo.

As he crossed St. Peter's Square to take a cab back to his office, he reviewed in his mind what had transpired.

"How big a threat will this scheme present to the holy father," the camerlengo had asked him. "What can be done to stop it in its tracks before it gains momentum?"

Paolo was convinced the threat was significant, and aggressive action was indicated. "We must move quickly," Paolo had insisted, "and luck is on our side. One of the group's members is Theodor Keitz, who owns a prominent detective agency in Frankfurt – Apollo Protection and Security. The plan is to have this firm involved in the investigation. One of their detectives is Raoul Maltese, a man indicted for fraud and embezzlement eight years ago in Milan. I was able to get the indictment vacated, and with his record clean, he was hired by Apollo. He is indebted to me. He will be our source of inside information – I am sure of that. I will contact him right away."

Paolo enjoyed a feeling of substantial satisfaction as he exited St. Peter's Square on its eastern end. *What a smart decision I made to affiliate with this Working Group. With this sort of inside information, we may be able to clip the wings of their project before it even gets off the ground!*

Chapter 35

Andreano's concern for Pope Pius XIII's welfare was deeply rooted, going back many decades. Like Antonio Ruggieri, he was born and raised in Cosenza, and the affairs of his family, like the Ruggieri's, were intimately intertwined with the Mafia who prevailed in the Calabria region. Paolo attended the same high school as Antonio, and got to know him well.

"Paolo, you and I think so much alike," young Antonio would say to him. "Our careers will probably be different, but we must always stay in touch. I think we're going to need each other."

Paolo's father, Cesare Andreano, could be described as a corporate farmer. Over the years, he launched or purchased several farms producing a variety of crops, including figs, eggplant, bergamot oranges, several cereal grains, and olives. These agricultural enterprises expanded so much over the years, thanks in part to his father's Mafia connections, that members of the local farming community typically referred to the conglomerate as the "Andreano Empire."

Cesare's connection to organized crime was especially pronounced in products created from olives and bergamot oranges. His olive oil was shipped to the U.S. and distributed by American Mafia families with close connections to Calabria's criminal organizations. Perfumes made from the rinds of Andreano's bergamots were also controlled by the Mafia, who made sure other suppliers never out-competed them.

Roberto, Paolo's older brother, was groomed to take over the family business. Paolo attended law school, and afterwards oversaw the family's business interests in Rome, the distribution hub for most of their products. As a side line, he watched out for Antonio Ruggieri's legal interests as he ascended the Vatican hierarchy. Several times, he was able to remove regulatory obstacles for Antonio and deflect even the slightest suspicion his activities were not above reproach.

"Antonio, you have so much on your mind, so many irons in the fire," Paolo often reminded him. "Any time you feel one of your activities might raise eyebrows, talk to me first. There's always more than one way to approach a problem. Some are safe, others are not and will cause problems." Ruggieri regularly repaid him by using his curial influence and position to benefit the Andreano business interests.

Prior to the Conclave that elected him pope, Paolo's counsel proved especially valuable to Ruggieri as he pressured vulnerable cardinals to vote for him. Paolo coached Antonio on how to lean on these churchmen in such a subtle manner that no one could later prove he had coerced them.

Paolo Andreano also ingratiated himself to many of the top-ranking prelates of the Holy See, offering legal advice and providing them with products from the Andreano empire as gifts. He was trusted by most, and frequently taken into their confidence. Because of this, he was often able to provide Ruggieri with valuable intelligence about what was transpiring in other Vatican departments.

After Ruggieri became Pope Pius XIII, Andreano was aware several prominent Catholics had approached the former secretary of state, Cardinal Sanjay Patel, to express their frustration about the Carabinieri's lack of success in its investigation of Francis Xavier's murder and their desire to see that justice was done.

In order to find out what was going on, Paolo also offered his services. "Cardinal Patel, this is terrible," Paolo asserted dramatically and convincingly. "The murder of Francis Xavier must be solved. Perhaps I can help."

When the Working Group was finally organized, Paolo was delighted to be in a position to learn, first hand, about any actions being taken that were not in the pope's best interests, and let him know on a timely basis.

After the Snowmass meeting, Paolo Andreano was convinced the pope needed to render the Working Group powerless as quickly as possible, before it gained momentum. Paolo decided it was his responsibility to make sure that happened.

Chapter 36

April, 2048
Frankfurt

Fred arrived at the Frankfurt Airport mid-morning on April 5. Outside the customs area, he was met by a limousine driver from Danube Industries, holding a sign with his name on it. The driver sped down the autobahn to the center of town and dropped him off at the Hilton Mainz, just blocks from the *Kaiserdom Sankt Bartholomäus,* Frankfurt's Catholic cathedral. After checking in and freshening up, Fred went to the lobby to join Danube Industries' president Theodor Keitz, and Adolf Klein, head of its Apollo Protection and Security subsidiary. Then the three took another DI limousine to a luncheon meeting at the unique Main Tower Restaurant and Bar.

As Fred entered the restaurant with Keitz and Klein, he couldn't help thinking of two classic cartoon characters. *I believe I've come to Frankfurt to work with Mutt & Jeff!* Theodor Keitz was about six feet tall, thin, well-dressed, with a neatly-trimmed mustache and a full head of dark-brown hair. Adolf Klein, in contrast, was at least six inches shorter with a beer-belly, thick glasses, bushy mustache and just a fringe of graying black hair. His black suit and bow tie looked like he had bought them at a second-hand store. A green eyeshade would have completed his image as a back-office bookkeeper rather than the head of a prominent detective agency, but his appearance probably was an advantage in his line of work.

Adolf was a plain-spoken man, serious, offering very little evidence he had a sense of humor. For the most part, he listened to what Fred and Theodor had to say, and joined in the conversation only when he had a substantive contribution to make. Fred considered this to be an asset, given the nature of what they planned to accomplish together. On the downside, Adolf was a habitual smoker. Fred hated cigarette smoke, and considered this reality a definite liability.

"Adolf has been briefed on the Working Group – how it was formed, who the members are, and what our mission is," Keitz informed Fred as he opened the conversation. With a wide smile, and a pat on Klein's back, he added "This man is completely trustworthy. I would trust my life to him – as a matter of fact, I have on several occasions, and I'm still here to tell you about it." This triggered a little laughter, and was a nice ice-breaker for the serious matters they needed to discuss.

Keitz outlined in detail their cover story, which was straightforward and with few apparent hitches. Fred was on assignment at Kirkland & Ellis' Frankfurt office to assist with legal matters involving the acquisition of an American chemical company by Palatine Chemicals, an Italian subsidiary of DI. Nothing unusual about that scenario. Apollo was already engaged in providing security for Palatine's main facility outside of Rome so, at least initially, there should be no obvious or overt activities to draw attention to Fred or Apollo.

"Theodor, you've planned this exactly the way we need to operate," Fred acknowledged. "Nothing out of the ordinary should occur to focus a spotlight on what we're really doing. It would be ideal if we could maintain this level of anonymity during our entire investigation to help ensure not only our effectiveness, but also our personal safety."

During the next few days, Fred toured Danube Industries' expansive Frankfurt facilities, covering a 60-acre plot of land. He met with the principal executives, and familiarized himself with their operations. This is exactly what he should be doing prior to launching into the issues involved in Palatine Chemicals' acquisition of the American company.

Fred spent a fair amount of time with Adolf Klein, presumably discussing security issues that might be exacerbated by the acquisition, but in reality, planning what they needed to do to develop leads in this stalled murder investigation. From previous investigations, Adolf had excellent connections with several senior Carabinieri officials who would be valuable sources of information and would also help them avoid being placed in a competitive posture with the Italian authorities.

***

Raoul Maltese felt very beholden to Paolo Andreano, more than Andreano could ever have imagined. Maltese's 2040 indictment in Milan, vacated through Andreano's machinations, would have proved disastrous if he had gone to trial. The discovery process and the testimony of witnesses would have uncovered several other serious legal violations for which Maltese had never been charged, leading to more indictments, guilty verdicts, and a long prison sentence. Raoul was more than happy to supply Andreano with whatever information he could garner.

"Paolo, I have little I can tell you at the present time," Raoul admitted to Andreano in a phone conversation a few days after Fred's arrival. "Nothing special seems to be going on. Since Whitaker's arrival, he's been looking around, meeting with all the big shots, talking with our lawyers – nothing surprising. I got to meet him, asked him about what he was doing. Nothing strange. I did find out he would leave for Rome in two days to visit our Palatine Chemicals Company subsidiary."

"Keep your eyes and ears open, Raoul. Somebody has got to know something. Ask questions but don't be nosey – don't draw attention to yourself, or cause suspicion. Let me know if you find out anything. Important people at the Vatican need to know what's going on."

CHAPTER 37

Autumn, 2047
Chicago

Martin Ramsey, creator and head of the Ecclesia Vera Society, believed the time was ripe for more aggressive action.

With Antonio Ruggieri elected Pope Pius XIII and Tom Costello now archbishop of Chicago, he was ready to move the Society forward. Although he could act with autonomy in setting the Society's agenda, Ramsey believed prudence dictated he consult with the leaders of other cells in the country to make sure his decisions were fully supported. In light of Tom Costello's elevation, he considered him to be first among equals and he made an appointment to see him in Chicago.

"I'm so pleased for you, Tom! Your elevation as spiritual leader of one of the most important – if not *the* most important – archdioceses in the country is not only good for you, but for the Chicago church and for the work of Ecclesia Vera. I have a number of plans – aggressive plans – for Ecclesia Vera that I want to pursue, and I want to talk to you about them first.

"There are dioceses and archdioceses initiating progressive programs, exactly the kind Pope Pius XIII disallowed in his Apostolic Letter. This must stop! Certain lay groups are putting pressure on their bishops to make ecclesiastical changes antithetical to Catholic doctrine. This is not acceptable!"

Tom Costello's elevation to archbishop of Chicago not only stunned other American prelates, but practically everyone who knew him. But for the election of Antonio Ruggieri to the papacy, Costello would have gone no farther. He had reached the height of his career as a Chicago auxiliary bishop – an appointment partly due to support from Cardinal Ruggieri who had been his mentor ever since Costello was his student at the Gregorian University decades earlier.

Costello wasn't even a competent auxiliary bishop. He was clearly a sycophant, and along with the Ruggieri connection, had advanced his career through his ingratiating mannerisms, insincere support rendered to his superiors, and glib style of communication. He talked a good game, but didn't play one.

Costello never stuck his neck out, never took a chance. When the hard decisions had to be made, he would procrastinate endlessly, hoping the problem would go away or someone else would take care of it. When Ecclesia Vera, at the behest of Cardinal Ruggieri, commissioned the Chicago cell to emasculate Pope Francis' Voice of the Laity mission entrusted to Fred Whitaker, Costello dumped all of the hard work into the lap of Roméo Hayek, the heavy-handed president of Streeterville Construction. Hayek was action-oriented, and often ruthless. Costello preferred not to even know what Roméo was doing.

The newly-elected Pope Pius XIII was well aware of Tom Costello's shortcomings, but he felt he would be useful as Chicago's new "ordinary" – the bishop who heads a diocese or archdiocese. Costello was very conservative, wouldn't question the pope's directives, and wouldn't introduce any innovations that reflected the post-Vatican II era. Rather, he would help Pius XIII reinstate the doctrinaire and inflexible environment of the past.

After mulling over Ramsey's proposals for a minute or two, Costello finally spoke. "Martin, as always, you have good ideas, and they're very imaginative. But I think you're moving too fast. Your plans would focus too much attention on Ecclesia Vera cells in too many parts of the country, and could get them in trouble. We're still fearful here in Chicago the authorities will uncover evidence in the death of Cardinal Rooney implicating our local operatives. You should be very careful as you put pressure on local bishops to undo some of the ill-conceived changes that came about after Vatican II. Work slow, but sure!

"In Chicago, I plan to make certain our seminary professors are teaching in a traditional manner, and to appoint only parish pastors who have good conservative credentials. I want to make sure, before I'm through, that Chicago is a showcase of conservative orthodoxy."

Martin returned to Southern California, very disappointed in Costello's cautious approach.

After what Chicago has been through during the Whitaker travesty, I suppose Tom has reason to be careful. Still, I think we can shake up the progressives in other cities more aggressively. I'd like to have his agreement, but I don't work for Tom. I'll move ahead on this, in my own way!

Chapter 38

April, 2048
Chicago

Elaine Whitaker was torn. She couldn't figure out how to pull this off.

Before Fred's departure to Frankfurt, she had told him, in no uncertain terms, that she was determined to participate in doing what the Chicago Police Department and the FBI had so far failed to do – solve the mystery of the mayhem, the murders, and the threats to their family's safety. While Fred was attempting to unravel the plot in Europe, Elaine was focused on making her mark, contributing to the local effort to untangle the Chicago connection.

The trouble was she had a full-time job, a very busy full-time job, as a senior manager at the Muscular Dystrophy Association. During Fred's mission for Francis Xavier, she had taken time off from the MDA on two occasions – about four months in total – to assist with the structure and analysis of the opinion survey of current and former Chicago Catholics. The executive director was very supportive of her efforts, especially in light of the courage and determination the Whitaker family had demonstrated in the face of substantial personal risk.

Things are different now, however. I can't tell the executive director or anyone else about the Working Group's mission. Even if I could, he might be reluctant to give me more time off. I'm not sure how I should handle this.

One option was to retire from MDA – something she had considered when Fred retired from Kirkland & Ellis. They had big travel plans, so retirement seemed to make sense. Then, practically – out of nowhere – came the pope's summons, and travel plans went on indefinite hold.

Before leaving for Frankfurt, Fred recommended she talk to Brett Higgins, head of Great Lakes Security, about the role she might play in this drama. The starting point, Elaine decided, was to talk to Brett about how she might contribute to the effort, and then determine what to do about her work at MDA.

Chapter 39

Great Lakes Security's office, on North Clark Street in Chicago's Uptown neighborhood, was about as unassuming as a business address can get. It was in the middle of a block with small store fronts in one- or two-story buildings, many establishments poorly signed, and some identified only by the address plate on the door. Great Lakes was one of them.

Somehow this all seemed very appropriate. It was an out-of-the-way location – away from the hustle and bustle of the Loop – and had an entrance door you would totally miss if you didn't have the exact address. For an organization often engaged in secretive, low-profile assignments, this place of business seemed consistent with its work.

Elaine arrived at the address for her appointment with Higgins about 20 minutes ahead of time, since she had given herself some leeway in case of traffic problems. She thought she must have come to the wrong address, and she double-checked the firm's business card Fred had given her. Being early, she wandered along the block to see what else was there – a yoga studio, a paint store, a smoke shop, a window blinds store, a real estate agency.

The door to Great Lakes was locked, so she rang the bell; the receptionist buzzed her in. A minute or so later, Brett Higgins came out of his office and greeted her, the first time she had ever met him. Elaine, just five feet, four inches tall, was used to looking up at most men, but Higgins was barely two inches taller. He was perhaps in his 40s, brown hair, a short salt & pepper beard, and a well-developed physique that gave evidence of serious body-building. Elaine was surprised to see him casually dressed – sport shirt, blue jeans and sneakers – since all of the agents providing protection for the Whitakers during the past three years consistently wore coats and ties. He ushered her into his office, a tastefully appointed space that belied the expectations one might have, having seen the building's exterior.

"Mrs. Whitaker, before Fred left, he mentioned I would probably hear from you. He told me about the great contributions you made to Pope Francis Xavier's assignment. Eric Johnson, your family's security detail head, told me how impressed he is with you – especially the way you handled things when the stresses on your family's safety were most intense."

All this was true, but it belied Brett's reservations about having Fred's wife involved in such a sensitive and potentially hazardous undertaking. He was used to the danger that was always a part of such clandestine operations — it came with the territory. His agents, some of them women, were as well. But they were highly trained, and most were former local or federal law enforcement officers.

This is Fred Whitaker's wife! What if something happens to her on my watch? It will be my responsibility! She's a business woman – what qualifies her to do dangerous investigative work? I can't visualize any way I can use her.

"Mr. Higgins, ever since Fred left for Europe, I've been considering what I could possibly do that might be of value to the project. Obviously, I have no training or background in law enforcement or criminal investigation, and I'm not a lawyer. I'm a manager and a good one. I also have a very good mind for detail. I've been really thinking about my involvement for the past few days, and I want to make some suggestions."

Higgins felt a sense of relief, since Elaine seemed to be a realist. She didn't fancy herself as a latter day Nancy Drew or some kind of Wonder Woman. He wanted to hear what sort of ideas she had.

"Call me 'Brett,'" he requested. "and may I call you 'Elaine?'"

"Of course you may," Elaine responded.

"There are a couple of things I can do that may help develop leads that might otherwise be overlooked. I know you're aware of the opinion survey of Chicago's Catholics and non-Catholics Fred conducted when he was a lay cardinal, working for the pope. The survey had statements with which a person could agree or disagree and indicate how important those statements were, just by placing check-marks in boxes.

"At the end of the survey, there was a page where respondents could write opinions, questions, problems or amplifications – in fact, anything they felt was important to make the survey form a better reflection of their opinions. We received hundreds of thousands of these hand-written additions, and had to categorize each one of them according to the survey's parameters.

"But just pigeon-holing these additions according to fixed parameters left a lot of information unaccounted for – complaints about certain clergymen, hearsay, attitudes fellow parishioners exhibited that the respondent found troubling, and so on. I think a detailed re-analysis of these hand-written comments might point to some patterns, some clues to get us closer to the perpetrators."

Higgins smiled, folded his hands on his desk and leaned forward. "I think I see where you're going with this, Elaine. You have the experience with the data, and the expertise to perform such an analysis."

"That's exactly what I'm thinking," Elaine responded. "Not only that, but I have a team of two good analysts to help me—analysts who are familiar with the data. One is Fred's executive assistant, Rachel Fischer, who was invaluable to our project last year. The other is my son Chris, a junior in high school who sees things from a very different perspective. Both of them know about the Working Group, and both of them are without question reliable, and will keep everything totally confidential.

"I can't say what we'll come up with. But out of hundreds of thousands of hand-written responses, we are bound to discover something of value."

Brett got out of his seat, came around the desk, and warmly shook Elaine's hand. "You're on! When can you start?"

Chapter 40

April, 2048
Rome

Adolf Klein accompanied Fred Whitaker to the offices of Palatine Chemicals Company outside of Rome. There was nothing unusual about Adolf's visiting Palatine. Apollo had a security detail there and every few weeks he would make a site visit to make sure everything was being handled properly.

While still in Frankfurt, Fred and Adolf had mapped out a strategy they believed would help them be productive.

"Our first priority is to meet with Divisional Colonel Carlo Laurenti of the Carabinieri," Adolf informed Fred. "We've cooperated over the years on some very demanding problems, some involving serious crimes. We've avoided conflict by communicating clearly and honestly."

Fred knew from his experience as a litigator that nine-tenths of the battle was good communications, but still he was quite incredulous.

"I can't help but believe this situation is distinctly different from the other situations in which you were involved with the Carabinieri, Adolf. We're talking about an open case –an extremely high-profile case – which the Italian authorities have been unsuccessful in solving – the murder of a pope! The pressures on the Carabinieri must be intense, the embarrassment they're experiencing overwhelming.

Then in comes a German detective firm with the temerity to believe it can contribute to the resolution. And not only that – the director of this effort is an American lawyer! I wouldn't be surprised if your Colonel Laurenti kicked us out of his office in less than five minutes!"

Adolf gave a tight-lipped smile with his eyes closed, squeezed his cheeks with his left hand, slowly shaking his head. He took a puff of his cigarette, placed it on the rim of his ash tray, folded his hands in his lap and looked at Fred. "Everything you say is rational, I can't deny that. But I don't think it will play out that way. Every time my agency has worked with Colonel Laurenti and his department, we've kept a very low profile. We've also made it a point not to take credit for the results, so there is never any embarrassment or competition. Of course, we would like to get credit more often, but this way we have the cooperation of perhaps the best law enforcement organization in Europe. And we get the job done."

"That's great!" Fred responded. "Without a doubt, you have the right formula for working with the Carabinieri successfully."

I've seen so many instances in the past, he thought to himself, *when, instead of cooperating, agencies in the U.S. get into jurisdictional disputes, with the result that nobody is effective in getting the job done.*

Their first two days at Palatine Chemicals precisely followed the official "script" for the trip. Fred met with Palatine's officers and in-house counsel to discuss the issues regarding the upcoming acquisition of the American firm, and Adolf got together with the agents assigned to the company to discuss any security problems they were facing.

On the third day, Fred and Adolf went to Colonel Laurenti's office in downtown Rome. Laurenti, a man in his early 50s and of medium height, rotund, balding and sporting a bushy white mustache, greeted them warmly, invited them to be seated on a sofa in a small sitting area, and offered them tea or coffee.

Adolf initiated the conversation. "Colonel Laurenti, you already know a little about our project from the phone conversation we had a few days ago, but I'll let Mr. Whitaker fill you in on the details. He'll tell you why we need to share our mission with you in complete confidence."

Given what Adolf had told Fred about Apollo's relationship with the Carabinieri, Fred had prepared his presentation for Laurenti carefully, avoiding any statement that might intimate the Working Group intended to steal law enforcement's thunder. He underscored that what he was about to tell Laurenti was strictly confidential, totally privileged information. Laurenti agreed.

Fred described the mission in detail: Cardinal Patel's role in creating the Working Group; the group's organization and funding; their suspicion that Francis Xavier's murder was the result of an internal Vatican plot; the possible connection with Cardinal Rooney's murder in Chicago; concerns about how the current pope was elected; and, finally, the group's belief that, operating out of sight, it would be ideally placed to uncover important information the perpetrators had hidden from the Carabinieri, the Chicago Police Department and the FBI.

In his presentation, Fred told the colonel how he was selected to be the first lay cardinal in centuries, his mission, and the violence it triggered. He finished his narration by telling the officer: "It seems highly likely to us that a common thread runs through all this mayhem, and that solving one murder will lead to the solution of the rest. Cardinal Patel believes even the murder of Cardinal Christian Bauer eight years ago may be connected."

"Gentlemen," Carlo Laurenti stated after Fred had finished speaking, "I am impressed by the initiative you have taken, especially since, as you know, it is not without danger. Several months ago, our crime lab found an unusual protein in the heart muscle of Pope Francis Xavier. We asked the Munich authorities to exhume

Christian Bauer's remains and examine his heart for the same protein. We also asked the Chicago Police Department to do the same with Cardinal Rooney's remains. With both requests, we included small samples from the pope's heart. Both Munich and Chicago recently informed us the identical protein was found in Bauer and Rooney's hearts.

"There is no question there is a connection among the murders. Something was injected into their hearts, but we have no idea what it was. None of the examining laboratories have ever seen anything like this – it has to be something new. If we knew what it was, and who made it, that might lead us to the killer or killers."

"Is there no residue from the substance, no unusual chemicals somewhere in the body?" Adolf asked him.

"That's what's so strange," Laurenti replied. "No foreign substance is found anywhere in the bodies. And the protein itself is not abnormal – it just isn't normally seen in the heart muscle."

"It's a little bit like shooting in the dark, but it does provide a starting point," Fred commented. "It's certainly better than nothing. Someone, somewhere in this world, besides the killers, knows about this substance, and where it came from. Out of the eight billion people on earth, we've got to find out who that is. We'll go to work on it, and keep you apprised of our progress."

Colonel Laurenti rolled his eyes and shook his head. "I don't expect to hear from you very soon!"

CHAPTER 41

Fred personally took on the task of searching out the origin of this deadly substance. He was sure his investigative abilities, honed over years as a litigator, made him the logical person to pursue what seemed like a hopeless task. Meanwhile, Adolf had several informants who had first-hand knowledge of the comings and goings of the organized crime families in Rome and its environs, and he surreptitiously tracked them down in a manner that wouldn't blow their cover. Even an iota of a lead, no matter how tenuous, might point to something bigger.

Scotty had informed the members of the Working Group that Fred had gone to Frankfurt to meet with Theodor Keitz prior to going to Rome with the head of Keitz's security firm. Andreano, of course, knew that already, and since he had Fred's cell phone number, he phoned him in Rome to find out what he was doing, and how he could be of help.

Fred had serious reservations about Paolo – something about him didn't ring true. During the Snowmass meeting, Paolo had little to contribute to the discussions, which troubled Fred. Here was a man who traveled half way around the world for a critically important gathering, but had little to say. Moreover, he was the only one who hadn't honored his financial contribution immediately and was, in fact, still in arrears. A call from Paolo made him uncomfortable.

Paolo exuded enthusiasm: "Fred, welcome to Rome! I see you are wasting no time in pursuing the goals we established at Snowmass. That's excellent! How are things progressing, and what can I do to help?"

Pay what we agreed to in Colorado would be a good start, Fred felt like saying.

"Everything is going well, Paolo. We're generating possible leads. It'll take time to follow up on them, but it's a start."

"What kind of leads?" Andreano asked. "And who are you talking to? I'm sure that, with my Roman connections, I can be of help."

Somehow, his eagerness to "help" didn't appear genuine. Adolf and Fred had agreed they wouldn't discuss the details of their activities with anyone, including Working Group members, except on a "needs know" basis. He would put Paolo off.

"We're engaged in several things, Paolo, and as they pan out, we'll have more to say. I appreciate your offering to help us. If we need assistance, I'll be sure to call you."

"I'm really anxious to help" Paolo insisted. "I know my way around Rome. I have a multitude of valuable contacts. I'm sure I can be of great assistance to you during this phase. We must get together and talk about how we're going to proceed. When can I see you? Perhaps later today, or tomorrow? What will be the most convenient time for you? I can work around your schedule."

Red flags were running up all over the place. "I'll let you know when I need to talk to you, Paolo. I have to run now. Thank you for your interest." Fred hung up before Paolo was able to respond.

Fred joined Adolf for lunch at a restaurant near Palatine Chemicals, and filled him in on his earlier conversation with Andreano. "Adolf, I never thought I would be asking you to investigate a member of our

Working Group, but I have serious misgivings about Andreano. See what you can find out about him – his background, his activities in Rome, his business connections – everything you can. Something's not kosher here, and the sooner we know what it is, the better."

CHAPTER 42

Fred was not sure where to start his investigation. He thought of searching out Italian research chemists to see what they knew, but he gathered from their discussion with Colonel Laurenti that the Carabinieri had been down that avenue already, without success.

He phoned Frank Ryan, the Chicago police superintendent whom he knew well and who had personally supervised the investigation of Cardinal Albert Rooney's murder. Scotty and Fred had taken Ryan into their confidence, just as Adolf had done with Laurenti, and had gotten Ryan's support for their strategy.

"I'm not sure whether our crime lab has contacted appropriate research chemists," Ryan admitted. "I'll follow up on that, and will also touch base with the FBI crime lab."

Fred was stymied as to what to do next. Then it occurred to him an Internet search of scientific journals might be productive. But search for what? The protein residue was normal. Searches for poisons had already been conducted by the law enforcement agencies. What would he search for?

He decided to look for muscle paralyzers. Since they're used in surgery, maybe somebody had developed something new – an improvement over previous compounds. Fred began a search of scientific databases.

It was tough-going. Some of the descriptions were terribly technical, but Fred could plough through, partly because his undergrad degree was in chemistry, and he had worked for a pharmaceutical company. He remembered enough terminology to give him an edge over the average lay person. None of the citations he found had anything to do with muscle paralyzers.

Finally, he found an interesting abstract from a scientific journal. Although the articles in the journal were written in German, the abstracts, fortunately, were in both English and German. A scientist with The Swiss Alpine Laboratory in Bern, Switzerland – a man named Eric Schmidt – had developed a muscle paralyzer which was quickly metabolized by the cells of the muscle and left no trace, except minor protein changes. Other than the paralysis, there appeared to be no side effects to any other part of the body. However, since its effects were permanent and non-reversible, it wasn't applicable for surgery or most other medical procedures.

Fred found the original article in German, made a copy of it, and asked Adolf to translate it for him. The only additional relevant information Adolf found was Dr. Schmidt's opinion the formulation might be a more humane technique for slaughter houses to use when killing animals, since once injected into an animal's heart, it caused instant death with no bleeding or toxic residue.

Could this substance have been the cause of the deaths of these three churchmen? And if so, how did it get into the hands of the perpetrators?

Adolf and Fred decided to take a trip to Bern.

CHAPTER 43

May, 2048
Bern

Dr. Schmidt was perplexed, and concerned. Sometimes government authorities contacted him regarding current Swiss Alpine products. Usually the inquiries were related to contracts the laboratory had with the Swiss military or with other governments. These calls were just part of being in business – authorities checking on sensitive projects, timetables, and possible information leaks on classified assignments.

He had never before heard from a commercial firm, such as Apollo Protection and Security, that wasn't doing business with them. Also, they wanted to talk to him about his article published nine months ago? Why?

Of course, the compound he described in his paper wasn't his creation, but nobody knew that – nobody except the eccentric Sister Sophie who actually developed it. Before he had submitted his paper, he checked to see if she was currently conducting research. He discovered she was running a routine hospital laboratory and performing standard medical analysis. He thought it highly unlikely she was now reading any scientific journals as esoteric as the one in which his paper had been published. Even on the outside possibility she claimed the compound as her own discovery, who would believe such a crazy woman? But then again, why would a detective agency want to see him?

Schmidt didn't want anyone at Swiss Alpine to see him with these men, so he suggested that they meet in the lobby of their hotel. Fred and Adolf greeted him there and they retired to the hotel's restaurant for coffee. After a few pleasantries, Adolf got right to the point.

"Mr. Whitaker and I have been retained to look into some murders which have remained unsolved for several years. We believe a common denominator among them is the injection of a lethal substance into each of the victim's hearts which killed them, but left no trace.

"Searching the literature for a clue – however remote – we came upon your paper in the *Fachzeitschrift der Chemie* describing a compound you developed that can paralyze a muscle but leave no abnormal trace. This substance might be the culprit we're looking for."

Schmidt was relieved. Their visit had nothing to do with the insane Sister Sophie. "Gentlemen, I know of no one outside our lab who has access to this substance. And, as I mentioned in the article, since this is a dangerous compound, I left out one of the key ingredients in my paper. Without this ingredient, no one can reproduce the compound. I considered this omission a necessary precaution."

"Dr. Schmidt, your organization obviously needs to license its innovations in order to produce an income," Fred remarked. "Could it be possible a licensure occurred which didn't come to your attention?"

"This is highly unlikely," Schmidt responded, and, since he was no longer concerned about bringing these men into his lab, he suggested "Let's go back to Swiss Alpine and check our records."

Schmidt drove Fred and Adolf in his car to Swiss Alpine. He took them to a large room filled with file cabinets, where five women were sitting at computer terminals and a man was removing an accordion folder crammed with files from one of the cabinets and bringing it to his terminal.

"Klaus, I'm interested if any licensing activity has taken place involving compound 57WS4982. Can you look that up for us?" (Schmidt had deliberately avoided using the name Serum-C that Sophie had given the compound and instead used its research identification number.)

Klaus looked at Schmidt with a quizzical expression: "Dr. Schmidt, this couldn't have been licensed without your knowledge or approval."

"Look it up anyway, Klaus. It's quite important."

Klaus directed his attention to his terminal, opening a folder, then an imbedded folder, and finally typing "Compound 57WS4982." He scrolled through several dozen paragraphs of data, describing the details of the compound, its development, effects and precautions, until he got to "Licensure."

"As I expected," Klaus informed them, "there's no activity here."

Below "Licensure" was an entry for "Inventory." Schmidt's eyes bulged. He moved his head close to the screen, and read an initial stock of 18 vials was recorded, but the current inventory indicated only 12. Six vials were missing.

"Six vials are missing, Klaus! What's the reason for that?"

Klaus scrolled further down to the next section labeled "Comments" and found a memo that read "Six samples supplied to Carne di Qualità Meat Packing Company as a courtesy by Kaspar Bieber."

"That's our executive director," Schmidt informed Fred and Adolf. "I'll phone him and see what this is all about."

"A problem, Kaspar," Schmidt said when he got Bieber on the line. "Six vials of 57WS4982 are missing from our inventory. It says you gave these to an Italian meat packing firm. I'm concerned since the substance is so lethal."

"Don't worry, Eric. Carne di Qualità's owner Rico Pacelli wanted to test 57WS4982 to see if it was effective as a more humane way to kill animals for slaughter. If it meets their requirements, they plan to license it from us. I fully explained the precautions to his nephew."

"His nephew?" Schmidt responded.

"Yes, he was Pacelli's currier—a young priest named Gustavo Bivona."

CHAPTER 44

May, 2048
Frankfurt

Upon leaving Bern, Fred Whitaker and Adolf Klein returned to the Danube Industries offices in Frankfurt – Adolf to follow up on other projects Apollo Protection and Security was involved in, and Fred to discuss with Theodor Keitz the progress of Palatine's U.S. acquisition. Although the acquisition was Fred's "cover story" for the secret Working Group project, in fact he was actually involved in the related legal matters.

In the meantime, Fred did an Internet search for Gustavo Bivona, and discovered he was currently an administrative aide to Pope Pius XIII and previously his secretary when the pope was still a cardinal. He also searched for Rico Pacelli, and found nothing of interest other than what he already knew – he owned Carne di Qualità Meat Packing. Whether Bivona was actually Pacelli's nephew he wasn't able to determine.

Fred and Adolf decided a visit with Pacelli at his factory in Milan was called for, as well as a meeting with Father Bivona.

No one employed by Danube Industries had been given any information about the Working Group's existence. However, Adolf saw no harm in asking one of his Italian agents if he knew Pacelli or Bivona, or anything about them, obviously without telling him why he wanted the information. So he called Raoul Maltese into his office.

"Raoul, some things came up," Adolf told Maltese, "while Fred and I were at Palatine Chemicals that may involve Rico Pacelli and Father Gustavo Bivona. You've spent time in both Rome and Milan, and I thought you might have some knowledge of them." Adolf continued by telling Raoul who these people were.

"I'm afraid those names aren't familiar to me, Adolf. However, if I remember something later, I'll be sure to let you know."

Raoul could hardly believe his good luck. He departed from Adolf's office and immediately returned to his own and phoned Paolo Andreano.

"Paolo, I finally have some information for you! Whitaker and Klein are leaving for Rome and Milan to interview two people, one of whom worked for Cardinal Ruggieri before he became pope. Maybe you should warn him."

CHAPTER 45

May, 2048
Milan

Fred and Adolf were only three blocks away from Carne di Qualità Meat Packing in Milan's outskirts when the two men became nauseatingly aware the meat preparation facility was close by.

"I've never been to a slaughter house before," Fred confided as he held his nose to underscore his displeasure with the ambiance. "Are they all like this? The smell could easily turn me into a vegetarian!" By this time, Fred was getting used to Adolf's cigarette smoke, but was sure he could never learn to tolerate the pungent odor emanating from the meat packing plant.

Klein laughed. "It's been some time since I've visited a slaughter house. I don't remember such a pungent odor. I suspect this company may have some sanitary issues."

As usually happens in such cases, eventually the sense of smell becomes somewhat numbed or acclimated to the environment, but not entirely. When they entered the plant's office building, they were thankful to discover the air-conditioning effectively filtered out the overpowering stench of the factory.

"Thank you for making the time to see us, Mr. Pacelli," Fred addressed the factory owner as he shook his hand. "I know you're familiar with The Swiss Alpine Laboratory in Bern and have licensed compounds they developed for use in meat preparation and preservation."

"Yes, I have," Pacelli responded. "They are very 'cutting edge' as far as our industry is concerned. Without their innovations, we wouldn't be able to prevent otherwise unavoidable meat spoilage."

Given the horrible smell that welcomed our arrival this morning, Fred was tempted to insert into the conversation, *you certainly couldn't prove that by us!*

"Swiss Alpine's head, Kaspar Bieber, told us," Adolf commented, "he gave you some samples of an advanced compound they refer to by its research designation, 57WS4982 – a substance that may be a more humane way to kill animals than the current slaughtering procedures. We were anxious to know if you found this a useful and improved method for your business, so we could give Mr. Bieber some feedback on its value, and your possible interest in using 57WS4982 at your plant on a regular basis."

This scenario, of course, was a complete fabrication but Fred and Adolf needed to present a plausible reason for their visiting Pacelli.

"It may be," Pacelli responded, "but I'll have to get more vials of the compound to determine its value. I had just one vial, which was enough to kill two cows, but I'll need more to conduct a definitive test."

"Only *one* vial?" Fred remarked with amazement. Bieber had told them he gave six vials to Father Bivona.

"That's correct. My nephew picked up the compound for me, but he said five of the vials unfortunately broke in transit. I'm planning to ask Bieber for several more. If this experiment is successful, then I'll license the compound and use it on a regular basis. It seems more humane, and definitely less messy."

"Who is your nephew?" Fred asked, to confirm the information he and Adolf already had.

"He's a young priest with the Vatican – Father Gustavo Bivona. When he was in the seminary, he worked in the plant to help pay for his education. He's the son of my wife's sister."

Chapter 46

May, 2048
Rome

Rico Pacelli informed Fred and Adolf that Father Bivona's office was "extraterritorial" – on the Via della Conciliazione – since the Vatican City State was not large enough to provide office space for all Vatican administrative personnel. It was close to the Apostolic Palace, so Bivona had just a short walk to the pope's offices when he was needed there. Before his guests left, Pacelli gave them Bivona's address and phone number. The two men called him and made an appointment for ten o'clock the next morning.

A number of Vatican departments and officials had offices in the same building as Bivona's. When Fred and Adolf arrived for their appointment, a central receptionist greeted them and said Father Bivona was expecting them. She told them to take the elevator to the fourth floor and informed them that Bivona's office – at the end of a long hall – was the only office on that floor.

When they got to Bivona's office door, they knocked, but there was no response. They knocked again, even louder, but no answer. The transom above the door was open, and they could see lights were on. After a minute or two, they made the assumption Bivona had stepped out, and, if the door was unlocked, they would go in and wait for him. Fred turned the knob, and the door opened easily.

The room was tastefully appointed, but not elegant. On the wall, several framed prints of famous paintings were color-coordinated with the carpet and the upholstery. A small sofa, two chairs and a coffee table comprised a sitting area in one corner. The stainless steel desk, a modern design with a walnut grain finish, had only one sheet of white paper and a computer on it.

From the ceiling, in the middle of the room, hung a large chandelier with many small flame-shaped bulbs, and a long leather strap was strung through the decorative chain that attached it to the ceiling. In a loop at the end of the strap hung the lifeless body of Gustavo Bivona.

Chapter 47

May, 2048
Chicago

Elaine Whitaker wasn't at all sure what she should do. She was in a quandary.

Although she knew, without a doubt, she needed to get busy on the opinion survey's hand-written statements, she realized the project would take a huge amount of time, even with help from Rachel and Chris. Since she couldn't discuss the Working Group with Ralph Morrison, the Muscular Dystrophy Association's executive director, she didn't know how she could ask for a leave of absence, and she really didn't want to resign from the MDA.

As she was staring out her office window, mulling over this conundrum, Morrison stopped by.

"These last few days, you've seemed to have a lot on your mind, Elaine. Is there anything I can do to help?"

Elaine was brought up short by Morrison's observation. She didn't realize her preoccupation was so obvious.

"I'm sorry, Ralph. There is something on my mind – a problem – but I'll have it ironed out soon. It's not getting in the way of my work."

"Fred's out of the country, isn't he Elaine?"

"Yes, he is," she replied, feeling unmistakably uneasy over his even asking the question.

"Are you concerned about his assignment, what he's doing, his safety?" Ralph asked her, looking intently into her eyes.

"I can't discuss his assignment," Elaine responded, almost on the verge of tears, and suddenly realizing she'd already said more than she should have. She totally forgot to use the agreed on "cover story" of Fred's legal work for Danube Industries in Frankfurt.

Morrison was leaning against the wall, with his hands in his pockets.

"How long have we known each other, Elaine?" he asked her.

"A long time, Ralph – about twenty years I think."

He walked over and took a seat opposite Elaine at her desk.

"I'm very sensitive to what's going on with you. I don't claim to be clairvoyant, but when you're troubled, or when you seem to need time for something important, I think I know. I remember seeing, first-hand, the traumas you and Fred went through when he was working for the pope, and you were helping him. I'm sensing he needs your help again. Is that true?"

By now Elaine was in tears. "He does, Ralph. He needs my assistance very badly. I love my job at MDA. I don't want to give it up!"

Ralph got up, went around the desk, and put his hand on Elaine's shoulder.

"Your value to MDA is incredibly great – I can't possibly describe its importance. We don't want to lose you. There's no doubt in my mind Fred's project is important, probably essential. If he needs your assistance, you should give it to him."

"It may be for many months," Elaine quickly added.

"Take as long as you need to take, Elaine. But please, don't resign! When your work with Fred is finished, your position will still be here. That's a promise!"

As Ralph left her office, Elaine experienced a wave of relief and relaxation. He had solved her problem for her, and she felt as though she was now able to "have her cake and eat it too."

Soon after, Elaine arranged to take an extended leave of absence from MDA. She could now begin to start analyzing the hundreds of thousands of hand-written comments on the opinion surveys. She was certain some valuable information was there, but she had no idea about the surprises in store for her.

CHAPTER 48

Before leaving for Frankfurt, Fred had briefed Scotty on Elaine's probable need to use his office and have Rachel's assistance while he was out of the country. So Scotty wasn't surprised when Elaine informed him about her meeting with Higgins, and her need to spend some time at K&E. Rachel Fischer was also prepared, and eager to get her hands on the surveys again. Rachel thoroughly enjoyed her participation in the project almost two years ago, and was actually excited about the challenges this undertaking presented.

"When we analyzed the hand-written comments back in 2046, Elaine, it was merely a matter of categorizing them according to a format with several headings – either the comments fit the headings, or they didn't. What we're going to do now is more like detective work. What's hidden in these statements? What's being implied, but not actually stated clearly? It's like looking for needles in a haystack."

"It's worse than that," Elaine responded. "We're not just looking for needles in a haystack – we're looking at a whole field of hay, with no guarantee that needles even exist. It may be very frustrating!"

"I really enjoy challenges, Elaine."

"They'll be no lack of challenges, Rachel, but if we can't discover any leads, we may be bored to death. However, with the hand-written comments running into the hundreds of thousands, my opinion is we're bound to find something of value."

Fred's office was still arranged as it had been in 2046, when Elaine and he worked on putting the survey together.

At one end of the room were two desks, and, at the other end, was a large table. When they, along with Rachel and their sons Chris and Bob, were analyzing the survey comments back then, they often had three or four people working at the table at the same time.

To the left of the table were several file cabinets containing almost a third of the 1,300,000 survey forms submitted by current and former Chicago Catholics. The rest of the forms were boxed and stored in the building's basement and would be retrieved as needed.

For starters, Elaine and Rachel pulled out a few survey forms to re-familiarize themselves with the format. There was a cover letter signed by Cardinals Rooney and Whitaker; instructions for using the form; 14 pages of statements, each statement followed by boxes where the respondent could check both level of agreement and importance; and finally one or more blank pages where the respondent could write additional opinions or comments. It was these last pages – the hand-written opinions and comments – to which Elaine and Rachel, and ultimately Chris, would direct their attention.

Chris was chafing at the bit to get involved in the project. His spring semester allowed him flexibility to schedule his electives, so he arranged to have two free afternoons a week to work with his mother and Rachel. As soon as the school year ended, he could then be on hand all day every day.

In addition to the massive amounts of hand-written comments to be analyzed, Elaine soon realized she had entirely overlooked another source of open-ended comments. To assist him in developing the survey questions, Fred had requested ideas from a cross-section of 180 Chicago archdiocesan parishioners, 150 of whom had sent him emails in response – some with fairly lengthy suggestions for the survey, others with favorable and unfavorable impressions regarding the Catholic Church's ability to meet the needs of the laity.

Elaine's recall of this original source of laity input would prove to be crucial to the project's success.

CHAPTER 49

May, 2048
Rome

Fred and Adolf froze in their tracks, hardly able to believe their eyes as they looked up at Gustavo Bivona hanging motionless from the chandelier. Adolf was the first to regain his composure. He took out his phone, and called Colonel Laurenti. Fred went to Bivona's desk to check the sheet of paper lying in the middle of it. It turned out to be a typed suicide note signed by Bivona.

As Adolf finished his call, Fred gestured to the note. "Adolf, look at this!"

> Writing this note will be the last thing I will do in my life. I have served the Vatican for over 10 years, first as secretary to the prefect of the Congregation for the Doctrine of the Faith, and then as an administrative aide in the office of the pope. I have not been a faithful servant. Unbeknownst to my superiors, I have been involved in smuggling illicit drugs and other contraband for criminal elements. I did this because I needed the money to pay for my gambling habits, and for prostitutes that I visited regularly. It is time to end my worthless existence.
>
> Gustavo M. Bivona

"I hope you didn't get your finger prints on this note, Fred."

"I avoided that, Adolf. I haven't touched it."

In less than two minutes after Adolf's phone call, sirens could be heard as the Carabinieri converged on the building. It seemed like moments later their footsteps could be heard coming down the hall, and then through the door.

"Do not disturb anything," the officer-in-charge ordered. "We need to take pictures of everything before the forensic investigators arrive." Adolf informed the officer about the suicide note, and told him they hadn't touched it.

A few minutes later, the medical examiner and forensic team arrived, and shortly after, Colonel Carlo Laurenti. Although a divisional head rarely came to the scene of a suicide or even a murder, it was not surprising in this case, since in all probability, it was related to the ongoing investigation of the yet unsolved murder of Pope Francis Xavier.

"This is a strange suicide note," Laurenti observed. "Bivona shows contrition, but doesn't mention the names of any criminal elements. He talks about working at the Vatican, but again doesn't give the names of his superiors. Very strange."

"Bivona apparently worked for only one man," Fred informed him. "Antonio Ruggieri was the prefect he served, and was also Bivona's most recent boss, Pope Pius XIII."

When forensics finally took the body down, the medical examiner determined the probable cause of death was strangulation from the noose.

After being questioned by the investigators, Adolf requested that Laurenti permit him and Fred to examine the files – electronic and hard copy – Bivona had in his office.

The Carabinieri planned to notify appropriate papal administrators of the suicide, and question them for any information they might have regarding Bivona's motives and activities.

Fred and Adolf returned to Palatine Chemicals to go over what happened, where this left them, and what to do next.

The next day, Adolf received a phone call from Colonel Laurenti. "Mr. Klein, would you and Mr. Whitaker come by my office for a discussion? Gustavo Bivona did not commit suicide. He was murdered!"

Chapter 50

Fred and Adolf arrived at Laurenti's office an hour later. While driving over, they expressed their surprise, confusion, and a certain amount of frustration. "Adolf, you and I had hammered out a new line of attack after discovering Bivona's apparent suicide. Now it looks like we can throw that plan out. The ground has shifted under our feet. We thought we knew what to do next, but evidently that's not the case."

"Gentlemen," Laurenti greeted them, "we've discovered a lot since we last saw each other. Several findings not only make a suicide questionable – they make it impossible. Significant contradictions present themselves.

"To start with, Bivona would have needed a tall ladder to attach the leather strap to the chandelier. The only such ladder available was in a maintenance area in the basement. Furthermore, it would take two men to bring it up to Bivona's office.

"And the hanging? To hang oneself, one needs to stand on a chair or stool, and then kick it away. There wasn't anything like that near the chandelier.

"And, of course, the victim's hands would be unrestrained. You saw his hands were free. However, we found rope burns on his wrists. His wrists had been tied and he struggled against the restraint.

"Finally, the suicide note. It was not produced on his printer, but clearly on someone else's. The signature at the bottom is indeed his – not a forgery – but it's not the way he usually signs his name. He added a middle initial – the letter 'M.' We think the addition was a signal from him that he signed the note under duress.

"Many contradictions! An unprofessional murder, poorly executed! This could not have been a suicide."

Fred and Adolf sat in silence. Carlo Laurenti picked up the pipe on his desk and filled it with tobacco. As he lit it, Fred spoke:

"We formed the Working Group to assist authorities, such as the Chicago Police Department and yourself, in solving two murders – Pope Francis Xavier and Cardinal Rooney – and now we should probably add the murder of Cardinal Christian Bauer. We feared this investigation could lead all the way to the halls of the Vatican, and we might be putting our own lives in danger. We were willing to take that chance.

"Now it seems the perpetrators are willing to take the life of one of their own in order to cover up their plot. I think we underestimated the dangers we face – the unremitting resolve of an adversary that will go to any extreme to make sure we fail."

CHAPTER 51

May, 2048
Chicago

Sitting down at her former desk in Fred's office, Elaine accessed the 150 email files the two of them had analyzed to create the opinion survey in 2046. Since all the completed survey forms were submitted as hard copy via U.S. postal mail, she printed out the emails, each on a separate sheet of paper, so they could physically sort, organize and combine documents that seemed, in some way, to be part of a useful pattern. She also printed out the notes Fred made from his face-to-face interviews with parishioners who chose to meet with him personally rather than sending him an email during the survey development phase of the project.

These activities had all the potential of ending up as merely shuffling overwhelming mountains of paper – nothing short of a nightmare. Elaine, Rachel and Chris had a strategy session before rolling up their sleeves and getting to work. Chris became self-appointed team captain for this stage of their endeavor.

"Last semester, I took a course in project management and organizational structure. It was really cool. Some of the concepts I learned definitely apply to what we are doing." Chris' high school in Evanston was exceptional, with college-level electives open to the better-performing students.

Chris created a flow chart, indicating what happens to an email or survey form from the time they get their hands on it – what to look for, what decision they make about it based on their criteria, and finally, where it ends up.

"With this much stuff to go through," Chris advised Elaine and Rachel, "we've got to make sure we don't touch a piece of paper more than once, without an obvious reason to justify another look. And never more than twice unless it's something really valuable."

This boy's got a good head on his shoulders! Elaine told herself, with some sense of pride. *He definitely takes after his father. But when you think about it, his mother's not so dumb either!*

To begin the project, Chris, Elaine and Rachel would do an initial sorting. They would take a survey form, go immediately to the hand-written comments at the end, and decide whether or not they contained anything relevant. If so, the form would be put aside for a second look later. If not – and that would be far more than 99% of the documents – it would be put in a box for storage, not to be viewed again.

"Anything relevant" – they spent at least two hours defining what that meant, so they wouldn't be wasting time on unimportant information and, at the same time, wouldn't be overlooking something that was potentially significant. They agreed that when one of them found a hand-written comment that appeared to be noteworthy, the other two would review it as well before they decided to put it aside for further evaluation.

To help them refine their definition of "relevant," they took a pile of survey forms, and read the comments at the end to find some examples of what they were looking for. Not surprisingly, they didn't find anything pertinent. They were well aware they might end up reviewing hundreds of thousands of survey forms, and find absolutely nothing. However, they could not afford to overlook, in that multitude of file cabinet drawers and dozens of storage boxes, a piece of information lying dormant that could provide a vital clue to solving the murder of Cardinal Albert Rooney.

Elaine also distinctly recalled seeing, during the coding of the hand-written survey comments two years ago, some respondents' statements that seemed to have absolutely nothing to do with the survey. Somewhere buried in this huge "field of hay" were hidden these few "needles" which might be valuable. It was critical to find them.

Elaine, Rachel and Chris finally agreed on the following six criteria for comments to be considered important:

- *A threat – actual or implied – made by the respondent.*
- *A threat – actual or implied –the respondent is aware someone else has made.*
- *An opinion expressed by someone that the respondent found to be disturbing.*
- *A rumor the respondent has heard that something bad or unpleasant is going to happen to the church or a church official.*
- *A prediction by the respondent that something bad or unpleasant is going to happen to the church or a church official.*
- *A negative or troubling experience the respondent has had with a representative or employee of the church, whether that individual was a cleric or a lay person.*

Starting with the surveys filed in the office, Elaine, Rachel, and Chris each took a separate file drawer and systematically reviewed every survey form. During their first hour, nothing was uncovered worth more than a quick perusal.

Then Rachel spoke up: "Here's a comment from a woman who says she's a cousin of Cardinal Rooney. She has always worried about his well-being – the stress of the job, his long hours of work. Take a look and see what you think."

Elaine read it and handed it to Chris. "It seems to me nothing more than normal family concern. There's no specific mention of any threats."

Chris looked at it and shook his head. "This doesn't seem unusual or disturbing to me either. Mom, you always told Dad not to work too hard, to take care of his health. This is the same sort of thing, don't you think? No big deal."

"I agree with both of you," Rachel commented. "I didn't think it was significant, either, but it's the first time something even remotely connected to Cardinal Rooney has come up in our search. I thought we all ought to look at it and make sure we're seeing things the same way."

CHAPTER 52

After more than three weeks, seven hours a day, of methodically examining thousands of survey forms, Elaine, Rachel, and Chris found nothing of interest or value. Their enjoyment of each other's company was the saving grace. They punctuated their days with two coffee breaks – sometimes three – and spent their breaks telling stories about their lives, what they were reading, interesting things they had seen on TV. Chris was a good story-teller, and had really hilarious anecdotes about things going on at school. The three got to know each other very well – better than ever before – and Elaine picked up insights into her son she never had previously. Other than the socializing, though, the task was extremely tedious.

One day, as Elaine took a minute's break to rest her eyes, she began considering what they were up against.

This seems like a thankless task – thankless and unproductive. We've been at this almost a month, and haven't found anything of interest. We may wind up completing this project with absolutely nothing to show for our efforts. I wonder if we're wasting our time, whether there's a better approach, something we may have overlooked.

She suddenly remembered that, when she and Fred were reading the email messages they had used as an aide in developing questions for the survey form, one of the emails bothered her quite a bit at the time, but she couldn't recall why. She shifted her attention to the 150 emails. In less than an hour, she came upon the message she was looking for. It was from a woman, a member of St. Barnabas parish on the Southwest Side, who wrote:

> I've had a lot of good experiences with priests during my life, but sometimes they are not as sensitive as they could be in dealing with parishioners. What really stands out in my mind is a priest – Father Thomas Costello – who was assigned to our parish many years ago.
>
> My 10 year-old daughter was a good girl, liked going to church and to the sacraments. After Father Costello had been at our parish for only a few weeks, her attitude changed. She no longer wanted to go to Mass or to Holy Communion. She said she hated Father Costello, that he was a terrible man, but she would never tell me why she felt that way.
>
> She's an adult now, and has left the church. Somehow Father Costello embittered my daughter. He didn't know how to deal with children. Maybe priests should be trained better when it comes to children.

"Chris, Rachel, I want you to look at this. Tell me what you think."

Rachel read it through, frowned and shook her head.

"Though the woman doesn't say so in so many words, I think her daughter was sexually abused by the priest." She handed the message to Chris.

"I recall that was my reaction when I first read this two years ago," Elaine responded.

Chris read the email, and his eyes bulged.

"Oh my God! That's the name of our new archbishop! Could it be the same man? Could Cardinal Rooney have known about this? Could Costello have known Rooney knew, so he did him in?"

Rachel began laughing. "Chris, your mind is going a mile a minute! You've come up with an identity, a motive and a perpetrator – all in 10 seconds! It sounds to me like you have the case closed, and it's now time for the jury's deliberation!"

Chris's expression turned from wild excitement to sheepishness, with a tinge of embarrassment.

"OK, so maybe I'm jumping to conclusions. And maybe there's more than one 'Tom Costello' in the archdiocese. But it may not be a coincidence. It may be important evidence that should be investigated."

"You're right, Chris," his mother commented. "It may be very important, or totally unimportant. We've got to classify this as a 'significant finding,' but it's premature for us to drop everything and follow up on it. We'll see if there is any – as your father would say – 'corroborating evidence.' At least, after three weeks of plowing through this avalanche of paper, we're not totally empty-handed. I find that encouraging."

It would be a gross overstatement to say the trio was "on a roll," but Elaine's discovery of the email had a positive effect on their morale. No matter whether or not they came up with more, they would consider their endeavor as successful.

It took them a mere two weeks to come up with more. This time it was Chris who made a discovery. One afternoon, he had arrived earlier than usual from school and was only 30 minutes into his pile of surveys, when he exclaimed:

"Wow! This is unbelievable! Rachel, Mom, take a look at this!"

The survey form was from a woman who expanded the "opinions and comments" section of the survey by attaching two pages of her thoughts. Her hand-writing was atrocious, and Chris struggled for almost 15 minutes to decipher it. He read it aloud to his mother and Rachel.

> Me and my friends think the church is getting too soft, too touchy-feely. The priest always tells us what we can and can't do. Why do this stupid survey? Too many people now a-days,

especially the kids, think they're smarter than the church. You start asking them their opinions, and all you'll get is more bitching – they already bitch too much. They think they can tell God what to do. What they need to do is follow the rules, and that's that.

My husband – him and his friends work in the construction industry. They get told what to do, and they do it. No ifs, ands or buts. They're good Catholics. They're mad as hell about this survey. He says they're going to figure out how to nip this thing in the bud. Me? – don't know how they can do that, but he says they're going to. That would be great as far as I'm concerned. But I tell him to stay out of trouble.

"The writer is telling us more than her pet peeves, and the gripes her husband and his friends have about the survey," Chris observed. "I think she's carelessly revealing a plot to stop the survey."

Elaine and Rachel acknowledged Chris for uncovering information that was potentially a "smoking gun."

"I don't know which one of us originally reviewed this survey two years ago," Elaine commented. "Maybe it was Fred or your brother. Given the difficulty you had deciphering her hand-writing, Chris, I'm not surprised we missed it."

The three agreed it was critical to find the woman who wrote these comments, and then have Brett Higgins or investigators of the Chicago Police interview her and certainly her husband and his friends.

There was a big problem, however. They had no way of identifying her name and address.

CHAPTER 53

Barkley Sylvester confronted the now unavoidable change in his life. He faced the inevitable events to honor him in the next few weeks with as much stoicism as he could muster.

He had known the day was not far off when he must clean out his desk, pack up his extensive files and the numerous books he had written, and leave his office at DePaul University for the last time. That day was just two months away.

There would be a special convocation to celebrate his career, accolades from the university president and fellow faculty members, parties in his honor, and interviews by the university newspaper, and probably the *Chicago Tribune*, the *Chicago Sun-Times* and *Crain's Chicago Business* – maybe even the *Wall Street Journal.* Sylvester had a stellar career as a professor of Industrial Psychology with national and international recognition for his publications.

He had considered putting in a few more years, but didn't want to someday retire because he absolutely had to – failing health, diminished mental acuity, lack of demand for his courses. His classes were still popular with graduate business students, and his past publications still relevant. However, his current papers were no longer of interest to refereed journals, and his previous publications were not being quoted.

Nor was he currently sought after as a consultant. The last time that happened was two years ago when Fred Whitaker, a former student and newly appointed lay cardinal, asked him to help devise an opinion survey for Chicago Catholics. This interesting and stimulating assignment ended tragically in the deaths of a security agent and Cardinal Rooney, and possibly led to the subsequent murder of Pope Francis Xavier.

Barkley was ruminating on all of this as he examined a folder of notes he would use in his class that afternoon, when, of all people, Fred Whitaker's wife Elaine phoned him.

"Elaine, what a coincidence! I was just thinking about the work I did with you and Fred two years ago. I was wondering what the two of you were up to these days."

"Hi Barkley! Fred and I talk about you often. A lot has been going on, and some of it has to do with the work you did for Fred. I need to see you. Can I meet with you soon?"

Conferring with Barkley had been something Elaine had discussed with Scotty. He agreed it was important – and safe – for Elaine to consult with him as long as she didn't reveal the existence of the Working Group or any critical details of their mission.

Elaine met with Barkley at his office the next morning. She wasted no time in getting to the reason why she wanted to see him so quickly:

"Scotty Campbell and Fred are still troubled about the lack of evidence in the murders of Cardinal Rooney and the security agent at our home, and are trying to do what they can to turn up any useful information. Fred's on assignment for a client in Germany, so Scotty asked me to help out in his absence by reviewing some of the comments that respondents wrote on the opinion survey forms to see if we can discover any leads. I've recruited Fred's executive assistant and my son, Chris, to help me, and we think we may have found something. The wife of someone who works in the construction industry wrote a comment suggesting her husband and his fellow workers may have been involved in a plot against Rooney.

The trouble, as you know, is there's no way I can identify individual respondents or where they live."

Sylvester looked very troubled and stared into Elaine's eyes for a few seconds before responding.

"Do the police know you're doing this?"

"Yes, they do, Barkley. Superintendent Frank Ryan knows about this and feels it may be helpful in their stalled homicide investigation." Elaine knew Fred had confided in Frank Ryan from the very beginning of the project, so they would have his approval, and unnecessary conflicts could be avoided. She also knew Brett Higgins had advised Ryan about this phase of the Working Group's project.

Barkley stood up, and walked over to the window, with his hands in his pockets. He turned to Elaine.

"As you know, Fred told me all he needed to know was the neighborhood the completed forms came from. I told him Condé Reproductions, who handled the printing and mailing, would insert an extra space between words – practically invisible – that would identify the neighborhood, and could be read by Condé's optical scanner when the form was returned."

He sat down again, his hands folded on his desk, and leaned forward toward Elaine.

"I did a lot more than that, Elaine. The program I wrote did a *lot* more than that. It is full of codes – spaces between words, forced line endings, subtle graphic variations, spaces between lines, a comma instead of a semicolon, the size of the dot over an 'i' – most of which are so small that it takes an optical scanner to see them. It's possible to read the name and address of each respondent!

"Why did I do that and not tell Fred? Was it dishonest? In the cover letter that Fred and Cardinal Rooney sent to each survey recipient, they said no one would be able to identify the respondent when the completed form was returned. Basically, that's true – nobody knew the identities, including me. And I was afraid it would bother

Fred if he knew it was available. Call it a mental reservation. Call it a white lie. Call it a damned lie!

"My experience over the years has proved the importance of having access to this information. Once a bomb was detonated in a factory, and if I hadn't included the hidden codes in a previous attitude survey, the perpetrator would never have been caught. As far as I'm concerned, solving a crime always trumps the guarantee of anonymity to the respondents."

Elaine smiled broadly. "You don't have to justify yourself to me, Barkley! Not to Fred either, I'm sure. I'm just relieved to know we can determine who wrote this on her survey form. It could turn out to be a key piece of evidence in helping to solve Cardinal Rooney's murder. It's good to know the time and effort we're devoting to reading all these comments is actually going to bear some fruit."

"Have you completed your project, Elaine?"

"Heavens, no! The three of us have been at this for just five weeks. We've barely scratched the surface. Conceivably, this will take a half year or more."

Barkley steepled his hands under his chin as he looked out the window. He returned his attention to Elaine.

"Are the two working with you absolutely reliable, without question?"

"I can swear to that, Barkley."

"Nobody but you, your team, Fred and Scotty must know what I am going to do. I want you to pack up all the survey forms – every one of them. If you haven't done this already, mark the one's you've already reviewed. I'll have a van from Condé Reproductions pick up the boxes. Condé will run the survey forms through the scanner, and identify all the names and addresses. The forms will be sorted according to neighborhoods, and all forms will receive a number. A separate list will be printed out with all names and addresses, and their corresponding form numbers.

"Give me the 'smoking gun' survey form separately. It will become '#1' in this very long series, and its neighborhood will comprise the first set of numbers in the sequence.

"That way, you can review the survey forms for everyone living near '#1.' Most likely, this is a working class neighborhood, probably ethnically homogeneous, with some residents working in the construction industry who are friends of the 'smoking gun.' You may even find some corroborating evidence. When you've completed your review, give me back the printout of names and addresses, and please don't make any photocopies of it."

Elaine could hardly believe the amount of information Barkley could provide. It was difficult to even estimate its potential value and contribution to the Working Group.

But there was a cost to be paid – additional anguish, suffering, and lives put in danger.

Chapter 54

June, 2048
Rome

The investigation sparked by the death of Gustavo Bivona was second only to the ongoing hunt for the individuals guilty of murdering Pope Francis Xavier, Cardinal Rooney and Cardinal Bauer. Colonel Carlo Laurenti assigned his crack forensics team the task of uncovering any traces of evidence, and following even the most remote leads, no matter how insignificant, unlikely or tenuous they might appear. He was convinced, as were Adolf and Fred, that Bivona's execution was tied to the other murders, and to unravel it would ultimately expose a trail leading to all the murders.

Colonel Laurenti requested Fred and Adolf come to his office for a briefing. He reviewed with them every detail of the Carabinieri's investigation, and their findings, or lack of same.

Every speck of dust in Bivona's office had been vacuumed for examination, every item dusted for fingerprints, every stain on the rug and upholstery chemically removed and sent to the crime lab for analysis. The ladder in the basement was subjected to the same kind of detailed attention.

Hair was found in the dust and dirt that didn't match Bivona's. Just two latent fingerprints appeared, missed by the killers who apparently had wiped down whatever they had touched. The prints were from the same hand, and the Carabinieri's database found a match with a known Mafia operative who had served prison time, but whose whereabouts were now unknown.

The leather strap turned out to be from the reins of a horse. It had bits of soil on it – soil found only in the region of Calabria where the Mafia operative was from.

Special attention was given to Bivona's computer. With whom had he been corresponding in the days leading up to his death? Was there any evidence of a motive for the crime?

"Gentlemen, Father Bivona's computer, like most computers, has folders for messages received and sent, and a variety of folders for documents he has created, or is currently working on," Colonel Laurenti informed Adolf and Fred. "That is, up until about 14 days prior to his murder. None of his document or email folders have any files dated more recently than two weeks ago. It's as if he hadn't touched his computer during that period, nor for that matter, had anyone tried to correspond with him. This is a clear sign that he – or someone – had erased all files that were more current than a half a month ago."

"I know that, even if a file has been erased, it isn't the actual file that's disappeared, but the directory for that file," Fred commented. "In other words, even if you can no longer see it or access it, it's still in storage as long as you haven't written over it as you subsequently create new files."

"Exactly," replied Laurenti. "My computer people found the files almost completely intact, which indicates the directories were erased shortly before Bivona's death. What we found in them was amazing, even shocking.

"There were a number of unremarkable files – normal and fairly uninteresting email exchanges you would find on any of our computers, and documents Bivona was drafting for curial members, or perhaps the pope.

"Then, about a week ago, he received an email from Mario Lusardi, the pope's camerlengo. It's the first correspondence from the camerlengo we found on Bivona's hard drive. Lusardi advised Bivona that the two of you would soon be contacting him for an interview, and that Lusardi should be advised about the scheduled meeting before it took place."

"A meeting with us?" Adolf sputtered with amazement. "A week ago, no one knew we planned to see Bivona!"

Adolf suddenly remembered, and with some chagrin. *I did ask Raoul Maltese whether he knew anything about Gustavo Bivona. Could it be he was part of the conspiracy?*

Laurenti continued: "Bivona replied to Lusardi asking why would Whitaker and Klein possibly want to see him? He wrote he found this unnerving. Lusardi didn't respond to that email. Then, the day before the murder, he received another email from Lusardi. Listen to this!"

> It has come to my attention, Gustavo, the German detective and the American lawyer have made an appointment to see you tomorrow. You are to tell them nothing! They're up to no good! In the best interest of his holiness and the Roman Curia, do not give them any important information. Tell them you write and edit documents – that's all you've ever done at the Holy See. Nothing else, ever! Period! Is that understood?

"Now listen to Bivona's reply to Lusardi:"

> Your Eminence, I find this situation quite frightening. Never have I been in any trouble. A detective or a lawyer has never questioned me about anything. Why are they planning to interrogate me? What if they're working for the Carabinieri?

What if they implicate me in something? I'm truly scared. What's going to happen?

The colonel paused long enough to reach for his pipe, fill it with tobacco from his tobacco pouch, and light it. "It seems clear the motive for Bivona's murder was to prevent him from showing his fear and being pressured into talking too much. He apparently knew enough to hurt people in high places, and had to be silenced. What he knew died with him. We've been through all his electronic files, cabinets and storage boxes for any significant evidence, but we haven't found anything."

"Colonel Laurenti, there's no doubt in my mind your investigators have been as thorough as humanly possible," Fred acknowledged. "However, sometimes there's value in having another set of well-trained eyes reexamine the data – sometimes an obscure clue will pop out unexpectedly. I believe my years as a litigator evaluating the usefulness of evidence might serve us well at this juncture."

"I have no objection, Mr. Whitaker. However, I have a question for you. Do you know the Italian language?"

CHAPTER 55

As they drove back to Palatine Chemicals, Adolf started laughing. "A lot of good it will do you to look at Bivona's computer files, Fred. I'm fluent in Italian, but I think you know just enough to order from a menu. It looks like I'll be doing the review by myself."

"I've got a better idea, Adolf. Even if I could speak and read the language, it would take forever for the two of us to go through all those files thoroughly. Let's assume the Carabinieri have already done a good job of that, and they still didn't discover any leads. All we really need are the names of the people with whom Bivona corresponded by email, or whom he mentioned in other documents. Then we can find out who these people are and their relationship to Bivona. Even not knowing the language, I can spot names and record them."

The next day, they were back at Laurenti's office. He provided them with two computers and two copies of Bivona's data storage. Adolf reviewed the emails, and Fred the other documents.

As they compiled their list of names, Laurenti's people were able to provide identifications – who these individuals were, where they worked and for whom they worked. One name came up several times in the emails – Gino Cogliano. The Carabinieri identified him as a porter at the Apostolic Palace. The correspondence indicated that he was a good friend of Bivona's.

"Fred, this last email is different than the rest – strange and troubling. It was sent the day before Bivona's death, shortly after he received Lusardi's message. He's asking Cogliano to stop by his office for an important discussion. He gives no indication of what the discussion would be about. Cogliano responded that he would be by later that day."

Fred rocked slowly in his swivel chair, arms folded, lips tightly pressed together, eyes staring straight ahead at the wall. His wrinkled brow reflected his intense concentration. Finally he spoke.

"This may be a blind alley, Adolf, but it's all we've got. Let's ask Laurenti to invite him in for questioning. No, not invite – insist that he show up at headquarters right away for interrogation. We'll create a scenario – a fiction – that Bivona wrote notes after their meeting, and we have read them. As a result, we now have reason to believe he was involved in the murder of Pope Francis Xavier.

"We'll scare the hell out of him! And maybe get some information."

CHAPTER 56

June, 2048
Chicago

It took almost two weeks for Elaine to get the detailed information Barkley Sylvester promised. After dozens of boxed survey forms were transported to Condé Reproductions, the firm had to un-staple each form – more than a million of them – and run them through their optical scanner for a second time, then re-staple them, organize them by neighborhoods, number them, and finally produce a list with all of the names and addresses. This latter document was the size of a large encyclopedia volume. It was an expensive operation, but Elaine felt it was necessary, and Scotty agreed.

While Elaine, Rachel and Chris were waiting for the return of the opinion survey forms, they searched through legal databases to find any cases where the Archdiocese of Chicago had been sued for any reason at all. In a city the size of Chicago, there are always law suits involving the archdiocese, usually quite insignificant. They retrieved the court documents and read them over thoroughly, but their main interest was to identify the parties involved – who they were, what they did for a living, their backgrounds, and especially if they had criminal records.

Finally the truckload of boxed survey forms were returned from Condé Reproductions. As Sylvester promised, the "smoking gun" was numbered "#1" and the immediate subsequent numbers were all from the same neighborhood.

A woman named Aniela Bobowski was "#1," and her husband, Pawel Bobowski, was "#2." His comments weren't nearly as provocative as his wife's, but he did complain the survey was un-Catholic and never should have been conducted.

The team focused their attention on other survey forms from the same Chicago neighborhood, and found comments in those similar to Pawel's. With help provided by Chicago Police Superintendent Frank Ryan, they discovered all but one of these respondents worked for the Streeterville Construction Company, and Pawel Bobowski and two others had minor criminal records – convictions for assault and battery. Pawel spent a month in jail, and the other two were given probation. A pattern was now immerging.

Interviewing the Bobowskis and the other Streeterville workers became a priority. But who would design the interview format? How would this group be made to talk, to tell the truth?

Chapter 57

June, 2048
Rome

Gino Cogliano had worked in Vatican City for 15 years, mostly as a porter at the Apostolic Palace. His responsibilities were varied, which made his job interesting and enjoyable. He never got bored. After greeting a visitor who had an appointment with the pope or another Holy See official, he escorted them to the office where they were expected, often giving him a chance to engage the visitor in conversation. Since the visitor might be a celebrity, royalty, or a head of state, he found these opportunities to be exciting. Visitors would sometimes ask his advice about where to dine, what museums to visit, or the best tours of the city to take. In effect, Gino fulfilled the role of concierge.

His education was limited – he was one year short of a high school diploma – and a job like this could hardly be better, given his limited educational background. The pay was modest, but enough to support him and his wife, and their two children. Gino considered himself a fortunate man and was happy with his work.

The Apostolic Palace was the headquarters of the Holy See, the ruling body of the Catholic Church. As with all large bureaucracies, there were political factions, some engaged in overt competition. An outgrowth of this political activity was an abundance of rumor mills among the employees working there. Throughout his career, Gino had distanced himself as far as possible from any involvement in this scuttlebutt – it distracted him from his responsibilities, and made him feel ill at ease. Since the election of Pope Pius XIII, the rumor mills had been working overtime, and the gossip was becoming quite disturbing to many employees, especially someone as sensitive as Gino Cogliano.

He minded his own business. As much as he enjoyed the company of his friend, Father Gustavo Bivona, he found it disconcerting when the priest shared confidences that Gino would rather not know anything about.

This was especially true the day before his death, when he begged Gino to come by his office for a private meeting. He talked to him about an investigation that frightened him. Father Bivona felt in danger, and feared he might have lost the trust of the higher ups at the Vatican. He didn't know what to do. Then the next day, he was murdered.

Now Cogliano had an order from the Carabinieri to come to their office for questioning about the murder of Pope Francis Xavier, and the conversation he had with Father Bivona the day before he was killed. Never in his life had he been in trouble. Never! Why had they singled him out?

What are they looking for? Is it possible they learned about what I told Father Bivona that day – the evidence about Francis Xavier's murder I had withheld all this time? Could they possibly know that?

CHAPTER 58

"Gino, what's troubling you?" his wife asked him the evening before his appointment with the Carabinieri. "There's something on your mind – I know it. I can tell when you're out of sorts. What is it?"

"It's nothing, Anna, nothing at all. I have an important meeting tomorrow morning, and my mind is a bit distracted. I'll be fine."

At the end of each day, Gino usually told his wife what he had done at work that day – the important people he had met, the problems he had solved, sometimes a verbal exchange he had with the holy father. What he shared was always upbeat and often quite interesting.

But he had never shared with Anna what he saw the morning Pope Francis Xavier was murdered. In fact, he didn't even understand what was going on, and was afraid to ask about it since it might jeopardize his job. He had tried to erase it from his mind, but it wouldn't go away. He shouldn't have said anything to Father Bivona, but he did. Could that prove to be a fatal mistake? Was that now coming back to haunt him?

His appointment at the Carabinieri headquarters was scheduled for 9:30 a.m. He arrived outside the building 30 minutes early, and finally went inside at 9:15. Waiting in the reception area was agonizing. Everything that could possibly go wrong went through his mind. Just a glance in his direction by an officer passing through the reception room was enough to convince him the authorities were preparing to prosecute him as an accomplice in the murder of Francis Xavier. He had never been so ill at ease, or so frightened.

"*Signore* Cogliano, Colonel Laurenti will see you now," the receptionist told him.

"Colonel Laurenti!" Gino gasped as he sat up ramrod straight. *I've heard his name he's the head man here, and he's going to interrogate me!* Gino's hands shook and he began to get dizzy. *I must be in big trouble! What are they planning to do to me?*

The receptionist took him into the colonel's office. Laurenti was studying a file on his desk, and didn't acknowledged Gino's presence for at least a minute. Finally, without looking up, he stated with a tone of authority: "*Signore*, sit down!"

Gino slowly lowered himself into a chair opposite Laurenti's desk. Fred and Adolf sat, unsmiling, on either side of the colonel. Neither of them acknowledged Gino's presence, but instead stared at him with unrelenting, steely glares. Gino was terrified.

Laurenti at last gazed at Gino, inspecting him like a piece of questionable, low-grade merchandise.

"I must tell you, *Signore* Cogliano, after your visit with Father Bivona the day before his death, he wrote a transcript of what the two of you talked about," Laurenti informed Cogliano. "What you said to him was most incriminating."

Adolf broke in: "You are in serious trouble for withholding evidence regarding the murder of Pope Francis Xavier. We consider you a suspect in this crime."

"We also think you might be involved in the killing of Father Bivona – a murder to ensure he never repeated the information you gave him that day," Fred added. "I would advise you, for your own sake, to give us a full disclosure of what you know if you want to avoid prison."

The scenario being played out in Laurenti's office with Gino was Fred's idea but orchestrated by the Colonel, who had coached Adolf and Fred in the roles they were to play in the performance.

Laurenti's years in criminal investigation had taught him to lean heavily on the most unlikely suspects, even those he was sure were innocent of any wrong doing, since blind fear of being entrapped in a web of unjust accusations and possible prosecution often resulted in the hapless target pouring out a stream of information. Although most of this information was irrelevant, it sometimes included clues ultimately leading to the solution of a crime.

The colonel's *modus operandi* was about to pay dividends.

Chapter 59

The interrogation dragged on for almost an hour. Laurenti fired questions, followed by Fred and then Adolf.

"Why did you withhold information when you were questioned after the death of Francis Xavier?"

"Who's paying you to keep silent about what you know?"

"What Mafia family do you work for?"

"Is Gino Cogliano your real name? Did you change it after being convicted of a crime?"

"What will your wife and children think when they find out you're in trouble with the law?"

Gino answered most of the questions by denying any knowledge or involvement in a crime. Perspiration dripped down his face, and he frequently mopped his brow with his handkerchief. He was petrified.

"We know what Father Bivona wrote after your meeting with him," Laurenti reminded him, "but we want you to tell us, in your own words, what you told him that day."

Gino slumped in his chair. "My mouth and throat are dry. Please give me some water."

There was a water pitcher and glasses on a sideboard. Adolf went over, poured a glass, and gave it to Gino.

"What I saw that day seemed very unimportant, and I put it out of my mind. Only when Father Bivona asked me to meet with him, and told me he felt threatened, did those unusual events the day Pope Francis Xavier was killed come to mind, and I shared them with him."

Colonel Laurenti realized his interrogation strategy was now paying off.

"Go on," urged Laurenti, "tell us what you saw."

***

Gino sipped the water, and put the glass on the desk in front of him. He mopped his brow again. His hands were shaking before, but now he was trembling all over as if he had chills.

"I have a small office just down the hall from the office suite occupied by the camerlengo, Cardinal Mario Lusardi," Cogliano began, his voice cracking. He held the arms of his chair in an attempt to control his trembling. "When I'm not greeting an important visitor or performing some other duty, I work in my office.

"I was leaving my office around 9:00 a.m. when I head voices down the hall. I recognized Cardinal Lusardi and saw – from their attire –he was with another cardinal and a nun. Since their backs were turned towards me, they weren't aware I was there. They entered the camerlengo's office.

"I proceeded to the floor above, where the papal apartments are located. I then went to the secretary's desk, situated outside the entrance, to check the pope's weekly appointment calendar so I'd know the times and places where I would need to be on hand that week. I was there for about half an hour.

"To my amazement, the nun I saw before came out of the door, said nothing to me or the secretary, and proceeded to the elevator. There is no way she could have entered the papal apartments without my seeing her. I was baffled and thought 'How could this be?'"

"There has to be another entrance," Fred interjected. "Do you know of any secret passages in the building?"

"I've heard there are many secret corridors in the building," Gino added, "but I only know where a few of them are located, and they have been closed – walled over or converted into normal entranceways. I don't think any of the remaining secret passages have been used for decades, maybe centuries. I believe they were built as escape routes in case the Apostolic Palace was under siege, but that fear is long gone."

"Did you ask the camerlengo about the nun, or how she got into the papal apartments?" Adolf queried Gino.

Gino sat silently for a few moments, a frown on his face, eyes cast down and hands clasped in his lap. Then he looked up at Adolf:

"I've worked at the Vatican for 15 years. There are lots of strange things that happen there. We're not supposed to question anything if we want to keep our jobs. I have a family to support, and there's no way I'm going to jeopardize my position. If I don't understand what's going on, and it's not part of my job, I put it out of my mind."

After Gino Cogliano was dismissed, the three men "debriefed" each other to ascertain if anyone was clear on what the next steps should be. None of them were. They agreed that Gino was an innocent bystander. They were certain the mysterious nun played a role in the crime, and the camerlengo as well. But they saw no way to proceed further without alerting guilty parties and putting the investigation at risk.

They were at a dead end.

Chapter 60

June, 2048
Chicago

Elaine, Scotty, Brett, and Fred held a weekly conference call on Fridays at 2:00 p.m. (9:00 p.m. in Rome) to discuss the Working Group's progress. When Adolf was with Fred, he was also included in the call.

At Elaine's request, another Working Group member, Marsha McGuire, was included in this week's conference call. Marsha, Executive Director of Rotary International, served on three advisory boards for the Archdiocese of Chicago, and since Elaine was planning to discuss Archbishop Tom Costello, she thought Marsha might have some helpful insights.

The Chicago contingent was completely mesmerized by Fred and Adolf's narrative about the interrogation of Gino Cogliano, and the inclusion of a nun and the camerlengo into the mix as possible suspects. They were still reeling from the account of Gustavo Bivona's murder the previous week, and marveling at the unfolding complexity of the investigation.

"We know a lot more now than we did a few days ago," Fred informed them, "with the camerlengo's probable involvement, and then this nun. Still, we're up against a substantial roadblock. For our investigation to be successful, we can't tip our hand. We can't question the camerlengo about the nun without alerting co-conspirators and effectively ruining the investigation. All major Vatican officials were interrogated shortly after Francis Xavier's murder, and the authorities didn't uncover any useful clues or information. We don't want them to know what we're doing now and put them on guard. At this juncture, the camerlengo doesn't know he was seen with the nun on the day the pope was killed. We're not sure what our next move will be."

"To complicate matters," Adolf added, "at Fred's request, I've had my detectives investigate the background of Working Group member Paolo Andreano, and have received some disturbing information about him. He's from a family in the Calabria region with close ties to the Mafia. There's reason to believe some of his current professional activities directly support Mafia interests."

"Andreano has hounded me for information about Adolf and my activities in Rome," Fred interjected, "but I have kept him at arm's length. I haven't told him anything."

Then Scotty commented: "Fred, there may be a way we can move ahead on our end, thanks to Elaine, Rachel and your son Chris."

Elaine provided the details. "We were frustrated and a bit discouraged by the total lack of leads or clues in the written survey comments, until Chris ran into a form from the Wicker Park neighborhood. A woman all but said her husband, a construction worker, and his co-workers were plotting some sort of action to stop the survey. The trouble, however, was we couldn't determine the identity of the woman. I met with Barkley Sylvester to discuss the problem, and, to my surprise, he said that type of detailed information was coded into the forms when they were printed."

"Why didn't Barkley tell us he had that kind of information?" Fred bellowed from 4,800 miles away.

"Because you only wanted neighborhoods, Fred. It's complicated – I'll explain it when you come back. Trust me – it's OK.

"Anyway, we found several other people in the same neighborhood with similar attitudes. Police Superintendent Ryan found they all work in the building industry – most of them for Streeterville Construction."

"Streeterville!" Fred stated with amazement. "Their president was the guy who offered to fly me to Rome in his private jet for my meeting with Francis Xavier! Of course, I didn't do that since we thought he might be up to something. This has got to be more than coincidence!"

"Like your situation in Rome," Scotty added, "we can't move on this right now. We don't want any of the suspects to know what we're doing, perhaps prompting them to circle their wagons, and preventing us from getting any concrete evidence.

"We have another avenue that may prove productive, and that's why we needed you to sit in on this meeting, Marsha."

Marsha was all ears. She knew there had to be a reason for her inclusion, and she was anxious to find out what it was.

"Remember, Fred, when we were developing the survey categories and you requested feedback from 18 parishes?" Elaine reminded him. "One of the emails you received was from a woman whose young daughter was alienated from the church by a parish priest, and you and I suspected the daughter might have been molested by this man. Do you remember the name of the priest?"

"My God in heaven!" responded Fred. "I do remember! It was Thomas Costello! It couldn't be our new archbishop, could it? The name is not uncommon."

"We've checked," Elaine informed him. "There's only one priest named Tom Costello in the Chicago archdiocese and he's our archbishop!"

Scotty jumped in at this point: "Fred, could it be Cardinal Rooney knew about this and was about to blow the whistle? Could Costello have found out and realized he had to do something to prevent Rooney from exposing him?

"Marsha, you attend committee meetings regularly at the Archbishop Quigley Center. I assume you see Costello frequently.

Do you have any insights to share, anything you think might be of help in light of where we're trying to go?"

There was silence for several seconds by all parties to the conference call. Then Marsha spoke.

"I really don't know Archbishop Costello well. I serve on three archdiocesan councils, one of which is the Council for the Prevention of Abuse to Women, which also includes several psychologists and lawyers. The archbishop sometimes attends meetings of this council, and shows considerable interest in the cases we're working on and the progress we're making."

Marsha turned to Elaine. "Do you know the name of the woman whose daughter was abused or the name of the daughter?"

"We know the name of the woman from her email, and her parish from our list of email requests," Elaine responded. "With this information, we identified her survey form fairly easily. Her form didn't add anything of significance. As yet, we haven't been able to determine who the daughter is. However, she has to be a grown woman now, probably in her early 30s. According to her mother's email, she left the church, apparently disillusioned and scarred by her experience with Costello."

Marsha commented: "Archbishop Costello is hardly the kind of guy who would be violent or do something criminal. He's pleasant and soft-spoken. Although he sits in on our meetings now and then, he never interferes. He just wants to know who the clients are we're working with, and how their cases are going. That's about it."

"Does he ever express an opinion regarding which cases you should select?" Scotty wanted to know.

"He never has. However, he has requested we never take a case without first letting him know who the woman is we're going to represent. I assume he has political reasons for doing this."

Adolf, in Rome with Fred, joined the conversation: "Maybe – just maybe – he is concerned that, after all these years, the mother of the abused child, will appear on the scene, asking for help. Maybe even the daughter herself."

Again there was silence, for almost half a minute as the parties digested Adolf's theory. Finally Marsha spoke again.

"I have an idea. If the mother can be encouraged – no 'pressured' might be a better word – to ask for assistance from the Council, I'm sure I can convince the Council to accept her case. She shouldn't ever mention the priest in question is now Chicago's archbishop, but she should inform the Council she's planning to go to the police. Then we can observe Costello's reaction when he discovers this woman is looking for help."

Elaine raised the question: "Won't the Council insist that the daughter is the one eligible to file a complaint, not the mother?"

"The Council will tell her that they need to meet the daughter as well," Marsha responded. "But often the parent is also a victim in these cases, and is equally in need of our assistance."

"We can't lose sight of why we're doing this," Scotty added. "We have to figure out how to get the mother and daughter on board after all these years, but without compromising our main objective. Ultimately, we need to determine who killed Albert Rooney, and why."

CHAPTER 61

Marilyn Rutherford was not happy about the role she was being asked to play.

She was a quiet woman, unassuming and shy. She couldn't handle conflict. In fact, her argumentative and outspoken husband never could understand Marilyn's tranquil personality, which ultimately led to their divorce years ago. Marilyn raised their daughter as a single mom, and did her best to inculcate strong moral principles and a deep appreciation of the Catholic faith in young Dianne.

Marilyn couldn't figure out why this woman had shown up on her doorstep, reminding her of a painful incident in the past, and asking her to participate in an effort to bring the perpetrator to justice. She knew she wanted no part of it. She was quiet and shy, but she had a breaking point. Moreover, she was distressed that – without a doubt – a confidence had been violated.

"Mrs. Whitaker," Marilyn sobbed with frustration and anger in her voice, "what is the meaning of this intrusion into my life, digging up a personal episode which is none of your business? Not only 'none of your business' – you read a confidential email I sent to your husband two years ago! That's immoral and unethical. How dare you!"

Elaine was taken aback. Marilyn was dead right. Elaine had a lot of explaining to do. But she couldn't tell her too much.

"There's an investigation by law officials going on, Mrs. Rutherford. It involves things that happened back when my husband was doing the opinion survey for Pope Francis Xavier. I don't understand all the details of it, but my husband and I have been asked to contribute certain relevant data, if we have it. Your email is relevant. If you decide not to register a complaint with the Council for the Prevention of Abuse to Women, no one will bother you.

"However, if you do decide to participate, it will be of considerable value to the authorities in their efforts to see that justice is done. Either way, we will see that your email is not given public exposure.

"It's important you not mention the name of Archbishop Costello as a possible perpetrator, at least for now. Also your daughter need not be identified to the Council at this time, maybe not at all. However, some of the investigators may want to talk to her.

"Should you decide to be involved, your contribution will be of significant value, both to the Catholic Church and to law authorities. I hope you decide to participate."

Marilyn Rutherford signed on.

CHAPTER 62

Roméo Hayek hung up the phone. He sat in his den, staring out the window with his elbows on his desk and cheeks resting on his hands, his gaze focused on nothing in particular. Roméo was bewildered.

Holy shit! Can hardly believe I'm hearin' from the archbishop. How many months has it been? With his highfalutin job, I thought he'd written ol' Roméo off!

Since Tom Costello had been appointed archbishop of Chicago by Pope Pius XIII, Roméo had neither seen the archbishop, nor heard anything from the new leader of Chicago's Catholics. This wasn't all that surprising – the archbishop's responsibilities were overwhelming, greater by several magnitudes when compared to Costello's former assignment as auxiliary bishop and vicar of Vicariate IV. Moreover, the archbishop was concerned his involvement with the Ecclesia Vera Society might become public, and bring with it undesirable if not disastrous repercussions.

So a phone call from Costello was unexpected. Even more unusual was the archbishop's sense of urgency. He not only said he wanted to meet with Roméo, but he needed to see him right away at Roméo's condo, not at the Archbishop Quigley Center.

Two people could hardly be more different. Tom Costello, a career churchman, inveterate sycophant and a smooth talker, was a procrastinator and not terribly talented. He avoided decision-making and aggressive action, and only received the appointment as Chicago's archbishop because the former Antonio Ruggieri, now Pope Pius XIII, mentored him years before, knew they shared the same ultraconservative philosophy and was certain Costello would do what he was told to do – he wouldn't rock the boat.

Roméo Hayek, the son of working class Lebanese immigrants, was rough around the edges, outspoken, uncultured but bright. He had worked his way up in the construction industry and was now president of his company. He was quick to jump to conclusions, and when opposed, he was inclined to shoot first and ask questions later.

Costello and Roméo's common bond was their conservatism, the ethical compromises they would make to achieve their reactionary goals, and their membership in the ultraconservative Ecclesia Vera Society. Although Costello was head of the Chicago cell, since becoming Chicago's archbishop he kept the organization at arm's length, which made Roméo effectively acting head.

Shortly after their phone conversation, Archbishop Costello arrived at Roméo's historic condo building in the Streeterville neighborhood on Lake Michigan. He was pale, looked very tired, and was obviously disturbed.

"Roméo, I must apologize for not getting in touch with you sooner. I don't think I've ever been so busy or worked so hard in my life. There's no end to the problems the Chicago archbishop must handle. I hope you understand."

"No need to apologize to me, Archbishop. It don't bother me a bit. You got a big job, I know. I'm just glad you're stoppin' by now. Been a long time, that's for sure. I can see somethin's troublin' you. Can I help?"

"A major problem, Roméo. There's a woman, a parishioner from St. Barnabas Church where I was associate pastor many years ago. I think she's trying to ruin me!"

"Tryin' to *ruin* you? What do you mean? What's she doin'?"

"The archdiocese has a service called the Council for the Prevention of Abuse to Women. It's a place where women who have been abused, or are in abusive relationships, can come, unburden their problems to receptive councilors, and get legal advice if they need it. She's petitioned them to take her case. She says her preteen daughter was abused by a priest at St. Barnabas during the time I was the associate there. The Council says they will take her case."

"And she named you?" Roméo asked Costello in utter amazement.

"No, she doesn't want to name the priest until her daughter agrees to join her in the complaint. I remember the woman – she hated me! I lectured her because she was divorced and living with a man who wasn't her husband. She said she would get back at me someday. I never touched her daughter!"

"Well then you're OK, Archbishop. No one's gonna believe her."

"If she gets her daughter to go along with this lie, Roméo, it might stick. When it comes to clerical sex abuse these days, everyone assumes the priest is guilty, and they believe the accuser, almost automatically.

"Do you know what that means, Roméo? My career will be ruined! All the hard work I have done, you have done, and Ecclesia Vera has done to bring the church back to it's traditional roots will be undermined; liberals will take advantage of the situation; the agenda of Pope Pius XIII will suffer a serious setback. We just can't let this happen! I need your help."

Roméo hit his beefy right fist into his left palm, hard enough and loud enough to startle the archbishop.

"We gotta nip this in the bud!" Romeo bellowed. "No broad who's got attitude is gonna mess with what we done in Chicago. Too much at stake. That make-believe lay cardinal – we scared the shit out of him. Cardinal Rooney too –we fixed his wagon. Any bitch who thinks she can call the shots is got a surprise comin'. What's her name? Where does she live?"

Costello shifted uneasily in his seat. True, he was there to elicit help, but the reality of Roméo's violent nature and unpredictable actions frightened him. He worried Roméo would slip up one day, bring the law down on his shoulders, and even paint a path leading to Costello's doorstep. The thought terrified him.

"I'll give you the information you need, Roméo, but avoid violence, or anything illegal. Get in touch with this woman, and try to convince her that since she is unable to prove her accusations, pursuing this ill-advised course of action will ultimately bring shame and embarrassment to her family. She may end up disgracing her daughter, ruining her reputation and causing her great unhappiness. You're a successful and persuasive businessman, Roméo. I'm sure you can convince her."

"You want a drink, Archbishop? I can use one."

Costello held up his palms and shook his head. Roméo went over to his wet bar, poured himself about three fingers of bourbon, and returned to where Tom Costello was seated.

"Listen, Archbishop. Have I ever let you down? Don't I get the job done? Do I know how to make things happen or what? You give me her name and address – oh, and don't forget the daughter's. You let me worry about how to handle this. I know what I'm doin'."

Chapter 63

Aniela had been married to Pawel Bobowski for 22 years and nothing about that man ever surprised her. He was quite ill-tempered, especially when he was drinking, and several times had been arrested outside a bar for assault and battery. Even at church he misbehaved – getting into shouting matches with parishioners after Mass when they disagreed with his ultra-traditional beliefs about what Catholicism should be.

But this was different, and appeared extremely serious. Two police detectives appeared at their door this evening, and told Pawel he needed to come down to headquarters for questioning – questioning about a murder.

If nothing else, this was a creative call on police Superintendent Frank Ryan's part.

Elaine had gone to Brett Higgins with the comments from Aniela's opinion survey form from two years ago – comments that suggested her husband and his fellow construction workers might be plotting to wreck the survey of Chicago Catholics that Fred Whitaker was conducting for Pope Francis Xavier. Brett took this evidence of a conspiracy – as thin as it might be – to Frank Ryan to see if he thought they could do anything with it.

"So far, we have no credible leads to Cardinal Albert Rooney's murderer," Ryan stated. "Yes, this is terribly slim. Guys over a beer or two will talk about the big things they're going to do to change the world, and it usually doesn't mean a damn thing! But, at this point, we have nothing else to go on.

"These guys work for Streeterville Construction. We did see a Streeterville company car – a silver Mercedes – in the driveway of the cardinal's mansion the morning he was killed. As far as I'm concerned, that very fact dictates we follow up on this woman's comments."

"Everyone who filled out a survey form was told their responses were totally confidential" Higgins reminded him. "I think we're obligated to honor that."

Ryan and Higgins explored options as to how this could be handled. They came up with a plan.

"What do you mean, me and my buddies got together to waste Rooney? What kind of guys do you think we are? You're talkin' through your hat! You can't prove this! How did you come up with a crazy idea like that?"

Ryan stood up, put his hands on his desk, and leaned forward. "Listen, Bobowski, we have our sources! We have undercover agents where you least expect them. The guy you think you can trust the most might be working for us. He'll end up in court testifying against you!"

The superintendant never read him his Miranda Rights and didn't really care whether what he said could be used against him. He wanted to determine whether there actually had been a plot, and get Bobowski to finger the ring leader.

"We'll see you spend the rest of your life at Statesville, Bobowski. You're obviously the ringleader of this outfit. You don't like the Catholic Church, and this was your way of getting back at it."

Brett Higgins, sitting in a chair on the opposite wall, observed Ryan's technique with some amazement, amusement, and even envy.

Pawel Bobowski was not the brightest star in the sky. It never occurred to him that Superintendant Ryan might not hold all the cards he said he had.

"Listen, Chief, I take orders, I don't give them! I'm not taking the rap for something I don't deserve! My boss, Roméo – he gives me and my buddies the orders and we obey them. He always knows what's best. You're talkin' to the wrong guy!"

Ryan then began to probe for details about what Bobowski and his "buddies" were told to do, and how they did it. But finally a light bulb went on in Pawel's head, and he realized he had said too much. He clammed up.

But Ryan and Higgins had all the information they were looking for.

CHAPTER 64

Six weeks into their review of the handwritten survey comments, Elaine, Rachel and Chris put aside an afternoon for a strategy meeting. As they were getting quite discouraged and frustrated, they needed time to assess their progress to date, and determine what, if anything, they could do to improve their productivity.

"We've been through thousands of these things, and have found just one 'smoking gun,'" Elaine grumbled, as she waved her arms at the file boxes of forms they had already inspected. "It may not even be a 'smoking gun.' Brett Higgins and Superintendant Ryan are trying to determine that now. And how many hundreds of thousands of forms are waiting for us in K&E's storage room? It boggles the mind!"

"I think I'm going snow-blind looking at this stuff hour after hour," Chris added.

Rachel, always positive and optimistic, chimed in: "I've got to admit that, after a while, every form begins to look the same."

"Mom, maybe that Bobowski comment I found *is* important. If it is, I guess it's worth all our time and effort. And don't forget the Rutherford email you found – it looks like Archbishop Costello is a 'bad actor.' Knowing Rutherford has gone public may force his hand, and who knows what will come up."

Sharing their frustrations that afternoon was cathartic. None of them was about to quit, but giving vent to their emotions actually increased their feeling of solidarity. They were in this together, and knew what they were doing, though far from glamorous, was both important and necessary.

After they unloaded their mutual annoyances, they agreed they had to improve their future line of attack, to make their work more focused.

"I think we've got to capitalize on the information we already have," Elaine suggested. "We've uncovered two potentially important items – Aniela Bobowski's comment about a possible plot by the construction workers, and Marilyn Rutherford's reference to the abuse of her daughter Dianne. What we haven't yet discovered is whether there are paths leading from what we know now to other revelations that might be even more important."

The other two sat in silence as they thought about what Elaine had just said. Then Chris spoke up.

"We know Pawel Bobowski's buddies – the other Streeterville construction workers who live in his neighborhood and submitted survey forms – and we know what they said. But we also need to find out if some Streeterville workers who live in other neighborhoods submitted survey forms. If so, we need to read them too."

"That's a wonderful idea, Chris," Elaine replied. "Frank Ryan's office can get us their names and addresses. Professor Sylvester can then search his database for those who are Catholic and responded to the survey, and where they live. It will be easy to find their forms, since each will have a unique number."

"I have another idea," Rachel added. "Maybe other parishioners at St. Barnabas had bad experiences with Tom Costello when he was associate pastor there. We need to examine their survey forms. Also, was Costello assigned to any other parishes before he became auxiliary bishop? If so, we need to pull out all the forms from those parishes and read them."

"This is just great!" Elaine enthused. "You two have terrific ideas on how we can proceed in a more focused way, and build on the information we already have. Let's get started!"

CHAPTER 65

Superintendant Frank Ryan instructed the Chicago Police Department's investigative unit to produce a list of all construction workers employed by Streeterville, along with their addresses. Barkley Sylvester compared the list with the opinion survey database and was able to identify those who had submitted survey forms. Since each form was in numerical sequence, Elaine and her team easily located the documents. They checked them to see who might have complained about the survey process. They discovered two complaints, and put them aside for possible follow-up.

They also examined the survey forms completed by parishioners at Marilyn Rutherford's parish, St. Barnabas, searching for any references regarding the parishioners' children, or any negative comments about the clergy. They found none about clergy, but did find one reference to a child.

One woman noted that when her primary school daughter became quite withdrawn and introverted, she discussed the situation with the associate pastor, Father Costello. Since he was responsible for working with the parochial school children, she hoped he could help her daughter, maybe talk to her. She said the priest told her not to worry – children went through various phases, and her daughter would surely outgrow it. Since this incident occurred years ago, her daughter would now be about the same age as Marilyn Rutherford's daughter Dianne.

"I've had several contacts with Marilyn Rutherford since I asked her to lodge a complaint with the archdiocesan Council for the Prevention of Abuse to Women," Elaine told Rachel and Chris. "I think she now understands the importance of what she's doing for us. I have no hesitation asking her what she knows about the woman with the problem child."

"Also," Rachel added, "you could find out the names of other parishioners who had daughters about the same age as Dianne at that time. It would probably work best if you see her in person, rather than speaking to her on the phone."

"Mom," Chris interjected rather emphatically, "if it's OK with Mrs. Rutherford, I'd like to go with you. Some of the kids at my school talk about their parish priests, and have younger brothers and sisters in parochial schools. These days, everyone is pretty sensitive to the possibility of abusive priests. Kids talk about this. I may hear something that rings a bell. Besides, having another set of ears with you might be helpful."

"I agree, Chris. I'll ask Mrs. Rutherford if you can come along."

***

The next morning, Elaine and Chris headed south on the Kennedy Expressway toward the Chicago Loop, past the Circle Interchange where the Kennedy changes its name to the Dan Ryan Expressway, and down to Beverly in the southwest corner of the city. Historically Irish-Catholic, Beverly had become one of the more ethnically and racially diverse areas of the city. Marilyn Rutherford's home – built in the early 20th century architectural style known as the Chicago Bungalow – was on Hamilton, a leafy street off 97th.

When they were several blocks from her neighborhood, they saw smoke billowing up from where they were headed. Two blocks away, they were stopped by barricades. There were police cars, fire trucks, and an ambulance ahead. Peering down the street, Elaine could see the smoke was coming from Marilyn Rutherford's house.

Elaine and Chris jumped out of the car, and ran ahead to a police officer manning the barricade.

"Officer, we're heading to that home for a meeting with Mrs. Rutherford who lives there," Elaine stammered, trying to catch her breath. "Is she OK?"

The officer held on to the barricade, frowning. "No she isn't, ma'am."

"Is she badly burned?" Elaine paused, and with a look of dread on her face, asked: "She's alive, isn't she?"

"She didn't get burned, ma'am, but she's not alive. We found her on the living room floor with her throat slit."

CHAPTER 66

Elaine and Chris stared at each other in total disbelief. Finally Chris blurted out "Mom, Mrs. Rutherford's daughter, Dianne!"

Without another word spoken, they both turned and ran for the car. The tires squealed as Elaine turned around and raced to 97th Street, turned west and sped to Western Avenue, zipped south to 115th Street, drove west to Maplewood, and right to Dianne Rutherford Moffat's home in the Morgan Park neighborhood – an address Frank Ryan had given her.

As they careened toward their destination, Chris got on the phone and called Brett Higgins to inform him of Marilyn Rutherford's murder, and told him where they were now headed.

"Chris, you and your mother stay in the car! Don't go near the house! I'll let the police know what happened, and they'll be there in a matter of minutes."

Elaine parked a half a block from the house.

"The police should be here momentarily, Chris. We'll wait in the car for their arrival."

"Mom, she may be in grave danger! We can't just sit here! I've got to warn her to get out of her house!"

With that, Chris swung open the car door, and began running toward the house. Elaine stuck her head out the car window.

"Chris, come back! The murderers may be in there already. Don't put yourself in danger!"

Chris headed toward the front door at a dead run. There was a gunshot from one of the front windows, and Chris fell to the sidewalk.

Almost at that very moment, the sound of sirens wailing in the distance could be heard, heading for Maplewood. Several squad cars screeched to a stop in front of the house. Seeing Chris lying on his back near the front door, and bleeding, the officers piled out of their cars, guns drawn, and took up positions around the house.

"You are surrounded!" a voice boomed from one of the squad car's loudspeaker. "Drop your weapons and come out with your hands up!"

As the police waited, two officers, at considerable danger to themselves, crawled toward Chris to move him to a safer place. The sound of an ambulance siren blared in the distance.

Elaine was horrified seeing her son gunned down. Without even thinking, she jumped out of the car and ran toward where Chris had fallen. Before she got far, an officer restrained her. She was hysterical.

"My son – I've got to help my son!"

"You can't go any further, ma'am, without putting yourself in the line of fire. We're attempting to move your son to safety. An ambulance is on its way. There's nothing for you to do at this time."

In less than five minutes, the front door swung open, and a man walked out with his hands up. A few seconds later, two more men appeared in the doorway, their hands above their heads.

"Are there more in there?" shouted the officer in charge.

"No one but the woman," responded the first man who came out – Pawel Bobowski.

With their guns still drawn, four officers cautiously entered the house. In the kitchen, they found Dianne Rutherford Moffat on the floor, unconscious but alive, her face badly bruised.

Paramedics found Chris was still alive. He had a bullet wound in his chest, and had lost considerable blood. With his mother at his side, the ambulance took him to the Emergency Room at the nearby Little Company of Mary Hospital. He fluctuated between consciousness and unconsciousness during the trip as Elaine held his hand and prayed that God would spare him.

Chris was in surgery for five hours. The bullet had passed through his right lung and lodged close to his spine. Significant arterial damage had to be repaired. After surgery, he was in serious but stable condition. Elaine stayed with him all day and all night. It was over 24 hours before she returned home to get some rest.

CHAPTER 67

"My God, Elaine," Fred shouted. "Is Chris OK? Scotty wasn't able to reach me until a few minutes ago. I'll catch the next plane home!"

"Don't do that, Fred. There's no need. Chris is fine. The surgeons were able to remove the bullet and repair the damage. Chris is not in danger. He'll be in the hospital for about a week, and then convalesce at home for several weeks.

"I called Bob at Stanford, and also told him not to come home. But as you know, he's really close to his brother. He phoned back a couple of hours later, said he talked to the dean, and got a two-week leave to come home. The dean promised him he would be brought up to speed on anything he missed. Your sons are as stubborn as you are, Fred!

"Mother will be here as well. She's going to move into our guest room to help out as long as necessary. I know you are urgently needed in Rome at this stage of the investigation – more than you're needed here at this time. Don't worry about Chris."

"I'm not only worried about Chris – I'm damned mad! Why did that kid put himself in such danger when Brett Higgins specifically told him not to?"

"He's only 16, Fred. When you're 16, you think you can do anything – you're invincible! We had no evidence the killers were already there. It was an expensive lesson for our son, but thankfully, not a fatal one."

"And you say the suspects are all employees of Streeterville Construction?"

"That's right. Of course they're in custody. Scotty, Brett and Superintendant Ryan met this morning to determine what the next steps should be. They suspect that Roméo Hayek, who heads Streeterville, is the mastermind behind the murder of Marilyn Rutherford and the attempted murder of her daughter, but Ryan doesn't want to move until they've conducted a thorough interrogation of the men they've apprehended. He has plainclothes officers staking out Hayek's place, and monitoring his movements."

CHAPTER 68

August, 2048
Southern California

Bishop Martin Ramsey was a cool and collected individual, virtually unflappable. His disposition made him the ideal person to have created and organized the Ecclesia Vera Society, and plan its nationwide schemes, attempting to dismantle and destroy the liberal and progressive elements in the U.S. Catholic Church.

Now, however, his face was flushed, his blood pressure rising, and beads of perspiration were forming on his forehead and running down to his chin. No phone call could be less welcome than the one he was dealing with at the moment.

"Tom, are you out of your mind? Calling me at this time is totally insane! Your line may be tapped. You're putting me in danger! The Ecclesia Vera Society is secret, and furthermore, I'm not supposed to – and don't want to – know anything about what's going on in the Archdiocese of Chicago!"

The personalities of Bishop Martin Ramsey and Archbishop Tom Costello had a number of similarities. Both men were smooth talkers, ingratiating, politically astute, and more deceitfully calculating than might appear on the surface. On top of this, Tom Costello was a life-long sycophant, a trait that contributed to his advancement in the Catholic Church hierarchy. At this moment in time, Costello was as disturbed as Ramsey, probably more so.

"Martin, we've got a major problem on our hands – a problem that's on the verge of turning into a catastrophe!"

"Don't give me this 'we've got a problem' bullshit, Tom! What's happening in Chicago is no concern of mine. You know that! I set policy for the Society. It's up to the individual cells to decide how to implement policies and get results. I don't want to know how it's being done!"

"You can't hide behind that wall this time, Martin. What's coming down may prove to be the ruination of the Society, and more important, the ruination of you and me!"

Archbishop Costello went on to describe how Roméo Hayek was supposed to convince Marilyn Rutherford and her daughter not to tell a "lie" about Costello sexually abusing the daughter back when he was their parish priest. He apparently had his thugs murder the mother, but before taking out the daughter, they were caught.

"These brutes will surely lead the police to Hayek. You've met him, Martin. You know he's volatile. His mouth gets in motion before his brain is fully engaged. The authorities may tie him to the death of Archbishop Albert Rooney. To save his own skin, he may implicate me – and you!"

"Implicate me?" Ramsey screamed over the phone. "I wasn't involved! No one can connect me with that crime. I don't want to hear anything more about this!"

"If they get to Hayek, he may link me, and you as well! I need your help, Martin – we've got to nip this thing, and nip it now."

Martin Ramsey slumped back in his chair, his head spinning. He had structured the Ecclesia Vera Society specifically to distance himself from the activities individual cells chose to accomplish the Society's objectives. He didn't want to know what they were doing. And he certainly never asked any of his operatives to kill. Now, due to apparent blunders in Chicago, he was being dragged into their mess against his will. The situation was threatening everything he had worked for. He had no choice but to cooperate.

"What are you proposing I do, Tom?"

CHAPTER 69

August, 2048
Chicago

Chicago hosts a 96 acre jail campus – the largest in the country. The Cook County Jail is located at 2800 South California Avenue, southwest of the Loop. The facility has been cited by the U.S. Department of Justice on several occasions for various violations, some due to poor management or questionable practices, and some probably unavoidable due to its size, housing almost 13,000 inmates. Being incarcerated at Cook County Jail is an experience that has made many criminals wish they had chosen a life of virtue.

The three suspects arrested at Dianne Rutherford Moffat's home were taken there in separate police vans, isolated from the rest of the inmate population and with no contact with one another. They didn't even know if their co-detainees were at the same location.

For Superintendant Ryan to imprison them this way, there was a "method in his madness." He wanted to ensure there was no communication among these men, no opportunity for them to devise a "story." Furthermore, he wanted each of them to feel cut off, and perhaps forgotten.

The next day, he had them brought separately to police headquarters at 3510 South Michigan Avenue, and taken to different interrogation rooms. Each suspect was read his Miranda Rights, and told his attorney could be present during the questioning. Surprisingly, one of the men waived his right to have an attorney present, saying he didn't trust them and didn't need one. Ryan told the interrogators to concentrate on this particular man. His name was Charlie.

The interrogators spent the first few minutes making small talk with Charlie, asking about his family, even joking with him. Then the lead investigator shifted gears rather abruptly, throwing Charlie off-base.

"Charlie, we don't think you're the guy who planned this thing. How did you get mixed up with this crowd?"

"I had nothin' to do with wastin' that woman in Beverly. It was the other guys. I just showed up to help them lean on the gal on Maplewood, get her to stop tellin' lies."

His response was naïve, and quite damning. The interrogator had said nothing about Rutherford's murder, but Charlie did.

"We put out the fire before the house burned down, Charlie. We found your fingerprints in several places. We think you were there alone and killed the woman."

Charlie began to panic.

"Look, the other two guys were there. Bobowski planned the whole damn thing. He dragged me into it. I ain't the guy who snuffed that broad – he is!"

The interrogators left Charlie and entered Bobowski's room. His attorney was sitting next to him.

"My client has nothing to say to you, officer. He was at the Hamilton address, where you apprehended him. He was not in Beverly, did not kill that woman or start that fire."

The lead interrogator, ignoring the lawyer, glared at Bobowski.

"Look, Pawel, don't lie to us! One of your cohorts is willing to testify you planned this whole thing, and you killed Marilyn Rutherford. They're going to put you away for good!"

The attorney stood up and was about to speak, when Bobowski, hands trembling, blurted out:

"Listen, no one's going to frame me – we were all in this together. And I didn't make the plans!"

As the lawyer began to protest, the lead investigator shouted loud enough to drown him out.

"The other day, you told us that you take your orders from Hayek. Did he plan this? Did he also plan the murder of Cardinal Albert Rooney?"

"This is outrageous!" the attorney yelled, banging the table. "How dare you attempt to ensnare my client by insinuating his involvement in a murder years ago! You are blatantly engaged in a fishing expedition, and at my client's expense!"

He turned to Pawel: "Mr. Bobowski, say nothing more! Let me handle all of the officer's questions and unsubstantiated allegations."

Pawel Bobowski grabbed the arms of his chair, his knuckles white, his face ashen. He was clearly overwhelmed by the current situation. Shaking his head, he mumbled:

"Hayek's the boss – I do what I'm told!"

Chapter 70

Martin Ramsey's past trips to Chicago usually included an evening at Lyric Opera or the Chicago Symphony, or both. However, these diversions were the last thing on his mind as he removed his suitcase from the carousel at O'Hare, and went outside to catch a cab for the Loop.

What in God's name can I say to that Neanderthal to convince him to keep his mouth shut? Ramsey asked himself as the cab navigated the southbound traffic on the Kennedy Expressway.

Ramsey knew he had made it crystal clear to Ecclesia Vera cell members in all parts of the country he didn't want to know how they accomplished the Society's goals. Nevertheless, he had no doubt that the church shoot-up, the car bomb killing a Whitaker security guard, and the murder of Cardinal Albert Rooney were all the work of the city's cell, which Tom Costello controlled with Roméo Hayek as his "heavy." Costello as much as told him this earlier in the week when they spoke on the phone. Furthermore, the one time he had met Hayek, the man bragged about the strong-armed tactics his thugs used to accomplish their goals.

Too much was at stake for Ramsey to let this situation spin out of control. He felt sure the authorities had no hard evidence implicating anyone in the Chicago cell with the past violence. Otherwise, charges would have been leveled and arrests made months ago. Consequently, he needed to make it clear to Hayek he had nothing to fear, no matter what empty threats the police were now making. That is, as long as he denied knowing anything, and said as little as possible.

As a precaution, Ramsey determined it was too dangerous for them to meet at Roméo's condo, since it might be under surveillance. Better to have them meet in his hotel suite at the Drake.

Martin Ramsey was a smooth and fairly effective speaker, quite adept at arguing his point-of-view. Even with a coarse and uncouth specimen like Hayek, he felt he could make a strong case: protecting Hayek's reputation, the security of his family, the continued success of his construction company, and, of course, the avoidance of spending the rest of his life in prison.

He stopped by the archbishop's residence to discuss the strategy he would use with Hayek. Costello was plainly nervous, and showed signs of stress. Ramsey assured him he'd be successful with Roméo at their meeting the following afternoon.

CHAPTER 71

"You got good taste, Bishop. There probably ain't a better hotel in town."

"Good to see you, Roméo. Can I have room service bring you up something to eat or drink?"

"It's been a hard day, Bishop. A double bourbon on the rocks would hit the spot. Old Fitzgerald bonded if they got it. Otherwise, Maker's Mark."

Martin ordered a scotch and soda for himself.

While they were waiting for their drinks and some hors d'oeuvres, Roméo went on and on, in some detail, about the problems he was having with one of the builders with whom he had spent the morning.

"Some of these guys make life more difficult than it needs to be, Bishop. Don't know what it's like bein' a church official, but in construction, sometimes you're walkin' a tightrope with these developers who think they know more about how to build than the construction people who have to do the job."

After the drinks were delivered, and the waiter had left, Martin got down to the reason he was in Chicago.

"You talked about walking a tightrope, Roméo. That's a pretty good analogy for the situation the Chicago police are probably putting you in at this time. I've heard three of your employees have been implicated in a murder and an attempted murder a few days ago. When people get in that kind of trouble, they sometimes try to put the blame on someone else, thinking this will save their skin. They might try to do this to you, since all of them work for you.

"I've heard these three men have all had brushes with the law in the past – criminal records – and one actually went to prison for a couple of years. Whatever they claim now – if they try to shift blame to someone else – it would never hold up in court, given their records. You can't let them pull a fast one on you, Roméo. It's your word against theirs. Whatever they say, no one will believe them. You're an upstanding citizen, a successful businessman with a fine reputation. You can't let them drag your name in the mud.

"And I hardly need tell you, you mustn't say anything to implicate Archbishop Costello in this mess. He's an outstanding churchman, a leader with whom the pope has entrusted the spiritual life of two million Catholics in the Chicago area.

"Should these three brutes, in an act of desperation, attempt to sully the good name and reputation of this holy man, hand-picked by Pope Pius XIII to shepherd the faithful, you need to do all you can to protect Archbishop Costello's sterling reputation. You must make it clear the perpetrators are desperate liars, unreliable and not to be believed, even for a second!"

Ramsey's main worry was not what the three construction workers might say to the police, since he assumed they had no idea, and certainly no evidence, that would point a finger at Tom Costello. His whole focus was keeping Hayek from folding if it turned out he was brought to police headquarters for questioning.

Roméo took a big swig of his bourbon and coughed as it seemed to irritate his throat a little. He smiled at Ramsey.

"You know and I know that Costello ain't so lily-white, Bishop. Me and him have been as thick as thieves, and you're no innocent bystander either. We're all in this together. As the top guy in Ecclesia Vera, you told us to pull the rug out from under Whitaker's project, and we done a pretty good job o' that. I hope you're not tellin' me you got complaints. And besides that . . ."

"Look, Hayek, I never told you or Costello to engage in violence!" Ramsey interrupted Roméo in mid-sentence, his voice growing louder as he shook his index finger at him. "I didn't even want to know what you were doing. I just told you and Costello to stop the Whitaker operation any way you could. And what did you do? You engaged in a lot of violence, and the project continued. Is that what you call a 'pretty good job?' And now there's more violence, and your goons get caught."

"The archbishop didn't want these two broads lyin' about him. He told me to convince 'em to stop. As you said, we got to protect the archbishop's reputation."

Somehow, this wasn't going the way that Martin Ramsey had planned. He didn't want to revisit his instructions of two years ago to dismantle Whitaker's mission. Somehow Hayek dragged him into that scenario before he knew it. He needed to get this meeting back on track.

"The point I'm making, Roméo, is we must not do or say anything to compromise the integrity and position of Archbishop Costello. There's much too much at stake."

"It's too late, Bishop."

"What do you mean 'it's too late?'" Ramsey muttered, almost in a whisper.

"Let me put it this way, Bishop. You're a day late and a dollar short!"

Ramsey slumped back in his chair, hands planted firmly on his thighs and eyes widening as he stared intently at Hayek.

Romeo took another gulp of his drink, got up and walked to the window. He turned around and faced Martin Ramsey.

"Here's the deal, Bishop. The cops brought me down to headquarters yesterday to ask me a few questions. Turns out they leaned pretty heavy on my boys after they caught 'em red-handed. Seems they were scared outta their wits. The cops told 'em they could work a deal if they told 'em everything. One of the guys not only admitted to their snuffing that broad and setting fire to her house – he spilled the beans about all the other stuff two years ago, figuring he could save his skin. The goddamned sonofabitch then fingered me as the brains behind all this."

"Don't let the police intimidate you, Roméo! They can't prove a thing! They have no evidence. Remember what I said before – these men have criminal records. Their word can't be trusted. If you keep your mouth shut, you have nothing to worry about."

Ramsey was hoping against hope that Hayek hadn't already admitted his involvement, or worse yet, implicated Tom Costello.

Roméo returned to his seat, and finished off his bourbon on-the-rocks. He leaned back in his chair, and clasped his hands behind his head.

"I couldn't believe what these bums told the cops, Bishop. They know details about what happened two years ago that only guys that done the work – shootings, bombings, stuff like that – could know. They sang like canaries. Cops told 'em they might be able to work a deal if they cooperated. Even their lawyers went along with this. Turns out the DA and the top cop are lookin' for the big fish, so these jerks fingered me. The cops already knew too much – I had to spill the beans. Didn't even bother to call my lawyer."

The room began to swim before Martin's eyes – he thought he was going to pass out. He struggled to regain his equilibrium. Finally, he stood up and threw his hands in the air.

"Hayek, you fool!" he stammered. "You let them get the better of you – pull the wool over your eyes! Call your lawyer right away! If your lawyer wasn't there, they can't use any of that against you. And for God's sake, don't implicate the archbishop under any circumstances! The damage to the church in Chicago, and maybe even throughout the United States, would be beyond calculation!"

"It seems to me, Bishop, they want to hook fish a lot bigger than me. They told me I could work a deal too, as long as I played ball with 'em."

"Good God! You didn't tell them about Costello, or the Ecclesia Vera Society, did you, Roméo?

"Told 'em everything I could, Bishop. Told 'em I'd be seeing you today, so they gave me a wire."

Ramsey literally fell into his seat again, and buried his face in his hands.

"You've been *recording* all this?"

"Not me, Bishop. The cops are recording it. Or maybe it's the DA."

Martin Ramsey struggled to his feet, and pointed toward the door.

"Get the hell out of here, Hayek!" Ramsey shouted. "I never want to see your face again! You'll burn in Hell for all eternity for what you've done – to the church, the archbishop, to me!"

Roméo slowly lifted himself out of the chair, picked up his coat that was draped over another chair, and headed for the door. He turned around and looked at Ramsey.

"As I said before, Bishop, you're a day late and a dollar short."

Chapter 72

A bishop who is an ordinary has many duties beyond his administrative responsibilities. These other duties tend to be ceremonial and pastoral, and include such activities as presiding at liturgical events, attending fund-raising affairs, dedicating and blessing newly renovated churches, and serving as the principal Catholic representative at civic affairs and interfaith gatherings. At these times, the bishop is usually expected to deliver a speech, or at least make appropriate comments, and socialize with those attending.

For many bishops, pastoral activities are considered an important part of their mission, and they look forward to fulfilling this role – to be an apostle of Christ, spreading the Gospel and reaching out to the faithful and the rest of the community. Tom Costello had no desire to do any of these things.

Costello was a rigorous traditionalist. As archbishop, his goal was to bring the church in Chicago back to the purity enjoyed by Catholicism in the 19th and early 20th centuries. He wanted to enforce its former discipline, when the priests followed the directives of their bishops to the letter, and the faithful looked to the priests in their parishes for guidance and didn't question the rules and regulations laid down by the church in Rome. He knew his commitment to this goal was the reason Pope Pius XIII had appointed him Chicago's archbishop. Yet, it was a daunting task to get his priests, many of them all too liberal, to become more doctrinaire, more effective disciplinarians, and better role models for the people in the pews.

He wasn't looking forward to the evening's activities. A parish on Chicago's Southside was celebrating its 75th anniversary with a Mass at which Costello was presiding, followed by a banquet, with the archbishop as guest-of-honor, and at which he was expected to make a speech. The evening would include much socializing with the parishioners. He dreaded such evenings.

As he was preparing to leave his residence for the event, he received a phone call.

"Tom, this is urgent," he heard Martin Ramsey's voice, breathlessly informing him. "I saw Roméo Hayek this afternoon, and we're too late!"

Ramsey told him in detail what had happened during his meeting with Hayek, Roméo's total folding when questioned by the police in hopes of a plea bargain, and the incredible reality that he was wearing a wire to entrap Ramsey during their meeting.

Tom Costello had never felt the degree of panic he was now experiencing. His hands shook, and he dropped the phone.

"Tom, are you there? Are you OK?"

"What in hell are we going to do?" Tom screamed after he retrieved the phone. "The police are going to be at my front door any minute now! I'm ruined!"

"You told me you were leaving in two days for a meeting of the International Theological Commission at the Vatican. Don't wait two days – leave now! Now! Since Pius XIII was your mentor when he was cardinal, he'll protect you. The Holy See has no extradition treaty with the United States. You'll be safe there, but you must leave now!

"There's absolutely no evidence I knew anything about what was going on in Chicago two years ago. I can protect myself. But you must leave for Rome right away – before it's too late!"

That's it! Costello was quick to grasp the urgency. *I'll say the pope called me to Rome, and I can't make it to the anniversary celebration this evening. I'll make a reservation on the first flight to Rome that's available tonight.*

He had his secretary reserve his flight and told him to make the proper excuses, that he had to leave for the Vatican immediately. After grabbing his already packed suitcase for his planned departure in two days, he went out to his car, and told his driver to take him to O'Hare.

***

The trip to the airport was slow. It was the height of the evening commute, and the traffic was stop-and-go. The 18-mile trip took about 20 minutes in light traffic, but this evening, it would be well over an hour.

That didn't worry Tom Costello. His flight to Rome, with a plane change at JFK, was due to leave in four hours. After 15 minutes on the expressway, he was finally beginning to relax. The circumstances were not good, but not hopeless. Granted it would have been considerably preferable if Martin Ramsey could have met with Roméo Hayek before the police got to him, but from a positive point of view, he now had the information that Roméo had divulged everything, had put him in jeopardy in an effort to save his own skin – not only implicated him, but compromised the Ecclesia Vera Society and linked Ramsey to the Chicago schemes in a way Martin may not be able to shake off.

But Tom was on his way out of the country and even the long arm of the law wouldn't be able to grab him at the Vatican. He felt certain the pope would protect him and might even give him a permanent assignment with the Roman Curia.

The pope clearly owed him a debt of gratitude. Everything Hayek and his "gang" did on Tom's behalf was specifically done to accomplish the objectives of Cardinal Antonio Ruggieri prior to his election to the papacy. After all, didn't Ruggieri come to

Chicago, and personally give Tom a vial of serum, along with detailed instructions on how to take Cardinal Albert Rooney out of the picture?

Tom was not a violent man. All of this mayhem made him very uncomfortable, but he agreed with Ruggieri that getting the church back on the right track was essential, and a few compromises were necessary. In general, Costello didn't believe the end justified the means, but there were exceptions, and with the stakes so high he knew this was one of them.

Tom didn't like the heavy-handed tactics used by Roméo and his crew. However, they got the job done, and Tom avoided getting his hands dirty.

As the car left the Kennedy Expressway and headed to the airport's international terminal, he breathed a sigh of relief.

I have no doubt the holy father will take care of me. Yes, the way things have turned out is far from ideal, but it could be a worse – a lot worse!

***

Once in the terminal, Costello went to a kiosk to print his ticket. He checked his suitcase, and proceeded to the security gate, where he presented his ticket and identification to a TSA officer who was directing passengers to the proper lines. Since he was traveling first-class, he knew his line would be short, and he would have plenty of time to stop at a restaurant for a drink and something to eat before his plane took off.

As Costello proceeded to the first-class security check-in line, two Chicago police officers approached and asked him to step aside.

"Sir, we have some questions we need to ask you. We want you to come with us to a room off the lobby."

A wave of fear raced through Tom's torso and legs. His knees began to shake. *Don't trouble trouble 'til trouble troubles you,* he recalled his mother telling him when he was a child. Suddenly he remembered he hadn't cancelled his original flight scheduled for two days later, and holding two flight reservations might have triggered an alarm in this age of ultra-tight security. *That's it! Don't panic! This is probably nothing.*

"Gentlemen, can we make this very brief? I have a flight to Rome this evening, and I'm on my way to get something to eat before I board. If you have a question, perhaps you could ask me here so I won't be delayed."

The officers looked at each other for a moment, and then one of them addressed Costello.

"You won't be catching that flight to Rome, sir. Come with us. You're under arrest."

CHAPTER 73

The highly charged atmosphere in Scotty's office before the Friday conference call was hard to characterize – intense, excited, eager expectation, probably all of the above. Elaine, Brett Higgins, Marsha McGuire and even Chicago Police Superintendant Frank Ryan were there for the session.

At 2:00 p.m. precisely, the call was connected with Fred and Adolf at Palatine Chemicals. Before Scotty was able to introduce those present, Fred began speaking.

"Elaine, tell me how Chris is getting along."

"He's doing fine, Fred. As you know, Bob flew home from Stanford as soon as he could, and went directly to the hospital. His brother's presence did wonders for Chris. Instead of staying in the hospital for a week or more, he was released in five days. He's so anxious to get back to work on our opinion survey project and keeps insisting, quite accurately, our work has moved the investigation ahead by leaps and bounds."

"That brings us to the big news," Scotty quickly added, "and why the entire 'A-Team' is in my office this afternoon."

He went on to acknowledge everyone in the room. This included Rachel who had proved herself indispensable. She had very effectively handled follow-up for both Higgins and the Superintendent while Elaine was devoting her time and energy to caring for Chris.

"Our combing through the hand-written comments on the survey forms has been slow and tedious, with little to show for our efforts," Elaine related, "until Chris uncovered the Streeterville connection, and we got poor Marilyn Rutherford (God rest her soul), the mother of the girl whom Costello molested years ago, to file a complaint with the archdiocese's Council for the Prevention of Abuse to Women, and Marsha got the Council to accept it. These events triggered a big unraveling."

"'Big unraveling' is a major understatement," Brett Higgins was quick to add. "Tragically it led to Rutherford's murder, but thanks to the quick thinking of Elaine and your son, the hoodlums were apprehended, and another murder was prevented."

"Everyone was trying to save their own skin," Superintendent Ryan commented. "The thugs pointed fingers at Roméo Hayek. Hayek implicated Archbishop Costello, not only in the plan to kill Rutherford, but in the death of Cardinal Rooney two years ago."

Fred was flabbergasted.

"I can't believe what you're telling me! It sounds like Albert Rooney's murder is all but solved!"

"There's more," Ryan added. "A lot more!"

***

"We arrested Costello as he was about to leave the country for Rome. During our interrogation at headquarters we told him Marilyn Rutherford's daughter Dianne, who had just avoided becoming a murder victim herself, agreed to file charges against Costello for sexual abuse 20 years ago. Costello was terrified when we brought him in, but when we told him that, I thought he was going to have a heart attack!

"He started off by claiming he wasn't guilty of anything, probably on the advice of his attorney who was present. But when he found out how much we already knew, and we confirmed Ramsey's meeting with Hayek was recorded, he decided to join the 'Save Your Own Skin Club' along with Hayek and his boys.

"He asserted whatever happened two years ago was all the doing of Hayek and his underlings. They were responsible for the rough stuff, which he absolutely disapproved of. Moreover, Ramsey was the mastermind – he was the one calling the shots."

"Not only that," Higgins interjected. "He said Ramsey took his orders from Cardinal Antonio Ruggieri at the Vatican. Costello painted himself as a victim of circumstances. Not a conniver, not a schemer, certainly not a murderer. Someone who's as 'pure as the wind-driven snow!'"

"Antonio Ruggieri!" Fred gasped. "The man we now call Pope Pius XIII?"

"That's the guy," Brett added. "I was there during the interrogation. The investigator went on to say they already knew about the vial of serum Ruggieri gave Costello. Costello said he passed this on to Hayek and had no idea what Hayek did with the stuff. Pure as wind-driven snow indeed!"

"The archbishop promised more information if he could avoid indictment or incarceration – at least for a while," Ryan added. "He claimed the scandal would hurt the Chicago faithful irreparably, and the American church beyond measure. He wanted to make suitable preparations at the chancery office and archdiocesan headquarters before the word was out.

"The DA said OK, but with the stipulations that Costello was not to go anywhere other than his residence and the Quigley Center, and must not discuss the case with anyone in person, on the phone, or in writing. And, of course, surrender his passport. You've heard about the newly developed ankle bracelet that's a GPS, sensitive to the sound of human conversation and will pick up the electronic signals from both sides of the wearer's phone conversations. He agreed to everything, including the bracelet. The media has no knowledge of his arrest."

"It's essential the media not be informed at this time," Scotty added. "We must not tip off the perpetrators at the Vatican, and elsewhere."

"We brought Ramsey in for questioning as well," Ryan informed Fred and Adolf. "Although we're not sure whether he was involved in plotting Cardinal Rooney's murder, we wanted to prevent his communicating with the Vatican and tipping off the perpetrators. We obtained a court order to muzzle him as well, put an ankle bracelet on him, keep him in Chicago, and lift his passport. Hayek's wearing a bracelet as well. We're trying to be as careful as possible."

"We're at a dead-end in Rome," Adolf commented. "At the moment, my undercover investigators and those of the Carabinieri have no more leads to investigate in solving the murder of Pope Francis Xavier. Ruggieri's connection to Chicago two years ago appears to be a significant breakthrough."

"The breakthrough got wider as the archbishop supplied more information," Scotty informed Adolf. "Ruggieri unwittingly explained to Costello the origin of the serum. Some relative of a church big-wig, identity unknown to Costello, developed the muscle paralyzer which operates without leaving a trace . . ."

Fred jumped in before Scotty finished.

"Was this relative a scientist with The Swiss Alpine Laboratory in Bern, Switzerland?"

"I don't think so," Scotty continued. "He says she runs a medical laboratory in Munich. She's a nun."

Chapter 74

September, 2048
Mumbai

A messenger from the Kirkland & Ellis resident partner in Mumbai delivered a note to Sanjay Patel, stating his nephew needed to speak to him. Patel almost expected this. Every week or so he got this message – a signal from Fred Whitaker to phone him in Rome, or wherever he was at the time. At first, Sanjay would use the phone of a friend to ensure these calls were not tracked. But after a couple of weeks, he decided to purchase a disposable one-time use phone as an extra precaution. He had one, and dialed Fred's number.

"Cardinal Patel, much has happened in the past few days – let me fill you in." Fred went on to describe in detail all the extraordinary activity in Chicago – the murder, the arrests, the information the suspects had divulged that, beyond a doubt, provided a breakthrough in their investigation.

Patel was elated – things were moving forward at a more rapid pace than he had hoped for, or could have even imagined. When he instigated this initiative and recruited Fred Whitaker and Scotty Campbell to run the show, he was optimistic their efforts would bear fruit, but he didn't expect so much, so fast.

"I can hardly find words to express my pleasure about hearing the good news, Mr. Whitaker. We are well on our way, thanks to you and Mr. Campbell's excellent planning and effective leadership. It pains me to say this, but I'm really not surprised Ruggieri was an instigator – perhaps the chief instigator – of these tragic events. Somehow it's consistent with his life's pattern – an expression of the demons that clearly drive him. If the evidence proves he planned and executed these unspeakable tragedies, those who know him well will be the first to believe it's true. A sad commentary."

"Like everything we have done to date, Cardinal Patel, this penetration must be kept totally secret. We must avoid alerting Ruggieri or anyone connected with him about our project, and especially our progress. Otherwise, we compromise our achieving a successful outcome. I know you understand that"

"I understand completely, Mr. Whitaker. I have shared nothing with anyone, except with Paolo Andreano and Raj Magar, who of course are members of the Working Group."

"You've been *sharing* with Andreano?" Fred responded, gasping to catch his breath. He suddenly realized he had failed to alert Patel about his doubts regarding Andreano's trustworthiness. "What have you told him?"

"Andreano comes to Mumbai now and then. He and Magar are long-time business associates. Andreano has money that, for some reason, he can't invest in Europe. So Magar finds Indian opportunities for him."

How could I have missed this? Fred wondered in amazement, berating himself for letting this happen. *Adolf has evidence Andreano is not trustworthy, and now I find out he's doing business with another member of our Working Group, who perhaps is laundering money for him. This could spell disaster!*

"Cardinal, tell me what they know!"

"I met with Andreano and Magar just yesterday. I told them there was evidence Chicago's archbishop may have sexually abused a child when he was a parish priest. And also a possible plot by Chicago construction workers to dismantle the opinion survey project you were pursuing for Francis Xavier. Andreano complained you seemed to be too busy to give him feedback on the Working Group's progress, so he welcomed any information I was able to provide. I assumed there were no secrets among members of the Working Group."

"There's a problem with Paolo Andreano, Cardinal Patel, and from what you've just told me, maybe Raj Magar also." He went on to describe, in detail, what Adolf had discovered about Paolo's background, and the manner in which Andreano had pumped him for information. "There's a probable leak here, and we must do all we can to stem it."

Patel and Whitaker reviewed the situation thoroughly, and explored their options. They agreed Patel was not to contact either man, though they both expected to hear from Patel. When they finally phoned him for information, he would say there was nothing new. The evidence the Chicago members of the Working Group thought they had didn't pan out. The authorities there were back at square one and looking for new avenues to explore.

"Scotty and I have taken a 'needs know' approach to sharing information with other members of the Working Group. I should have informed you," Fred admitted, still kicking himself for his oversight.

"Don't worry about it, Mr. Whitaker. I'm sure no significant damage was done."

CHAPTER 75

September, 2048
Vatican City

"I've been waiting for a call from you, Paolo. It's been many days. Why haven't I heard from you sooner? Haven't you been able to find out anything?"

Mario Lusardi, camerlengo of the Holy Roman Church, was hardly a patient man. On top of that, he had strict instructions from the pope to make sure Paolo Andreano obtained – as soon as possible – all the information from the Working Group's investigation that threatened him.

"I apologize for not contacting you sooner, Your Eminence. It's been very difficult to find out anything of importance. Fred Whitaker is not including me in the process, or telling me what's going on. However, I now have something. I was in Mumbai to see Raj Magar, and we met with Cardinal Patel. It seems Archbishop Costello is in trouble, and perhaps some operatives of the Ecclesia Vera Society as well."

"I told you his holiness suggested you contact Bishop Ramsey, the head of that society, to see if he could be of help. Have you done that?"

"I was just coming to that, Your Eminence. After the Mumbai meeting, I called him. The call was timely. Bishop Ramsey informed me Archbishop Costello requested he come to Chicago and meet with Roméo Hayek – the other Ecclesia Vera member there. Some of Hayek's workers were arrested for a woman's murder, and the archbishop was worried these workers would implicate Hayek. His main concern was Hayek might not only be implicated in this recent killing, but also delineate a trail leading back to the archbishop's involvement in the murder of Cardinal Albert Rooney."

There was a long silence on the phone. Finely, Lusardi spoke.

"I will pass this information on to the proper people. It is essential this Chicago investigation go no farther than Chicago. We must bring the Vatican portion of the Working Group's investigation to an end. Think, Paolo! What can be done to end this evil activity threatening the church at the very highest levels?"

"I have a plan, Your Eminence. I will implement it right away!'

CHAPTER 76

September, 2048
Flight from Rome to Bern

The day after their conference call with the Chicago group, Adolf Klein and Fred Whitaker booked the first available flight to Bern, Switzerland.

"This is becoming more and more mind-boggling, Adolf," Fred opined, almost incredulously, as the plane took off from da Vinci for the one-hour flight to Bern. "New pieces of the puzzle keep appearing, but God knows how they fit together."

"Could it be this nun independently created the same serum Dr. Schmidt developed at The Swiss Alpine Laboratory?" Adolf asked.

"Or perhaps Schmidt is in cahoots with the perpetrators," Fred added, "one of whom may be the nun – the same nun, undoubtedly, the porter Gino Cogliano saw leaving the papal apartments.

"How can we get the information we need when we see Schmidt at Swiss Alpine? We need to motivate him to tell us what he knows without alerting the folks at the Vatican we might be on to something."

"I think I know a way, Fred. It's a bit risky – we could blow our cover – but I believe there's a good chance we can ferret out what we need to know without tipping our hand. As you know, after the conference call yesterday, I had an investigator check to see if other meat packers had licensed the serum. Since our previous visit with Schmidt, he discovered Swiss Alpine has signed up four meat packers, in addition to Carne di Qualità, to use the serum in their operations. This fact will prove vital to our strategy."

***

"Gentlemen, this is outrageous!" Dr. Eric Schmidt practically shouted at Fred and Adolf. "There's absolutely nothing wrong with serum 57WS4982! For several months now, the serum, which we have branded as 'Sarenol,' has been used in the meat packing industry with no problems. Sarenol is a humane way to kill animals – much more humane than slaughtering them in the brutal manner used by humans for thousands of years. What do you mean 'it's defective?' How dare anyone make that claim? The Swiss Alpine Laboratory has never licensed a substance that hasn't undergone rigorous testing, and met all regulatory requirements."

"Dr. Schmidt," Adolf informed him, "we have no involvement or stake in this investigation. We're passing this information on to you as a favor. When we saw you months ago about the criminal investigation involving Sarenol and the samples you gave Father Bivona, we promised you we would give you any feedback we thought would be helpful.

"One of your customers – we're not permitted to give the name – has a very serious issue," Fred continued. "The meat from cattle killed using Sarenol has caused malignant liver tumors in certain consumers. The packer sent the serum to a lab for testing, and found a carcinogenetic molecule created by the synthesizing of the drug. The meat packer has been sued for using Sarenol without government approval. But the packer claims your lab should have gotten regulatory approval prior to licensing the serum.

"Furthermore, they claim the inventor of the substance should have known this side effect, and it never should have been marketed. They feel duped. They've requested a criminal investigation, and you, of course, will be at the center of the probe. We wanted to warn you."

All of this was a fiction that Adolf developed on the flight to Bern, and Fred said he'd go along with it. Given the disclosure

Costello made about a nun as the architect of the paralyzer, they had to do something to smoke out the truth.

That goddamned nun! Why did we ever bring her aboard as an intern? Eric Schmidt's mind was churning.

He was in a "Catch-22." If he didn't admit he had stolen the formula from Sister Sophie, he would be subject to a criminal investigation. If he did disclose he took credit for someone else's work, he would be fired and his professional career would be ruined. These men had forewarned him, thank God! Maybe if he was candid with them, they might help him find a way out of this dilemma. He would take the chance – he saw no alternative.

"I don't know how to tell you this," Schmidt admitted, as he started his story. "I'm embarrassed beyond measure. We had this nun as an intern a few years ago. She was very bright and very creative. And she was crazy as a hoot-owl! She had invisible friends. More than that – she said she gets messages directly from God!

"She came up with this substance we now call Sarenol. It was lethal, and dangerous if it got into criminal hands. It would have been irresponsible on my part if I gave an insane woman the right to do with it as she pleased. I demanded she destroy all her working papers and give me any remaining samples of the compound. I thought that's what she had done."

"Can you prove this story?" Adolf interjected.

"I saved the original memo she sent me, in which she included the chemical formula, and the process by which she concocted it.

"Although Sarenol can be misused, so can a gun or a knife. I felt if our firm kept a tight control over who would have access to it, we could prevent abuse."

"So, as a matter-of-fact, you made money from this woman's creativity, and she got nothing for her efforts. Isn't that true?" Fred stated.

"This wasn't an ideal situation," Schmidt admitted. "We'll never make a fortune from this drug, but it did present a viable alternative for the meat-packing industry. If our exploiting the work of this nun becomes an issue, I feel sure our management would be willing to donate the profits to charity. However, if what you say is true – the serum morphs into a carcinogen – there will be no profits, only liabilities."

Dr. Schmidt continued, "I'm worried about my career, and the future of The Swiss Alpine Laboratory. I need any helpful ideas you may have in this regard."

Fred and Adolf looked at each other for a few seconds. Adolf spoke.

"I can assure you, Dr. Schmidt – we'll see to it the damage is minimal."

"But we need to know who this nun is," Fred added.

"Sister Sophie. She runs a lab division at the Medical Center of the Ludwig-Maximilian University of Munich. Also, you need to know her uncle is a very important churchman – the Vatican secretary of state."

CHAPTER 77

September, 2048
Vatican City

One of the salient features of Antonio Ruggieri's life was his single-minded focus. Ever since he was a teenager, he was determined to out-perform anyone in his chosen field of endeavor, and rise to the very top. His chosen field was the administration of the Catholic Church, and he had accomplished his goal completely and remarkably well. He was now Pope Pius XIII, the supreme pontiff of Catholicism.

To assist him in accomplishing his goal, he put in harness the efforts of quite a few like-minded churchmen, such as Dieter Kaufmann and Mario Lusardi, and laymen such as Paolo Andreano and senior operatives of the Mafia in the Calabria region. He was fully conscious of the ethical compromises – serious compromises – he had made to achieve his supremacy, but he was convinced the rulebook was written for the *hoi polloi*, not for exceptional people like himself who were destined to be outstanding leaders.

During his formative years, he had read the biographies of great leaders – men who had achieved remarkable things, but often cut corners and ignored widely accepted moral dictates in order to reach their objectives.

Anyone who imagines pure, unadulterated virtue will lead to a better world is hopelessly naïve, he would tell himself. *Virtue is its own reward!*

To make a difference in this world, you must do whatever it takes to come out on top and set the pace for the masses to follow. That's what makes the world go 'round!

The audacity of Sanjay Patel – galvanizing a secret group of "do-gooders" who are intent on solving murders that have alluded law enforcement officials on two continents – was despicable, Antonio fumed, finding this blatant personal threat beyond his comprehension. However, thanks to Paolo Andreano, he was able to keep track of what they were doing.

Not actually he – Mario Lusardi was charged with the task, and was to keep Dieter Kaufmann informed.

I don't want to even know what is happening! My mandate to these men is simple and clear – to make sure the Working Group's efforts are unsuccessful, and must not, in any way, pose a danger to my papacy!

***

"Dieter, Paolo called me," Lusardi informed Kaufmann. "He saw Patel in Mumbai, and heard distressing news about the Ecclesia Vera operatives in Chicago. There's evidence Costello is a pedophile. Also, three of Hayek's employees were arrested for murder. It seems the two situations are connected. Nothing has collapsed, but it's like a small break in the dike – it's troubling. As he gets more information, he'll pass it on. In the meantime, he's developing a plan."

"A plan? What sort of plan?"

"I have no idea, Dieter. He just said he has a plan and will implement it right away."

"Tell him to back off, Mario!" Kaufmann responded with a tone of urgency. "His job is to provide information, not execute 'plans.' He could end up making a bad situation worse. Tell him to make sure he finds out what's going on in Chicago, and especially what Whitaker and Klein are up to in Rome. Time is of the essence!"

Kaufmann was extremely worried about the unfolding situation in Chicago. Costello was no innocent bystander in the killing of Cardinal Rooney, Kaufmann realized. And Hayek was surely the man who carried it out. To have the authorities focusing on these two men – for any reason – was fraught with danger. On top of that, during his clandestine trip to Chicago, Ruggieri made the foolish error – the inexcusable blunder – of telling Costello that a nun, related to a senior church official, was clever enough to develop the muscle paralyzer.

Paolo Andreano was supposed to be a good source of intelligence on the Working Group, but lately had been able to provide little, if any, useful information. It seemed the Group had removed him from the loop, as if they considered him untrustworthy.

Do they know Sister Sophie's identity? Do they know about her work at The Swiss Alpine Laboratory? What if they are taping my phone conversations when she calls? This troubles me greatly.

Dieter couldn't think of any means of silencing her in a way that wouldn't create more problems than it would solve. He couldn't cut her down, but he could cut her off.

CHAPTER 78

September, 2048
Munich

Sister Eugenia welcomed the two visitors to her office, and invited them to be seated. The former principal of the Queen of Heaven Academy in Munich had been in her new role as superior of the Sisters of Mary Magdalene for just seven months. She was finally becoming adjusted to her position, and the duties that came with it.

One of her responsibilities was dealing with a host of government and business officials regarding regulatory concerns, contracts, and public relations issues. But these men were different. They were investigators who wanted to discuss the activities of a member of her congregation – Sister Sophie.

"Are you saying Sister Sophie has gotten herself into trouble?" she asked them incredulously. "There's no question she is a very strange woman, far from normal, psychologically. However, she is quite conscientious, pious and ethical. I've known her since she was a high school student, and I can't believe she would do anything wrong.

"She's in charge of a laboratory section at the Medical Center of the Ludwig Maximilian University of Munich, and the administration there has nothing but praise for the quality of her work. Everyone who deals with her knows she is quite eccentric, but they accept that – her virtues outweigh her faults."

"We are in no way accusing Sister Sophie of any wrong-doing," Adolf was quick to assure Sister Eugenia. "We are assisting law enforcement officials in Italy and the United States with the investigation of crimes involving a chemical developed at The Swiss Alpine Laboratory while Sister Sophie was an intern there. It seems she had a role in creating the substance, and we hope she can shed some light on the history of its development to help us with our investigation."

"I have asked Sister Sophie to be at our provincial offices today, as you requested. She is waiting for you in the parlor. I'm afraid she won't be of much help. Something's happened –I don't know what. She's not communicating with anyone. Maybe you can get through to her, but I doubt it."

***

Sophie sat alone in the ornate parlor of the provincial house, waiting for the guests Sister Eugenia told her had come all the way from Rome to see her. She had no idea why they wanted to meet with her. She didn't care, about that or anything else. She was in a state of confusion, and heart-broken.

How could it be that my Uncle Dieter, a man of God, no longer wants to talk to me?

Over the years he had given her guidance, told her what to do, and let her participate in his battle against evil men who were possessed by the devil. He told her it was God's will to destroy these men who were subverting the holy church, and she fully believed and trusted him.

Yesterday she phoned him, as she usually did once a month for his wise counsel, but this time, he cut her off abruptly, and told her not to phone him again. He screamed "Never contact me again!"

Then The Voice spoke to her:

> *"This is not a man of God, Sophie. He will lead you astray! You must find a new man of God!"*

Her invisible friends reinforced the message. Sophie was in a state of shock

Uncle Dieter, not a man of God? Has he led me astray? If he is not a man of God, is he the evil one? I don't know what to do!

As she sat there by herself, ruminating over the blow her uncle had dealt her, and the disconcerting message from The Voice, Fred and Adolf entered the room.

They introduced themselves. Sophie said nothing. Both men rolled their eyes, almost simultaneously, and seated themselves. Sophie never looked up. Finally, Fred spoke:

"We've come a long way to visit with you, Sister Sophie," Fred told her in a soft, soothing tone of voice. "We can see this is a hard time for you, and we think we can help."

Adolf looked at Fred quizzically, his eyes bulging. *What's he up to? What does he have in mind?*

The fact was Fred had no idea where he was going with this. It was a long shot, just an effort to break through.

Sophie looked at him, and began to sob.

"How can you possibly help me? I thought Uncle Dieter was a man of God. Now he won't talk to me. The Voice tells me I must search for a new man of God. Did Uncle Dieter lead me astray? Is he possessed by the devil? I don't know what to do! I need to talk to a true man of God!"

Since her slip with Eric Schmidt years ago, Sophie had not talked about The Voice with anyone, except Uncle Dieter. But she was overwhelmed by her emotions. Moreover, this nice man said he can help.

My God! Adolf thought to himself. *This woman is a genuine nut case! She's hearing voices that tell her what to do! And what role has her uncle, Dieter Kaufmann, had in this?*

Fred got up, walked over to where Sophie was sitting, and put his hand on her shoulder.

"Sister Sophie, The Voice is right; you must find a new man of God – a man who will guide you in God's way, who respects you and will help you undo any of the evil that Uncle Dieter may have led you to.

"I know such a man – holy, wise, a true man of God. He wants to help you lead a life that is fulfilling to you and pleasing to God. He wants to see you as soon as you are ready. Are you ready, Sister Sophie?"

At this point, Adolf figured there are two crazy people in the room! *What the hell is Fred talking about? How did he come up with this? I think he's painted us into a corner! How, in heaven's name, does he think he can deliver on such a promise? This shot in the dark is stupid and irresponsible on his part, and could even end up setting our investigation back – way back!*

"Yes, Mr. Whitaker – I am ready! I want to meet this man of God as soon as possible!"

CHAPTER 79

"Mr. Whitaker, it's good to hear your voice! Cardinal Patel has updated me on two or three occasions on your and the Working Group's progress. As I know he told you, I am available to assist you in any way I can. I don't think anyone at the Vatican pays any attention to what I do."

Fred's electronic directory had all the important phone numbers for immediate access, and Cardinal Stefano Paganelli's direct line was one of them. He was calling it for the first time.

"Your Eminence, I've often looked back with pleasure at the day Cardinal Patel and I spent with you before the tragic death of Pope Francis Xavier. Cardinal Patel told me he was sure you were willing to be of assistance if we needed you, and the time has come."

"Tell me what you need, Mr. Whitaker."

Fred proceeded to tell him everything leading up to their visit with Sophie – her connection with Sarenol, The Swiss Alpine Laboratory, and Dieter Kaufmann. In case Paganelli hadn't heard, he also mentioned the observations the porter, Gino Cogliano, made about a mysterious nun being at the Apostolic Palace.

"My request is an unusual one, Your Eminence. Sister Sophie not only is mentally unstable, but is exceptionally distraught at this time. She needs to talk to a new 'man of God.' We must find out what she knows, and what she has done."

"I get the feeling I have been designated to be a 'man of God,'" Paganelli observed with a bit of a chuckle, probably reflecting some nervousness on his part. He surely didn't think the situation was funny.

Fred didn't beat around the bush.

"Can you come to Munich right away? I think time is of the essence."

"I will get the first available flight," Paganelli responded.

As Fred hung up, Adolf stared at him, shaking his head, both hands firmly planted on the top of his head.

"No way in hell did I think you could pull this off, Fred! You're amazing. Not only that – you've really got guts!"

CHAPTER 80

The next morning, Fred got a phone call from Stefano Paganelli from the Munich Airport as soon as his plane arrived. They agreed to meet at the Sisters of Mary Magdalene Provincial House. Sister Eugenia contacted Sophie and told her what time to be there.

Cardinal Paganelli, accompanied by his secretary, Father Roberto Allegretti, met with Fred and Adolf prior to Sophie's arrival.

"Good to see you, Your Eminence. Thank you for being so agreeable, and coming on such short notice. As you are aware, the stakes are extremely high. We need to debrief Sister Sophie as soon as possible, and pray to God your meeting with her doesn't become known by anyone but us.

"Oh, us and Sister Eugenia as well. I made the decision to fill her in regarding our interest in Sister Sophie. She probably knows more about Sister Sophie's problems than anyone, and actually said she wouldn't be surprised if this poor soul had been manipulated. It's clear she is fond of Sophie. Sister Eugenia also gave me details of her family background and her childhood, to help complete the picture. I, of course, will share all of this with you.

"I am pleased to meet Father Allegretti, Your Eminence. But I don't understand why you brought him along."

"Roberto Allegretti is an invaluable aide, and I have confidence in him without reservation," the cardinal informed Adolf and Fred. "As you know, Mr. Whitaker, I was a litigator before I entered the priesthood, and involved in Vatican legal affairs after that. Too often, suspects want me to administer the Sacrament of Reconciliation – we used to call it 'going to Confession' – prior to my questioning them. But as a priest, I can't break the seal of Confession. So if they want to go to Confession, Father Allegretti is available, and I am not put in a compromised position."

"It seems you think of everything, Your Eminence," Adolf observed.

"I'm also wired for recording our visit. A judge I know well provided me with a court order yesterday. God willing, we'll never have to use this, but it's prudent to have it."

***

"How do I know you are a man of God?" Sophie asked after she and Cardinal Paganelli were seated. Fred, Adolf and Sister Eugenia had departed, leaving the two of them alone in the parlor.

"I have been thinking about you, even before I met you, Sister Sophie. I know you are a holy person, a pious person, a woman who always does her best and seeks to do God's will. God wants me to help you do this."

Paganelli knew from his legal experience that, to gain the trust of a client who questions his sincerity, it's necessary to make the case you believe in the individual's value and good intentions. He felt that applied in this situation.

He went on to discuss the fine things Sophie had done in her life, based on the information Sister Eugenia had given him. He told her God continued to have great plans for her.

She came to believe Cardinal Paganelli truly was a man of God.

Although Stefano Paganelli had faced many ambiguous moral situations, this one was especially troubling to him.

I am purporting to be a special "man of God" and this woman is putting her trust in me! Have I been sent by God? Maybe I have! She has been badly misused by others, perhaps even her uncle Dieter Kaufmann. I must find out what the truth is, for the sake of the church, and ultimately for Sophie's sake. I need to find a way to help her spend the rest of her life without being destroyed by others. She is not an evil person!

From Paganelli's extensive interrogation experience, he knew not to cut to the chase, but talk about what interested the "client" or "suspect," as the case might be. They spent several minutes discussing Sophie's lab at the hospital and what aspects of the work she enjoyed, the things that sometimes troubled her, her family in Mittenwald, The Voice that visited her every few days, and her invisible friends.

As she spoke, she sometimes giggled for no apparent reason, at times raised the volume of her speech in the middle of sentences, in no way enhancing what she was saying, and was constantly rubbing or wringing her hands. Paganelli marveled, not at this unusual activity, but at how a person so obviously unbalanced could have a track record of productivity, and creative abilities almost at the genius level.

"Tell me about your time at The Swiss Alpine Laboratory," Paganelli finally asked her. "You were very innovative, weren't you? You were able to come up with important discoveries."

"Oh, yes – many!" She went on to describe her more significant accomplishments, but never mentioned Serum-C (now called Sarenol).

The cardinal pressed on, "Did Dr. Schmidt give you good support?"

"Do you know Dr. Schmidt?" Sophie asked him with a tone of anxiety in her voice.

"I've heard of him. He's the developer of an important muscle paralyzer that leaves no traces."

Sophie jumped from her chair.

"Did he say that? That's a lie! I developed that!" She sat down, and related the entire scenario with Schmidt, along with his order to give him all the vials and destroy her notes. "But The Voice told me to keep some vials, so I did."

"Tell me what you did with the vials, Sister Sophie. Tell me everything. I can't help you unless you tell me everything. It is God's will that I know everything about what you did with Serum-C."

"I only did what Uncle Dieter told me to do. Was that wrong? Have I committed sin?"

"You always did what you thought was right, isn't that true, Sister Sophie?"

"Yes, yes! I thought Uncle Dieter was a man of God. He told me some people were possessed by the devil, and must be destroyed. Was that wrong, Cardinal Paganelli?"

"If you did what you thought was right, what you thought was the will of God, you committed no sin, Sister Sophie. You were true to yourself. At this moment, that's all that matters. Whether Uncle Dieter was doing the right thing is not the issue now. You were following your conscience. So I can assist you in discerning right from wrong, you must tell me what Uncle Dieter told you to do with the serum, and how you used it."

Sophie proceeded to describe her meeting with Cardinal Kaufmann, his disclosure that Father Ludwig Drescher, recuperating from heart surgery at the Medical Center of the Ludwig Maximilian University of Munich, was the devil incarnate, and must be destroyed. While she described this, she continued to wring her hands, occasionally giggle, and raise the volume of her voice for no apparent reason. Paganelli listened without reacting less he throw her off kilter, but his heart went out to this handicapped child of God who had been so badly exploited.

"Then Uncle Dieter phoned me one day, about two years ago. He told me the antichrist was on Earth, and was sitting in the Chair of Peter at the Vatican. My uncle said I must come right away!"

CHAPTER 81

September, 2048
Chicago

The Cook County states attorney, Philip Sabatini, was becoming more frustrated by the day. Roméo Hayek wasn't providing any additional information regarding his role in the deaths of Marilyn Rutherford, Cardinal Rooney, and Fred Whitaker's security agent, or the shoot-up at the church in Highland Park. Sabatini was positive all these events were connected – part of a master plot – but the evidence was still thin. Apparently Hayek's lawyer had gotten him to recant some of his previous confession, claiming it was forced testimony without his attorney present.

The state's attorney was especially anxious to learn how Hayek's goons were able to gain access to Cardinal Rooney, and who else was involved in the plot. Without details and some hard evidence, prosecuting him for murder would prove difficult.

Roméo's thugs had also clammed up. Although law authorities made sure there was no communication among the suspects, their lawyers were clearly talking to each other and advising their clients accordingly.

Martin Ramsey was still in town, under "house arrest" at the Drake Hotel, with a police officer outside his suite, ensuring the bishop didn't leave. Interrogations were conducted at his suite.

It was becoming clear to Sabatini that Ramsey had played no part in the Chicago crimes, and probably had no knowledge of what was going on. It was true he instructed Costello to bring Whitaker's opinion survey to a halt, but he hadn't been part of any plot to commit murder and create mayhem. However, Sabatini had to make sure Ramsey didn't communicate anything to anyone in Rome, possibly jeopardizing the international investigation, so he obtained a court order requiring Ramsey to wear the ankle bracelet and stay in his Chicago hotel.

Costello's situation was entirely different. This man was Archbishop of Chicago, the spiritual leader of over two million Catholics in Northern Illinois. No one yet knew he had been arrested. How to handle his upcoming indictment was still uncertain. For the time being, his movement and communications were limited, but the decision was made not to subject him to extensive interrogation. Rather, as Costello had requested, he was given time to prepare a scenario that would inflict the least possible damage to the faithful in Cook and Lake Counties.

***

All of the participants in Friday's conference call – when Fred and Adolf were informed about the Rutherford murder, the arrests of Hayek and his cohorts, the sexual abuse by Costello decades ago, and the apprehension of Costello at the airport – had been sworn to complete secrecy about what had been discussed. Sabatini and Superintendent Frank Ryan were now handling the timing of all forthcoming information. Ryan was in frequent contact with Fred and the Carabinieri. The stakes were high. All efforts were made to ensure the events in Chicago did not compromise the investigation of Pope Francis Xavier's murder in Rome.

A possible glitch in the strategy appeared – something that had been overlooked. Dianne Rutherford Moffat, who had been brutally beaten after her mother's killing, and possibly targeted as the next murder victim, wanted to take immediate action and file charges against Costello for sexually abusing her years ago.

"Scotty, what are we going to do?" Marsha asked. It was less a question than a plea for help. Marsha McGuire had rarely visited Scotty's office, so her appearance was clearly important. "She wants this man to pay for his crime, for the emotional and psychological damage he inflicted on her. The current Illinois statute of limitations will continue in her favor for some time, but given her mother's murder and threat to her own life, she doesn't want to wait!"

Marsha, a member of the Working Group and the archdiocese's Council for the Prevention of Abuse to Women, had convinced Dianne to bring her case – in complete confidentiality - before the Council. If Dianne went to the police now, her case would become public, and perhaps blow the lid off Sabatini and Ryan's strategy. Yet Dianne couldn't be told about the broader implications. It was a conundrum – how could it be handled?

Scotty sat with his arms folded, leaning back in his swivel chair, looking at the ceiling, thinking long and hard.

"As you know, we can't tell Dianne about the Working Group and the possible role Costello had in Rooney's murder. You should let her know, however, there's a broader investigation going on, which isn't public and will be compromised if word gets out now about Costello's sexual abuse."

"I've basically told her that," Marsha responded, "but she says she doesn't care! Her mother was killed; she was badly beaten and would have been killed; she thinks Costello is probably responsible for this since her mother went to the council. Dianne wants him to pay. She doesn't want him to slip out of this!"

"The archbishop knows he's in deep trouble, Marsha. Thanks to the state's attorney, he's not in jail yet. He has a temporary reprieve as he gets his affairs and those of the archdiocese in order before he's indicted and everything becomes public. We don't want any publicity yet, and neither does Costello. If Dianne Rutherford Moffat goes to the police now, we lose and Costello loses.

"In order to prevent this, I think Costello would be willing to give Moffat a signed confession, if she agrees to hold off. That way, she knows he will be held accountable, and can't possibly slip through the cracks. Talk to her, Marsha. See if she'll agree to a short delay if she has such a document in her possession. If so, I'll talk to the authorities. I think they'll agree to the plan. I'm sure Costello will."

Chapter 82

Tom Costello was a devastated man. He had spent most of his life in the service of the church, doing the right things politically, and rising in the hierarchy to become archbishop of one of the largest and most important archdioceses in the country. Now he was facing disgrace, shame, ridicule, and probably the rest of his life in a prison cell.

He paced the floor of his residence, something he was now doing so regularly he had almost worn grooves into the polished wooden surface.

Why did I ever get involved with the Ecclesia Vera Society? I thought it was a pathway to renewing the old traditions of the church, not an extreme fundamentalist faction. I was wrong!

And how did I ever get involved with Roméo Hayek and his gang of thugs? Why did I let him make the decisions about how we should do things? How could I be so stupid? I pretended I didn't know what he was doing – that way, I told myself, I was free of any guilt. My head was in the sand! This has brought dishonor to me, and will scandalize the faithful of my archdiocese. May God have mercy on my soul!

He dropped to the kneeler in the corner of his den, fingered the beads of his rosary, and sobbed uncontrollably.

***

Marsha got Dianne Rutherford Moffat to agree to a postponement of her criminal complaint against Costello in exchange for a signed confession from the archbishop. The state's attorney agreed to this arrangement, since it was essential to delay public knowledge of the Chicago investigation while matters were at a critical stage in Rome.

Police Superintendent Frank Ryan stopped by the archbishop's residence to explain the situation to Tom Costello. At first, Costello objected vociferously, but Ryan was able to demonstrate this solution was the lesser of evils. The archbishop, without a doubt, would be charged as a child molester, and other victims were expected to emerge when that happened. A delay was to his benefit, so they agreed Scotty's office would draw up the document, and then Scotty, accompanied by a notary public, would bring it to the archbishop for his signature.

Two days later, Scotty, the notary and Frank Ryan came to the archbishop's residence at the agreed upon time. They rang the doorbell, but there was no answer. After a minute or two, they rang it again, but still no response. They banged on the door, but no one came. Ryan took out his phone and called Costello's number but didn't get an answer. Ryan had his driver call the department's communication's unit, and learned that Costello's ankle bracelet indicated he was inside. They knew something must be wrong.

Another squad car arrived, and two officers with a battering ram broke the door open. They went room by room, looking for Costello. The parlor, the den, the dining room and kitchen, the bedrooms – everything appeared in order, but no Costello.

Then they arrived at the master bathroom and found Costello in the bath tub – dead. The water was still hot. They saw an empty prescription medicine bottle for sleeping pills and a half-filled water glass next to the tub. On the toilet seat was a typed six-page document which contained a complete narrative of everything Costello and Hayek had done from the time Martin Ramsey had informed him Cardinal Ruggieri demanded the mission assigned to Fred Whitaker by Francis Xavier be scuttled. He also confessed to the sexual abuse of Dianne Rutherford Moffat over 20 years ago as well as the abuse of other juveniles. It ended with a plea for God's forgiveness, and was signed by the archbishop.

Chapter 83

September, 2048
Munich

Stefano Paganelli's heart began racing. Sister Sophie was starting to tell him about a trip to Rome, at the behest of Cardinal Dieter Kaufmann.

Was she going to unravel the mystery surrounding the death of Pope Francis Xavier? Was she the nun the porter Gino Cogliano saw leaving the papal apartments the day of Francis Xavier's murder? I need to be extremely careful not to throw her off track as she relates what happened. I can't believe the immensity of this tragedy hasn't, at some level, sunk into her consciousness, even with her obvious mental problems. Telling me about it could overwhelm her.

"Did Uncle Dieter tell you why he wanted to see you?"

"No, he just said the antichrist was now at the Vatican, and something must be done. I wasn't to tell anyone about his call."

"Didn't you need permission from your provincial to make this trip?"

"I was already going to Rome for a meeting of hospital laboratory supervisors – new, improved techniques – all that. It just meant leaving a few days earlier. When I told my superior that my uncle the cardinal wanted to see me before the meeting, she said it was fine."

Sophie got up, walked over to the window, swinging her arms back and forth, her fists clenched, then turned around and faced Paganelli. She now looked pale, and was trembling.

"I'm no longer sure if any of this actually happened. My memory of it is fuzzy, like it was a dream - a very bad dream. I don't think I should tell you this, since I'm not sure it's true."

Stefano's fears about the impact of these memories on Sister Sophie were proving to be true.

"Don't be concerned if your memories are fuzzy, or it seems like a bad dream, Sister Sophie. If I'm going to fulfill my role as a man of God, it's important you share these memories with me. No matter what they are, I won't think any less of you, because I know you are a good woman, and you always want to do what's right. If Uncle Dieter made some mistakes, they are not your mistakes. I feel sure of that.

"Do you want me to ask Sister Eugenia to bring us some coffee or tea?"

Sophie smiled – something she rarely did. Then she giggled again.

"No, Cardinal, I don't care for anything. I'm alright. I'll tell you what happened, even though it's hard for me to even think about it. Like a bad dream."

Sophie sat down. She put her elbows on her thighs and head in her hands, wrinkled her brow, closed her eyes and pursed her lips.

"I am thinking, Cardinal. I am trying to remember everything. I don't want to leave anything out. Uncle Dieter talked and talked and talked about the man in the Chair of Peter, who called himself the pope. He was not a pope, Uncle Dieter said. He was the antichrist, a demon posing as the pope, and he was leading the church astray. Because of him, the eternal salvation of hundreds of millions of Catholics was in danger, and something had to be done. He had to be destroyed, just like the bad priest in the Munich hospital years before.

"Then he said to me, 'Here's a vial of your Serum C, and a case with a hypodermic needle and syringe in it. It is the Lord's will that the antichrist be eliminated, and cause no more harm to the children of God."

"Did you know this man who Uncle Dieter said was the antichrist, Cardinal? Was he really bad?" Sophie asked as she opened her eyes and looked at Paganelli with an expression that suggested she was pleading for support.

"Yes, I did Sister Sophie. I knew him well. I will tell you more about him later on. However, this is not the time for that – this is the time for you to reconstruct for me the events of that day, so I can understand and do the right thing for you. Please go on."

Sophie slowly nodded her head and sat back in her chair.

"He then took me to the office of a cardinal – his name was Mario something . . ."

"Was it Mario Lusardi?" Stefano asked, interrupting her narrative.

"Yes, that was his last name. He had a big, fancy office."

The camerlengo! Paganelli said to himself in semi-amazement. Only "semi," since – from the very beginning – Lusardi had, in effect, obstructed the investigation of Francis Xavier's death.

"Forgive me for interrupting you, Sister Sophie. Please continue."

"Uncle Dieter left. Cardinal Lusardi took me to a hallway in his office and pushed on a mahogany panel which suddenly became a door and opened up. 'Go up that staircase, and through the door at the top. You will find the pope sound asleep at his desk. He won't wake up. Do what your uncle told you to do. Then leave right away.' The cardinal went back into the hallway, closing the door behind him."

Stefano was aware there were a number of secret passages in the Apostolic Palace, used centuries before for various purposes. Many had not yet been discovered.

"It was like he said. The pope was in a deep sleep. I unbuttoned his cassock over his heart, and injected the serum, just like I had done with the bad priest in Munich at the hospital. I redid the buttons, went back to the door I came through, but it had closed. It all looked like a solid wall, and I didn't know how to open it. I left through the regular door instead. Uncle Dieter said I should leave the Vatican as soon as I was through, and not tell anyone I had been there. That's what I did."

There was a long silence while Sophie sat staring at the wall. Her eyes were now welling with tears.

"The next day I went to my meeting. Everyone was talking about the murder of the pope. Murder! A murder! Did I commit a murder? I couldn't have committed a murder! Murder is evil. Then I thought I dreamed I did this. I didn't do it – I dreamed it. I never talked about it to Uncle Dieter. Never! And he never said anything to me. It was a dream!

"Now he won't talk to me." She began to sob. "Now I thought, maybe it wasn't a dream. Maybe the pope wasn't the bad man. Maybe Uncle Dieter was the bad man. Maybe he told me to commit sin. Maybe he wasn't a man of God!"

Sophie and Stefano Paganelli had been talking for about and hour and a half. Initially, Paganelli had approached this task as a "necessary evil," something he had to do in order to find the parties who killed Francis Xavier. Now, 90 minutes later, his attitude had changed. He was developing a fatherly affection for this poor woman, along with a sense of anger that she had been so badly exploited.

"Sister Sophie, the things you did at the request of Uncle Dieter – did you think you were doing the right thing?"

"Oh, yes I did!" she said sobbing.

"Did you think you were doing God's will?"

"Uncle Dieter said this was God's will, and I believed him."

"You committed no sin, Sister Sophie. To sin, you must knowingly offend God. You didn't knowingly offend God – on the contrary, you thought you were serving Him. If there was sin, it was on the part of the man who told you to do these things. You were a good woman then, and you are still a good woman."

Cardinal Paganelli gave her a brief description of Pope Francis Xavier, as he promised he would, and how good a man he was.

"If Uncle Dieter is evil, does he still do bad things?"

"I hope not," Stefano responded, as he got up, walked over to her chair, and patted her on the shoulder. "He may have to answer to the authorities for this, and you may need to help the authorities. I will tell you what to do, and when to do it."

They finished their session, and Sophie left for the hospital to resume her duties. Fred and Adolf were waiting for Paganelli in a nearby room.

"This has been heartrending. I can hardly express my sympathy for the woman, and my anger at Dieter Kaufmann for the damage he has done to her.

"As you know, Mr. Whitaker, I am a licensed attorney. I haven't represented someone in a criminal case since I was a layman, but I'm going to be an advocate for Sophie Mueller. I will fight tooth and nail to see she doesn't go on trial for anything. She is clearly insane, and not responsible for the actions she performed on behalf of Dieter Kaufmann. On the other hand, Dieter – and his accomplices – should be subjected to the full force of the justice system for their criminal activities."

"Since she is insane," Fred asked Paganelli, "will her testimony be allowed, or mean anything?"

"Possibly," he responded. "She clearly is not responsible for her actions, but her recollection of the details – of what really happened – is quite complete and consistent. I think there's a way her testimony could be allowed, but it may take some doing. I plan to work on that. Also, my recording of our meeting will be useful in refreshing Sophie's memory, if and when she is called to testify.

"But that's not the relevant issue now, gentlemen. We have to find available evidence and identify the accomplices. Kaufmann was not alone in this criminal activity. Mario Lusardi has been clearly implicated. And also Antonio Ruggieri – Pope Pius XIII."

Chapter 84

September, 2048
Rome

After leaving Munich, Fred and Adolf headed back to Frankfurt for two days of meetings to update Working Group member Theodor Keitz, Danube Industry CEO and Adolf's boss. Then it was on to Rome and their office at Palatine Chemicals to consider what action was now required.

"Where do we go from here?" Adolf asked Fred, almost rhetorically, since it looked like another dead-end. "Stefano Paganelli's meeting with Sister Sophie was very productive – lots of incriminating evidence against Lusardi and Kaufmann, but it's probably worthless! The woman is crazy, and her accusations won't mean a thing. We still have little hard evidence, and nothing that implicates Pius XIII who's undoubtedly involved, if not the chief perpetrator. My detectives have been beating the bushes for weeks now, looking for some cracks, some weak spots we can exploit, but so far, nothing. What are your thoughts?"

Fred sat with his arms folded, and shook his head.

"I'll be damned if I know, Adolf! We have so little to go on. No 'smoking gun.' We've apprehended the perpetrators in Chicago and the murder of Cardinal Rooney is almost solved. But, although we know there is a connection between his death and Francis Xavier's murder, we have no way of proving it. At the moment, we have nowhere to go!"

As they were weighing their very limited options, the phone rang. It was Cardinal Paganelli.

"Mr. Whitaker, when I last saw you and Mr. Klein in Munich, I said I would work on where we can go from here with what we now know. I think I've come up with some options, and I need to see the two of you right away."

"We can come by your office at once, Cardinal."

"No, we shouldn't meet at my office. Everyone at the Vatican will learn about your visit. I want you to meet me at the law offices of Giuseppe Esposito. Tomorrow morning at 9:00 a.m. would be ideal. Can you do that?"

Fred and Adolf agreed to the time, and Paganelli gave them the lawyer's address.

CHAPTER 85

Esposito's office was unassuming, and not at one of the more exclusive addresses of high-priced corporate lawyers. The receptionist ushered them into his office – spacious, with a well-appointed sitting area, and a desk piled with legal briefs and petitions. Stefano Paganelli was already there. He made the introductions, and the four of them seated themselves in the sitting area.

"I've known Giuseppe for many years, all the way back to when he was fresh out of law school, and I was on the verge of leaving my legal practice and entering the seminary. We have stayed in touch, and as head of the Tribunal of the Rota Romana, I have utilized his expertise on several legal matters. They don't come any better than Giuseppe Esposito!"

Esposito smiled modestly at Paganelli, then laughed a little.

"With that kind of endorsement, gentlemen, Cardinal Paganelli gives me a lot to live up to! As always, I'll try to do my best.

"Cardinal Paganelli has reviewed with me the evidence you have so far: the exchange of emails between Father Gustavo Bivona and Cardinal Lusardi on the eve of Bivona's murder, the porter Gino Cogliano's claim he saw a nun coming from the Papal Apartments the day Francis Xavier was murdered, the Chicago perpetrator's statement a nun related to a high-ranking churchman developed the serum that killed Cardinal Rooney, and Dr. Eric Schmidt's admission that he didn't create the serum but, in fact, Sister Sophie did. And then, of course, there's Cardinal Paganelli's interview with Sister Sophie. Now, where do we go with all this?

"Sister Sophie has admitted she personally killed Pope Francis Xavier. I have listened to the recording Cardinal Paganelli made. He is convinced she is innocent by reason of insanity, and he believes, as her advocate, he can argue that successfully during a Preliminary Hearing. I'm sure he's right.

"Sister Sophie's interview with Cardinal Paganelli is an indictment of both Cardinals Dieter Kaufmann and Mario Lusardi. Based on her testimony and the other evidence, the strongest case we can make right now is against Cardinal Mario Lusardi. But there is a problem, and you know what that is. Sister Sophie will be ruled as legally insane, and her testimony will hold no weight, if it's even allowed, unless there's a way around this liability.

"I think I have that. I can't discuss that with you yet. I haven't even discussed it with my good friend and mentor, Stefano Paganelli. He fully understands."

"I fully support Giuseppe's judgment on this," Stefano added. "In the present situation, the fewer people who know his strategy, the less chance there will be of someone making an inadvertent and disastrous slip of the tongue.

"When I needed a court order to record my meeting with Sister Sophie, I went to Ceasario Baldassare, an old friend and one of Rome's most eminent judges. After returning from Munich, I asked him to review the evidence, and to issue a Notice of Closure which will formally make Cardinal Lusardi a defendant rather than a suspect. Baldassare has appointed Giuseppe as prosecutor, and the Notice of Closure will be delivered to Cardinal Lusardi today. All of the evidence, including the recording of my session with Sister Sophie, will be available to Cardinal Lusardi and his attorney, and a date for the Preliminary Hearing will be set as soon as possible."

CHAPTER 86

September, 2048
Vatican City

"What the hell is going on, Giacomo? A Notice of Closure, to a cardinal, a Vatican official? How dare they! Who does Judge Ceasario Baldassare think he is? The Vatican City is a sovereign state, and an Italian judge has no right to call me to a Preliminary Hearing."

Giacomo Sciarra, Lusardi's attorney, spread a sheaf of papers on Lusardi's desk, and then sat down in a chair opposite Lusardi's.

"Unfortunately, Cardinal, he does. You must remember, this has to do with a capital crime, the murder of Pope Francis Xavier. The Lateran Treaty gives Italy the authority to investigate such crimes, even though they were committed on Vatican, not Italian soil. We must comply.

"The fact is, we have little to worry about. I've been to court and obtained copies of all the evidence the prosecution has," Giacomo stated as he pointed to the papers he had put on Lusardi's desk. "The evidence is paper-thin, so much so that it amazes me Ceasario Baldassare even issued a Notice of Closure. This will never go to trial!

"The prosecution's principal evidence is also their weakest – the recording of an interview Cardinal Paganelli had with Sister Sophie in which she implicated you. As you know, Cardinal Lusardi, she is not sane. Her testimony would be worthless! I have spoken to her superior in Munich and her psychiatrist. If this should ever go to trial, we will have them testify. But it will never go to trial. I'm insisting Sister Sophie be present at the Preliminary Hearing so we can put her on the witness stand. I can shoot down her testimony in a matter of five minutes."

CHAPTER 87

October, 2048
Rome

A date for the Preliminary Hearing was set by Judge Baldassare, just three weeks after the Notice of Closure. Giacomo Sciarra strongly objected to the early date, claiming this did not give his client enough time to prepare. Baldassare retorted that this was only a Preliminary Hearing, and its purpose was to determine if the prosecution had enough evidence to indict a defendant. Should the judge determine there was sufficient evidence, then the defendant would have ample time to prepare a defense prior to a trial.

On the first day of the Preliminary Hearing, proceedings began promptly at 9:00 a.m. Present in the courtroom were Cardinal Lusardi and his attorney, Giacomo Sciarra, Fred, Adolf, prosecutor Giuseppe Esposito, and Cardinal Paganelli with Sister Sophie. Paganelli had traveled to Munich a few days before to spend some time with Sophie and prepare her for this ordeal. He then brought her back to Rome.

Esposito and Paganelli had agreed to first get the issue of Sister Sophie's guilt out of the way. Since Paganelli was accredited by the Italian court system, Judge Baldassare allowed him to present his case that Sister Sophie, though she may have killed the pope, was innocent by reason of insanity. He brought affidavits from Dr. Schmidt, Sister Eugenia, Sophie's mother and father, and her psychiatrist. Judge Baldassare ruled, if she indeed murdered Francis Xavier, she was not responsible for her actions. Therefore, there was no need to put Sister Sophie on the witness stand. Attorney Giacomo Sciarra did not object, since her insanity was key to having the recording of her meeting with Paganelli, and any in-person testimony at the hearing, disallowed.

Paganelli's presentation on behalf of Sister Sophie took most of the hearing's first day. On the second day, Giuseppe Esposito rose to make his case against Mario Lusardi as a conspirator in the death of Pope Francis Xavier. He discussed some of the circumstantial evidence, going all the way back to Lusardi's attempt to block the Carabinieri's investigation the day Francis Xavier was killed.

Then he asked the judge to enter into evidence the recording Cardinal Paganelli made when he interviewed Sister Sophie. As this point, Sciarra rose to his feet.

"Your Honor, I strongly object to this recording being accepted by your court! I also insist any testimony by this woman be disallowed. As Cardinal Paganelli so successfully argued yesterday, this woman is insane. She is not responsible for her actions regarding this case."

"Judge Baldassare, before you rule on attorney Sciarra's motion," Esposito interjected, "I would like to call a witness whose testimony will be directly relevant as to whether this recording should be entered into evidence."

"Very well," Ceasario Baldassare responded, "since you assure me it is relevant, I will allow it."

"Thank you Your Honor," Esposito responded. "I want to call Gino Cogliano to the witness stand."

The papal palace porter had come into the courtroom almost unnoticed when the proceedings began, and was sitting in the back of the room. Exuding an air of considerable uneasiness, Gino slowly walked up to the front of the courtroom, and took the prescribed seat. After being sworn in, and giving his name and his occupation, Esposito began questioning Gino.

"What are your responsibilities?" Giuseppe asked him. Gino described the duties of a porter, and informed the court he was the senior porter, the supervisor of other porters, and kept records and schedules.

"You say you keep records. Does that include information on the secret passages? I purchased a brochure about them in the Vatican Gift Shop." Giuseppe held up the brochure.

"Yes sir, I do keep those records," Gino responded. "Vatican City administration requires any secret passages discovered be either converted into regular entranceways, or permanently sealed off. Seven secret passages have been found; the last was located five years ago."

"Does this brochure list all of them?" Giuseppe asked him.

"Yes, it does," Gino responded.

"I don't see a secret passageway listed for the camerlengo's office suite of rooms."

"In Cardinal Lusardi's office? No sir. No passageway has been found there."

"So if a secret passage had been found and not reported, does this mean only the finder would know about it?"

"Your Honor," Sciarra interrupted, "this line of questioning is a complete waste of time! I objected to this recording being submitted as evidence since the nun is not a reliable witness. Mr. Esposito's line of questioning has no relevance to the issue. I again restate my objection to the transcript."

"Judge Baldassare, Mr. Cogliano's testimony has all the relevance in the world!" Giuseppe Esposito insisted. "He has stated that no secret passageway has been reported in the camerlengo's suite. Yet, in the recording in question, Sister Sophie claims Cardinal Lusardi took her to such a passageway, and he told her to use it to gain entrance to the papal apartments. She couldn't know about such a passageway unless she was there, and the cardinal opened it for her.

"If this is true, and if she indeed killed the pope, then Cardinal Lusardi is implicated in the crime. It is essential we determine if the passageway exists. If it does, it lends credibility to the rest of the recording."

"This hearing is recessed for 30 minutes," Baldassare stated, tapping his gavel on his desk.

In one-half hour, the Preliminary Hearing reconvened, and was called to order.

"I have determined," Judge Baldassare advised the parties to this hearing, "that if the passageway exists, the recording will prove to be a key piece of evidence.

"This session of the Preliminary Hearing will be in recess until tomorrow morning at 10:00 a.m., and will reconvene at the suite of rooms used by Camerlengo Cardinal Lusardi. Joining us will be three carpenters who will determine if the passageway exists.

"I am ordering you, Cardinal Lusardi, not to return to your office suite until tomorrow's hearing. You will stay at your residence until then. Further, you are not to communicate with anyone except officers of this court. A court official will accompany you to your residence now, and will stay with you to provide any services you may need, and to ensure you follow the directives I have just given you."

Chapter 88

Fred, Adolf, Cardinal Stefano Paganelli, Sister Sophie, Giuseppe Esposito, Camerlengo Mario Lusardi, Giacomo Sciarra, Judge Ceasario Baldassare, two of his staff members, and three carpenters (arranged for by the judge) assembled at Lusardi's office suite at 10:00 a.m. the next morning. Judge Baldassare also gave Gino Cogliano permission to attend, since he was responsible for keeping the log on the Vatican's secret passageways.

Extra chairs were brought in to accommodate everyone, and the judge sat at Lusardi's desk, making it the judicial bench for the hearing.

"Do you recognize this room?" Esposito asked Sister Sophie.

"Of course I do!" she responded with a tone of petulance. "This is where Uncle Dieter brought me before I carried out his instructions."

"And who was in the room?" he continued.

She pointed to Mario Lusardi.

"The cardinal was here," she replied.

"You told Cardinal Paganelli there was a secret passageway. Do you remember where that was?"

Sophie got up, and walked to a hallway that connects the camerlengo's office with a small meeting room.

"Somewhere on this wall," she said, shaking her head, "but I can't see where it is."

The hallway wall consisted of identical polished mahogany panels on both sides, each about three feet wide and separated by decorative trim. The panels appeared to be completely solid with no separations or gaps.

"I want the carpenters to examine this side where Sister Sophie claims there is an entrance to a secret passageway." The three men came forward to inspect the wall Baldassare had indicated.

Instead of banging on the panels to hear how they resonated, one of the carpenters produced an electronic device similar to a large remote control, and ran it along the wall, starting at one end and slowly continuing toward the other. After two minutes or so, lights began flashing on the unit, and it began beeping.

"This panel has no structural support behind it," a carpenter informed the Judge. "It's covering a hollow area."

Then the three carpenters began carefully examining the decorative trim – poking, twisting, pushing, pulling, banging, attempting to trigger something that would open a hidden door. After some 20 minutes, one of the carpenters pushed on a section of trim, and the panel over the hollow space receded and slid to the left, exposing a staircase.

"We need to climb this staircase and see where it leads," the Judge informed those present. He led the way to the top, where he pushed on the secret door leading into the pope's den. The door opened, and the room was empty. Baldassare's staff had found out in advance the pope was away.

Everyone returned to Lusardi's office. The Judge asked them to be seated again.

"This session started yesterday when attorney Esposito requested the recording of Cardinal Paganelli and Sister Sophie's meeting be entered into evidence. There is no way Sister Sophie could have known about the secret passageway unless she was here, as she said she was. This fact has been established in my estimation beyond a reasonable doubt, and it leads to the conclusion the contents of the recording are basically factual. Therefore, I am denying the defendant's request that the recording be excluded from evidence, and accepting it as an exhibit, as requested by the prosecution.

"Furthermore, this Preliminary Hearing has determined there is sufficient evidence to try Cardinal Mario Lusardi as an accessory to the murder of Pope Francis Xavier. In consideration of his high rank in the Holy See, he will be held under house arrest instead of incarcerated. He is to surrender his passport.

"It is clear Cardinal Lusardi is part of a conspiracy. I am instructing the prosecutor to continue his investigation and granting him any assistance he requires from the Carabinieri and any appropriate subpoenas he may need from this court.

"Today's session is adjourned. The Preliminary Hearing in this case is now completed."

CHAPTER 89

October, 2048
Chicago

This week's Friday conference call between Fred, Adolf, Scotty, Elaine, Rachel and Brett was nothing if not dramatic. Fred gave a monologue for over 20 minutes – a complete account of the Preliminary Hearing, Paganelli's successful argument on Sister Sophie's behalf, the testimony of the porter, and the ultimate discovery of the secret passageway Sister Sophie had described, which vindicated her.

"Something concerns me," Elaine chimed in. "This poor woman was sitting through this hearing being referred to as 'insane,' and 'incompetent to testify.' How did she handle this? It seems a bit cruel to me."

"Cardinal Paganelli has taken on her well-being, almost like a personal crusade. He spent several days with her in Munich prior to the hearing. She's very bright, and realizes she has mental problems. Paganelli has visited her psychiatrist, and she says that Sophie's invisible friends, and The Voice she hears are what allow her to keep her balance, and hold herself together.

"During their time in Munich, Paganelli prepared Sophie for what might be said about her at the hearing, and he helped her to understand why. Although she now knows what she did was wrong, she also understands that, since she intended to do good, she is not a sinful woman."

"What a blessing," Elaine exclaimed, "for Sister Sophie to have a man like Cardinal Paganelli in her corner!"

"He's even gone the extra mile," Fred responded. "There's a large orphanage in Rome which is run by a congregation of nuns. The orphanage has a small hospital with a lab. The cardinal has arranged for Sophie to be their one and only lab technician – a perfect situation for her. Her provincial in Munich has agreed to this. The court has assigned a detail to give her protection during this crucial investigation, lest any suspect or defendant tries to do her harm.

"Stefano Paganelli is providing the kind of care and counsel her biological father was never able to give her. In some ways, Sophie is still a child and needs this desperately. It's clearly fulfilling something in his life as well. As the saying goes, 'God works in mysterious ways.'

"The recording of Sister Sophie and Paganelli's meeting plus her testimony, if she is placed on the stand and it's accepted, will help criminally implicate Dieter Kaufmann. The prosecutor, Giuseppe Esposito, is hopeful Mario Lusardi will also implicate Kaufmann in hopes of reducing a possible life sentence."

"I have some positive news," Scotty interjected. "You'll recall we told you Tom Costello claimed he got the vial of serum that killed Albert Rooney from Antonio Ruggieri during the cardinal's secret trip to Chicago. Since Costello committed suicide, he can't testify to this. However, he mentioned this transaction in the long confession he wrote before taking his life.

"Even better, in an effort to keep Ruggieri's presence in Chicago secret, his meeting with Costello was held in Hayek's condo. Roméo Hayek witnessed Ruggieri giving Costello the serum, and, as part of his plea bargain, Hayek has agreed to testify against this man – now Pope Pius XIII - whether he faces trial here, or it means flying to Rome with federal marshals to testify against him there."

"That's certainly good news," Fred concurred. "A man capable of plotting the murder of the Chicago archbishop could also be capable of plotting Francis Xavier's murder. Maybe the two events can be tied together.

"However, we've got a big problem. Prosecutor Esposito says even if we get Lusardi or Kaufmann to implicate Ruggieri, the Italian government would be hard-pressed to indict and try him, since he's the sitting pope and a head of state. The obstacles are formidable. The hue and cry of Catholics throughout the world would be deafening."

There was silence as everyone was thinking. Then Rachel spoke up.

"What if you could get him to resign?"

CHAPTER 90

November 2048
Mumbai

This is just too important to handle over the phone, Fred thought. *Also too dangerous. We've taken precautions, but these days, how do you know who's listening in?*

I've got to meet with him in Mumbai. This may take us several hours, maybe a day or two. Here's a situation where we've got to get it right the first time!

Cardinal Sanjay Patel hadn't seen Fred Whitaker since that fateful meeting he had with Fred and Scotty Campbell the previous year at the Union League Club in Chicago. Amazing progress had been made by the Working Group that Scotty and Fred formed at Snowmass, and Sanjay was wondering if the end game was now in sight. Fred would arrive the next day, and Sanjay knew he was going to find out much more.

"Cardinal Patel, I needed to see you personally rather than have a long-distance phone call. As you know, we've accomplished a lot. We know who murdered Francis Xavier and Albert Rooney, murders we're sure are connected. Camerlengo Mario Lusardi has been indicted and will go on trial in the near future. Dieter Kaufmann, without any doubt, is guilty of complicity in the plot, and I believe will be indicted soon.

"Here's where we are right now. We need the identification and indictment of the 'mastermind' of the murders, whom we are convinced is the former Cardinal Antonio Ruggieri, now our pope. We can tie him directly to the death of Cardinal Rooney, but not to Francis Xavier's. Since Lusardi and Kaufmann know the truth, can we get them to implicate the pope? Can the Italian courts act when the defendant is the Holy See's head of state?"

"I have no doubt that Antonio Ruggieri orchestrated this entire thing, Mr. Whitaker. His life is full of moral compromises. He had much to gain from Francis Xavier's death. And he 'brow-beat' and threatened many cardinals to vote for him in the Conclave two years ago. He was determined to be the next pope – at any cost."

Fred and Patel explored options all morning, broke for lunch, and after that continued their exploration, to no effect. They were looking for a source of hard evidence, but could find none.

Finally, Fred slapped his forehead.

"How did I forget! There's one thing we haven't explored – something my assistant in Chicago suggested. Could we possibly get Ruggieri to resign the papacy? If he resigned, then the authorities could aggressively pursue him as a suspect, and other Holy See officials, no longer fearing his authority, could come forward with the truth. It might produce the break we've needed."

Cardinal Patel got up and slowly paced the floor with his hands clasped behind his back, saying nothing. Finally, he sat down again.

"It's hard for me to picture how we can create the kind of pressure to make him resign. His whole life has been devoted to getting this job, and I doubt if anything or anyone could take it from him."

"What if the College of Cardinals demanded he resign?" Fred suggested.

"I'm not sure even that would work," Patel stated, shaking his head. "Even if Cardinal Lusardi implicates Ruggieri in the plot to kill Francis Xavier, even that would probably not be enough – except . . ."

"Except what?" Fred asked.

"If Mario Lusardi was willing to testify the sitting pope was behind the conspiracy to murder Francis Xavier, and his testimony became public knowledge, I believe there are dozens if not hundreds of bishops who would then urge Pope Pius XIII to resign.

"During my career as a papal nuncio, and as secretary of state under Francis Xavier, I got to know many bishops around the world who disliked and did not trust this man when he was prefect of the Congregation for the Doctrine of the Faith, and trust him even less as pope, especially the many cardinals whom he blackmailed to vote him into office. They fear him now, but if he was publicly implicated in Francis Xavier's murder, they might feel safe enough to demand his resignation. Even that might not move him, but I think it's a possibility."

"From what you're saying, Cardinal, our energies should now be directed toward getting Lusardi to finger Ruggieri as the 'mastermind,' and, if and when that happens, to make sure it gets lots of media coverage. We've also got to make sure prosecutor Giuseppe Esposito works out an attractive plea bargain with the court, so he can make Lusardi 'an offer he can't refuse.'"

"Exactly, Mr. Whitaker. This is our best chance. If Lusardi cooperates, I'll be contacting bishops I trust and know well, whom I'm sure, in turn, would be willing to get in touch with other bishops they know, in our efforts to create a ground swell against Pope Pius XIII."

"I think we're off and running with this one, Cardinal! I'm optimistic. We've come this far. We're going to reach the finish line!"

CHAPTER 91

November, 2048
Rome

As soon as he arrived back in Rome, Fred updated Adolf on his meeting with Sanjay Patel. Then he made an appointment for them to see Giuseppe Esposito.

"Your request is a bit disconcerting, Mr. Whitaker. You want me to ask the court to show leniency to Cardinal Lusardi if he implicates the pope, which is something he might do anyway – even if the pope wasn't involved in the murder – just to get special treatment for himself."

"That's not true, Mr. Esposito. Like you, I am an experienced litigator, and have both prosecuted and defended individuals accused of capital crimes. If Lusardi makes accusations that can't be verified, then, of course, the deal is off.

"The former Cardinal Ruggieri has been implicated in the murder of Chicago's archbishop, which occurred prior to his being elected pope. He has exhibited a pattern of working on the margins of the law – just out of reach. We are convinced the people involved in Francis Xavier's murder – Lusardi, who has been indicted, and Kaufmann, who probably will be indicted – were operatives working under the direction of the principal instigator, Antonio Ruggieri, now Pope Pius XIII. If so, we must nail Pius XIII."

"I assume you are aware of the problems created by indicting a head of state, especially a pope," Esposito reminded Fred.

"Yes, I am. However, Mumbai's archbishop, Cardinal Sanjay Patel, believes if the pope's involvement in Francis Xavier's murder becomes public, he might be able to generate a ground swell among bishops, as well as laity, for Pius XIII's resignation. If the pope resigns, then he'd be more accessible to law enforcement."

Giuseppe drummed his fingers on his desk while fixing his gaze on the ceiling. Finally, he looked at Fred with a big smile.

"I think I have a plan!"

CHAPTER 92

Today wasn't Mario Lusardi's first trip to the Carabinieri's Rome headquarters since he was implicated in Francis Xavier's murder, but something was different this time. There was a greater sense of urgency – enough to unnerve him. Lusardi, accompanied by his attorney Giacomo Sciarra, wasn't meeting with a regular investigator in a normal interrogation room. This meeting was in the office of senior Carabinieri official Colonel Carlo Laurenti with an unexpected, if not unprecedented, gathering of noteworthy individuals, seated around a conference table: prosecutor Giuseppe Esposito, American attorney Fred Whitaker, head of Apollo Protection and Security Adolf Klein, Senior Cardinal Bishop Stefano Paganelli, Mumbai archbishop and former Vatican secretary of state Cardinal Sanjay Patel, and – to his total amazement – Italian Foreign Minister Agostino Spallino.

"This is truly an impressive assembly," Sciarra sarcastically observed after he and Lusardi were seated. "I am sure we are supposed to be impressed, if not frightened. You should know full well my client has nothing to say prior to his day in court. I fully expect he will be acquitted. In the meantime, he will not respond to any questions pertaining to the accusations against him."

Regardless of the bravado Sciarra was exhibiting, Lusardi indeed *was* alarmed – very much so. These men, as a group, knew more about him than he wanted anyone to know.

"I feel sure this was not the assemblage you expected to see this morning, Cardinal Lusardi," Esposito stated, initiating the discussion. "The seven of us have communicated a number of times these past few days, and we have arrived at some conclusions regarding your role in the murder of Francis Xavier."

"I'd like to share my observations first," Agostino Spallino interjected, interrupting Esposito, "since I was the official notified of the tragedy by Cardinal Patel, Vatican secretary of state at the time. I immediately requested Colonel Laurenti seal off the Papal Apartments and initiate a murder investigation."

"My officers did just that," Laurenti added, "but you, Cardinal Lusardi, did all you could to prevent it. Only when you were threatened with a citation for obstructing the investigation did you follow the officers' demands to leave the pope's residence."

"During the following days, you failed to contribute to the Italian government's investigation," Spallino added. "Not only did you fail to contribute, your actions could be considered an intentional effort on your part to block the investigation."

"The same can be said of your lack of cooperation when we investigated Father Gustavo Bivona's murder," Laurenti alleged. "We think there is a connection between that crime and the pope's murder, but you stone-walled us."

Then Fred spoke up.

"Your email exchange with Father Bivona, just before his murder, suggests he knew about your guilt, so you had him eliminated."

"You tried to have the recording of my meeting with Sister Sophie thrown out," Paganelli reminded Lusardi, "but the court denied your objection. This woman's accurate description of you, your office, the secret passageway and the details of Francis Xavier's study indicates, without a doubt, your culpability in the pope's death."

"We have reached the conclusion," Esposito informed him, "that you are the mastermind behind this plot. All of these gentlemen will testify at your trial, and without doubt, you will be found guilty, and spend the rest of your life behind bars."

After waiting a few seconds for Lusardi to absorb that possibility, Esposito continued, "The only way you can avoid a life in prison is to prove you were taking your orders from someone else – that you were a foot soldier in this conspiracy, and not the general. But you were indeed the general, weren't you? If so, it won't go well for you!"

Giacomo Sciarra spoke up for the second time.

"How dare you threaten my client this way! This is not a court of law! This is a bare-faced attempt at intimidation, and I will not . . ."

Mario banged his fist on the conference table, stood up, marched over to a corner of the room, and then whipped around, facing the table.

"Shut up, Sciarra, goddamnit! Let me speak for myself! I'm not so dense as to not realize the evidence they have against me is overwhelming. There is no way I'm going to take the rap as the instigator of Francis Xavier's death! There were two other people involved – Dieter Kaufmann, and Antonio Ruggieri. Antonio was the mastermind! I'm going to tell what I know!"

"Cardinal Lusardi," Sciarra pleaded, "I beg you not to say anything more before . . ."

"Not another word, Sciarra. I will speak for myself!" Lusardi came back to the table, and slumped into his seat.

Esposito looked at him with an expression that could be characterized as understanding and sympathetic. He spoke with a calm and soothing voice.

"Cardinal, I received a court order from Judge Ceasario Baldassare allowing me to record the discussion at this meeting. I haven't done so yet, and I could do it now without your knowing it. However, I'm only going to do so if you are in agreement."

Sciarra began to speak, but Lusardi held up his palm to silence him.

"Yes, Mr. Esposito, that's fine with me. I have a lot to tell you. It is truly shocking."

Chapter 93

The media went into overdrive as soon as news broke that the Roman Catholic pope and his secretary of state, at a Preliminary Hearing in Rome, were implicated in the murder of Francis Xavier. Dieter Kaufmann was indicted and put under house arrest. Pius XIII – the Vatican's head of state – was not indicted but was accused of being the architect of this conspiracy.

The recorded testimony of Lusardi's deposition was over an hour, and was replete with verifiable information that rendered the details he related irrefutable. A considerable amount of it ended up in the media worldwide. Catholics and non-Catholics worldwide were both shocked and scandalized. Calls for Pius XIII's resignation were widespread even before Sanjay Patel had the opportunity to galvanize cardinals and other bishops to pressure Ruggieri to resign the papacy.

And the pressure did indeed come, more than anyone could have imagined. Most of the cardinals petitioned the pope to abdicate for the good of the church. Diocesan and archdiocesan bishops, who otherwise would be reluctant to stick their necks out, reacted to the demands of their clergy and laity to do something and, usually through their country's papal nuncio, initiated appeals for the pope to step down.

The most strident demands for the pope's resignation came from the cardinals whom Ruggieri, aware of skeletons in their closets, had blackmailed to vote for him at the Conclave two years before. Now they had a legitimate way of getting back at him.

Three weeks after the news broke, there was still no reaction or acknowledgement from Pope Pius XIII. Nothing.

CHAPTER 94

December, 2048
Chicago

"Honey, when are you coming home? Your weekend visit three weeks ago seems like an eternity. You've solved the mystery of Francis Xavier's death – you're not still needed there, are you? Chris and I miss you, and Bob will be coming home for the holidays soon. It's time to return to Chicago!"

At the Friday conference call, Elaine was the first to speak. As she pleaded with her husband, Scotty, Brett Higgins, and Rachel were not only smiling broadly, but tittering a little. No question she was getting frustrated.

"I hope it's soon, sweetheart," Fred responded, "but there's a new problem on the horizon. As you know, the pope hasn't publicly reacted. It's almost is if he's oblivious to the uproar in the media. It seems this pope is not about to abdicate.

"Foreign Minister Spallino called the pope, but was only able to get his secretary on the phone. Spallino basically demanded the pope meet with him and four others –prosecutor Esposito, Senior Cardinal Bishop Paganelli, Colonel Laurenti of the Carabinieri, and me – to discuss the findings of the Preliminary Hearing. Patel is back in Mumbai and was not included. Even the pope can't say 'no' to such a request from Italy's foreign minister.

"All communication has been through his secretary. It was agreed the meeting should not take place at the Vatican, or in Spallino or Laurenti's office – too much public exposure – but at the papal residence in Castel Gandolfo. It's scheduled for tomorrow morning at eleven.

"You want a real surprise? The pope will be accompanied by his attorney – none other than Paolo Andreano!"

"Andreano!" Scotty exclaimed. "So your suspicions about that man were right. He was the Judas in our Working Group!

"What can possibly be accomplished at such a meeting?" Scotty continued.

"The worldwide outrage isn't abating. In fact, it's increasing," Fred responded. "And thanks to the over-the-top reporting of the media, there's a growing impression Italy can do something about this situation.

"Of course, that isn't practically possible. Vatican City is not part of Italy, and the pope is head of its government. Spallino wants the pope to give some sort of public reaction to the charges – really any reaction is better than none. Hopefully some sort of compromise can be worked out.

"Paganelli, of course, wants to push for the pope's abdication. However, when he is no longer pope, he becomes more accessible to Italian criminal law, so Paganelli aims to work out a deal with the Italian government that will soften the heavy hand of justice, and 'grease the skids,' so to speak, for the pope to resign."

"Wow!" Scotty exclaimed. "I'd give anything to sit in on that meeting tomorrow!"

CHAPTER 95

December 2048
Castel Gandolfo

The town of Castel Gandolfo is a mere 24 kilometers from Rome, but the scenic beauty of this rural area stands in stark contrast to the teeming bustle of Italy's largest metropolis.

Located in the Alban Hills on the shore of Lake Albano, a small ancient volcanic crater, Castel Gandolfo has a population of less than 9,000, and is a popular resort with many villas and summer getaways circling the lakeshore.

The Papal Palace of Castel Gandolfo dates back to the 17th century and has been used by many popes as a vacation site and a retreat from the summer heat of Rome. The Lateran Treaty of 1929 established the residence as part of the territory of the Vatican City State, and not of Italy. Popular with vacationers are tours of the palace's beautiful gardens.

The five men drove up together, arriving at the palace 20 minutes before their 11:00 a.m. meeting. They were greeted by a porter, who informed them the pope had not yet arrived. Although he was due a half hour earlier, apparently he was running late. The porter took them to an elegantly-appointed parlor, and suggested they make themselves comfortable.

The 11 o'clock hour arrived, but still no Pius XIII. At 11:15, the porter returned, and said he would phone the Apostolic Palace to find out the cause of the delay, and when to expect his holiness.

A few minutes later, he returned, looking quite worried.

"Gentlemen, I have been informed his holiness left for Castel Gandolfo at 9 a.m. with attorney Andreano, and should have arrived well before 10. This is most disconcerting."

Fred had Paolo Andreano's phone number and called his office. His office staff hadn't heard anything. Colonel Laurenti called his headquarters, and learned the Carabinieri had heard of no accidents or other trouble that could have caused such a delay.

The porter returned, much more visibly disturbed.

"The pope has a cell phone with him at all times for which only his secretary has the number. His secretary called the number, but there was no response."

The pope's visitors waited in the parlor for another hour. Carlo Laurenti's phone rang several times as his office kept him abreast of the Carabinieri's efforts to locate the pope and Andreano, and to find out what had happened to them. They were coming up with nothing.

CHAPTER 96

December, 2048
Rome

"Our investigative units are working overtime in our efforts to come up with something – anything," Colonel Laurenti told Fred on the phone two days later. "The pope and Andreano must have disappeared into thin air. No trace of them. No accidents, no sightings, no ransom notes, absolutely nothing. The Vatican has received no communication from the pope. Andreano's office hasn't heard a word.

"We've alerted all airports in the country, and tightened our screening of travelers. All ports of entry to other countries are on the lookout.

"We've also made a thorough audit of the pope and Andreano's phone records, and found something unusual. In the three days before our trip to Castel Gandolfo, both men made several phone calls to Cosenza and the wider region of Calabria – a pattern not evident in the prior weeks. The parties called were, for the most part, family members.

"We've spoken to several of the call recipients. They were vague about what the calls were about, saying they were just friendly contacts from relatives who are usually too busy to keep in touch. No explanation of why so many in a short period of time. No one said they expected to see these men any time soon. I have a sense these family members and friends know more than they are telling us."

"If they wanted to disappear, that part of the country would be ideal," Fred commented. "Both of them have strong ties to Cosenza and Calabria, and evidence suggests that Andreano, and probably Ruggieri, have long-standing Mafia connections."

"As I'm sure you know," Laurenti added, "there are few places in the country where the Mafia has as much sway as it does in Calabria."

While the public was still trying to digest news of Pope Pius XIII's complicity in the murder of Pope Francis Xavier, news of Pius' disappearance became the top media story throughout the world.

Speculation about what had happened was rampant. Was he kidnapped? Were family and friends, who were rumored to have close Mafia connections, providing a hiding place? Had he been spirited away on a fishing boat across the narrow Straits of Messina to Sicily? The theories went on and on, but the general consensus had him running from the law. As the days went by, there was no evidence of the pope and Andreano's whereabouts.

Chapter 97

"Cardinal Patel, you asked us to form a task force to solve the murder of Francis Xavier, and we did just that," Fred reported to Cardinal Patel on the phone. "Our Working Group, with assistance from the Carabinieri and others, identified the conspirators. And with the help of the Chicago police, we also solved the murder of Cardinal Rooney. We determined, without a doubt, a connection between the two murders, and it is clear to me that, because of my mission for Francis Xavier, my family and I were also targets in this unholy intrigue. We're lucky to be alive.

"Scotty and I discussed this on the phone earlier, and we feel we've completed our job, and the Working Group should now be disbanded. It's time for me to return to my family."

"Mr. Whitaker, your success in solving these crimes is just short of miraculous! The value of what you have contributed to the church through your efforts is beyond measure. Not just to the church, but to the rule of law. However, because of the secret, almost invisible way you and your group had to proceed, you will never get the full credit you deserve."

"I think all of us who worked on this can give ourselves a silent compliment for achieving what we set out to do," Fred responded. "I'm proud of the Working Group for their dedication and successful efforts. None of us will ever be quite the same again.

"The only thing that could make our sense of accomplishment perfect would be for Antonio Ruggieri to be apprehended and face his day in court. Maybe we'll see that happen."

"Your success, however, creates a new problem – an unprecedented problem – for the leadership of the Catholic Church," Patel informed Fred. "Antonio Ruggieri is probably still alive and is still Pope Pius XIII. How do we elect a new pope?"

CHAPTER 98

January, 2049
New York City

Never in his wildest imagination could David McLaughlin have conjured up the series of crises visited on the church he had served for the greater part of his life. The past two years seemed like a nightmare to the cardinal archbishop of New York.

First was the murder of his dear friend Albert Rooney, the cardinal archbishop of Chicago. Then, just a few weeks later, another long-time friend, William Bracey, who became Pope Francis Xavier, met the same fate. And the calamities didn't end there. An unpopular and generally considered unscrupulous cardinal, Antonio Ruggieri, was elected Pope Pius XIII. Rumor was he blackmailed some of the cardinals into voting for him.

The new pope confirmed some of McLaughlin's worst fears by undoing several significant reforms of Francis Xavier. He also appointed a totally incompetent churchman, Tom Costello, to be the next archbishop of Chicago. Not only was Costello incompetent, he was implicated in child abuse and the murder of Albert Rooney, and then committed suicide.

As if it couldn't get worse, Ruggieri was implicated in the murder of Francis Xavier, and subsequently disappeared, leaving no evidence of his whereabouts – no evidence whatsoever!

David McLaughlin pondered these tragic realities, and wondered what he could possibly do to bolster the strength and courage of his flock in these trying times. His ruminations were interrupted by a phone call.

"David, this is Stefano Paganelli."

"Stefano, I am so glad you called. It's been several months since we talked. Is there any news about the pope?"

"I'm afraid not, my friend. As you probably know, the search for him is now worldwide, but there has been no communication, no sightings. Nothing.

"This has created a leadership vacuum. If a pope dies or abdicates, the camerlengo is in charge until a new pope is elected. And if the camerlengo is indisposed, then the pope's secretary of state fulfills the role. We still don't know whether the pope is alive or dead. And both the camerlengo and the secretary of state are under house arrest – unavailable, to say the least!

"I've met with leading members of the Curia, and it's been determined that I, as the senior cardinal bishop, must fulfill that duty. What we don't know is where we go from here. To deal with this problem, I'm calling a meeting of three cardinals who are knowledgeable and trust each other implicitly - you, Sanjay Patel and me. We will work well together, and will be able to reach closure more rapidly than a larger committee. Once we know where we want to go, then we'll involve others. Time is of the essence!

"I need you in Rome, David. Now!"

CHAPTER 99

January, 2049
Vatican City

Since the camerlengo, Mario Lusardi, was under house arrest, his office suite was not being used. Once the Curia determined the senior cardinal bishop, Stefano Paganelli, should function as acting chief executive of the Holy See, Paganelli began using the space. As soon as Patel and McLaughlin arrived in Rome from Mumbai and New York, he met with them there.

"My friends, our meeting is unprecedented," Paganelli stated as they gathered around a small conference table, "and the problem we are facing is unprecedented. I know of no similar crisis in the two-thousand year history of the church. We have little to go on, but we must act, and soon."

They discussed at some length the possible options available, and they seemed few and far between.

"I've done some research," Patel volunteered, "and read about dozens of predicaments the church has faced due to misbehaving or completely evil popes, but nothing remotely similar to the situation now confronting us. We have a pope who has been engaged in unethical and criminal activities – activities so egregious that both clergy and laity have demanded his resignation.

"So what is his response? Nothing – absolutely nothing! Not only that – he disappears, either willingly, or unwillingly. He's either in Italy, or he's not. He's either alive, or he's dead. Since we have nothing to go on, we don't have the vaguest idea of what we are dealing with."

David McLaughlin had been listening to Paganelli and Patel, but doing little talking. Now he spoke up.

"In the U.S., we have a procedure by which we can impeach a president for cause – remove him from office, strip him of all his authority. Stefano, there is no one in the Catholic Church who knows canon law better than you do. Is such a procedure available to us?"

"The issue you've raised is a very good one, David. There may be a way. In America, you have a Supreme Court to interpret your constitution in light of specific situations. Although we lack that tradition in the church, I think the three of us can create it!

"If a bishop is indisposed or otherwise unable to carry out his responsibilities, he can be removed, and another bishop assigned to perform his duties. There is no such procedure for a pope.

"But the pope is Bishop of Rome. We can make the case that, *ipso facto,* the Bishop of Rome is now indisposed for some unknown reason, is unable to carry out his responsibilities, and must be removed. However, since the Bishop of Rome is the pope, it means we will need to elect a new pope."

They sat in silence for about 15 seconds.

"Brilliant," Sanjay Patel exclaimed, breaking the silence. "Absolutely brilliant!"

CHAPTER 100

January, 2049
Chicago

Fred's flight from Rome arrived at O'Hare in the early afternoon. He was exhausted, not just from the six-hour flight, but from all the energy he had expended during the past few weeks as he and Adolf brought their investigation to a successful conclusion.

He dragged himself down the long terminal concourse to the baggage area, where he knew Elaine would be waiting for him, along with his two sons. He was looking forward to heading home, having a drink, and bringing Elaine and his sons up-to-date on the conclusion of his work.

Elaine threw her arms around Fred and smothered him with several kisses.

"Fred, we're heading to the Kirkland & Ellis offices."

"Not today, sweetheart," he protested. "I want to go home."

"This is important, Dad," Chris interjected. "You'll see."

At K&E, the entire Chicago contingent of the Working Group – Scotty Campbell, Brett Higgins, corporate attorney Scott Partelow and Marsha McGuire – along with Police Superintendent Frank Ryan and Rachel Fischer were waiting to greet him.

"We're having a little party to celebrate your return," Scotty enthused. "Welcome home!"

The conference room was decorated with multi-colored streamers and party table cloths. A bar was set up at one end, and a buffet supper at the other.

"I wanted to invite everyone in Chicago who knows you," Scotty told him, "but given the secret nature of what we've been up to, it's got to be just the inner circle."

While they were socializing, Scotty's executive assistant Barbara came in.

"Mr. Campbell, Cardinal Paganelli in Rome is on the phone."

"Put him on the speaker phone, Barbara, so we can all hear." Once the call was put through, Scotty told Paganelli he was on the speaker phone and who was in the room.

Paganelli filled them in on the meeting he had with McLaughlin and Patel, and what they had decided.

"I took our initiative to the nine prefects of the Curia, and they endorsed the plan unanimously."

"How do you think the entire College of Cardinals will react to this?" Fred asked. "Won't you need their endorsement?"

"Absolutely," Paganelli responded. "As the Holy See's temporary administrator, I am sending a letter to all cardinals, explaining our rationale. Given their reactions to Ruggieri's crimes, there's no doubt the vast majority of them will enthusiastically approve. I'm calling for a General Congregation in about three weeks, followed by a Conclave to elect a new pope."

CHAPTER 101

February, 2049
Vatican City

All went as Stefano Paganelli predicted, even better than he had hope for. Of the 125 cardinals who were eligible to vote for the next pope, only three expressed concern for taking such an extraordinary action.

What if Pius XIII showed up and declared the procedure illegal? Would this establish a precedent that would give the College of Cardinals the power to impeach a pope, perhaps with little or no justification?

For cons, the procedure to elect a pope had not changed. First, there is a General Congregation at which cardinals gather to discuss the issues facing the church, the attributes the new pope should possess to address these issues successfully, and to set a date for when the Conclave should begin. The General Congregation can be quite short, or last for several days, depending on the complexity of the questions facing them, and how many points of views there are to be heard.

The actual election of the pope takes place at the Conclave that follows, with only those cardinals eligible to vote attending – cardinals under 80 years of age. In the past, those participating were locked in to ensure secrecy and prevent outside influences.

("Conclave" comes from the Latin "cum clave" – with a key.) The Sistine Chapel has been the site for all Conclaves since 1848.

During the Conclave, four votes are taken each day until a candidate, usually one of the cardinals present, receives two-thirds of the ballots, and is willing to accept the election of his brethren. After each round of balloting, the ballots are burned in a stove especially installed for the Conclave. If no pope is elected a substance is added to the fire, producing black smoke, which billows from the chimney high above the Sistine Chapel. If a pope is elected, an additive turns the smoke white, and the bells of St. Peter's Basilica joyously announce the good news.

The General Congregation was over in three days, indicating considerable agreement about the issues facing the church, and also reflecting a sense of urgency to select a new pope.

The Conclave followed without delay, and on the first ballot of the second day, a pope was elected.

With a multitude of the faithful crowded into the St. Peter's Square to greet their new holy father and receive his blessing, the senior cardinal deacon addressed the crowd from the Loggia of the Blessings Balcony of St Peter's Basilica with the centuries-old proclamation: "I announce to you a great joy! We have a pope! Sanjay Patel, Pope Francis Xavier II."

To most of the church's bishops, the election of Cardinal Patel was really no surprise. Although very few knew the details, most were now aware he had played a major role in uncovering the conspiracy leading to the murder of Pope Francis Xavier I. Many viewed him as the man of the hour – the individual who pulled the church out of the terrible morass created by Ruggieri and his confederates. Admired and trusted, nearly all felt he was the logical pick for the papacy.

The choice of his papal name was also no surprise. Not only was he honoring the man slain for his efforts to give a stronger voice to the faithful, Patel had fully endorsed the agenda of this visionary when he was his secretary of state. Sharing a long history of friendship, Patel's support for the former Jesuit General was unqualified. Assuming his name was a way to tell the world Francis Xavier I's dreams did not die with him.

Chapter 102

February, 2049
Chicago

Fred took a much-needed and well-deserved two-week break from anything remotely connected with work, but not – at least from Elaine's point-of-view – a real "vacation."

"You've been away for months, working night and day, putting yourself in danger, and all you want to do is to take two weeks off," she admonished him.

"I just need a short rest, Elaine, at home with you and the boys. There's lots of loose ends I've got to take care of at Kirkland & Ellis, and they're not going to go away on their own.

"I'll tell you what. Next weekend, let's go up to the Door Peninsula to that cabin at Egg Harbor we like so much – the four of us. We always enjoy that."

"That sounds great, Fred. But I want you to promise me we'll take a real vacation soon and go somewhere. We haven't taken a trip since before Pope Francis Xavier I gave you that big assignment three years ago. You owe it to yourself. And you definitely owe it to your family."

"It's a deal! Give me six weeks back at the office, and we'll be off for parts unknown. I'll let you do the planning."

Two weeks was all it took for Fred to recharge his batteries, and he was ready to go. It was hard to believe this was the man who retired three years ago, before Francis Xavier I tapped him to be the first lay cardinal in centuries, and gave him an assignment that precipitated murder and mayhem. Retirement was no longer a high priority.

In Rome, dates were established for the trials of Mario Lusardi and Dieter Kaufmann. Prosecutor Giuseppe Esposito was using Adolf Klein and his Apollo Security as a subcontractor for evidence gathering and organizing depositions. Stefano Paganelli, whom Francis Xavier II had appointed as his secretary of state, continued to take Sister Sophie under his wing, helping her to adjust to her new life, preparing her to testify at the trials, and assisting her in understanding it was her Uncle Dieter and not herself who bore the brunt of guilt in the killings of Father Drescher in Munich, and Pope Francis Xavier I at the Vatican.

"Killing these men was wrong, Sophie, but you were trying to do the right thing. You can't expect more of yourself than that."

Trial preparations for the Chicago murders – Cardinal Albert Rooney, security detective Tony Salera and Marilyn Rutherford – were not going as smoothly. Roméo Hayek had confessed to his role, but only as a lieutenant of Tom Costello. In the meantime, Costello had committed suicide, and the onus of guilt shifted to Roméo. Granted Costello left behind a signed confession, it was neither notarized nor witnessed, and the state's attorney planned to press the case that Hayek was equally guilty. Facing these new circumstances, Roméo Hayek withdrew his confession, claiming it was coerced, and entered a plea of "not guilty." His henchmen, accordingly, did the same – all three entered "not guilty" pleas.

K&E was working with the state's attorney to build an air-tight case that these four men were guilty beyond a reasonable doubt in all three murders, and Scotty assigned Fred the task of gathering additional evidence, crafting the arguments the prosecution would use in court, and, if possible, finding a way to turn one of the defendants around, thus putting the lie to the other three. Much easier said than done.

In the midst of all this came an unexpected and disconcerting phone call.

"Mr. Whitaker, it's good to hear your voice," the former Sanjay Patel greeted him. "With all my new responsibilities, you may wonder what prompts me to call you at this time."

Fred literally broke out in a cold sweat. He felt sure this was not a social call. His instinct told him the new pope was up to something that would translate to intrusions into Fred's life, and the life of his family. In two weeks, Elaine and he were due to take a cruise to the Baltic ports of Denmark, Norway, Sweden, Germany, Estonia, Finland and Russia. A delightful and restful fifteen-day getaway Elaine had carefully planned and was getting more excited about as the departure date drew near. Intuition told Fred this phone call was a threat to that plan.

"It's also good to hear your voice, Your Holiness," Fred replied somewhat disingenuously. "We are very busy here preparing the case against the apparent perpetrators who murdered Cardinal Rooney. There's much work to be done." Fred figured, rather naively, this piece of information might help deflect a request he was sure the pope was about to make.

"You must realize this is not a casual call. What you're doing in Chicago is terribly important. I would be reluctant to ask for your help now were it not of vital importance – important, not just for Chicago or the United States, but for the entire Catholic Church."

'You want to see me in Rome, don't you, Your Holiness?"

"Yes I do, Mr. Whitaker."

"Soon?"

"Very soon."

"I need to talk to my wife. If I see you, she will be with me."

"I would want you to bring her with you. Don't you want to ask me what I have in mind?"

"No, Your Holiness. I think I know!"

CHAPTER 103

March, 2049
En Route to Rome

After a lovely Baltic cruise, followed by a week at home to catch up on chores, Elaine and Fred were on a flight bound for da Vinci Airport in Rome. As the plane left North America behind, and soared over the vast expanse of ocean toward Europe, Fred stared out the window at the billowing clouds below, reflecting on the talk he had with Elaine and the boys after his summons from Pope Francis Xavier II. He could remember it, almost verbatim.

"This in no way will affect our vacation, Elaine," I assured her. "The pope wanted to see us right away, but I made it clear our cruise to the Baltic seaports came first. He understood that."

To my surprise, she threw up her hands in pure frustration.

"You're missing the whole point!" she hollered, really annoyed. "For a third time, the church is intruding on our lives. The first was when the pope made you a lay cardinal and gave you a project that killed others and almost killed us. Then Cardinal Patel turns you and Scotty into latter day Sam Spades – another dangerous project, and your son gets seriously wounded. Now Patel is back, this time as the pope, recruiting you to do God knows what. You retired back in 2045. What happened to your retirement and all the plans we had for the future? Is this what our life is going to be like until

they bury us – one special project after another to keep the church afloat? Is that all we have to look forward to?"

As he watched the plane soaring through the higher cumulus clouds and then back into the bright sunlight, he shuddered remembering how stressful that conversation was for him.

I am rarely speechless, but I wasn't sure of what to say next. Fortunately, Chris spoke up.

"Am I intruding by getting into this conversation?"

Elaine gave him an irritated stare that had "mind your own business" written all over it. I quickly jumped in.

"Of course you're not, son," I answered, greatly relieved to have Chris join the conversation.

"As you mentioned, Mom, I was seriously wounded by one of the bad guys, and I'm not totally back to normal yet. I've done a lot of thinking since this happened.

"When I study history in school, I read about these people who do cool things that really make a difference. Most of us never get to do that. But Pope Francis Xavier I gave Dad that kind of project, and Dad got the whole family involved. Then all hell broke loose, but we kept at it. The bad guys came out on top in round one.

"Then Cardinal Patel got Dad and Scotty to find out who the killers were, and they did that with your help and mine.

"Now Pope Francis Xavier II needs Dad again, maybe to finish the job he started with Pope Francis Xavier I. Can Dad say 'no' to him? How often do you get to make a real difference?"

As usual, Bob sat quietly and listened – Chris is always the talker. But while Chris was holding forth, Bob was smiling and nodding.

Thank God, I finally recalled something Elaine said when I returned from Rome after Francis Xavier I's murder. I was discouraged and depressed, and Elaine counseled me wisely. "Divine Providence is playing a role here, Fred. There's more for us to do, but as yet we don't know what that is." I reminded her about what she said to me.

Fred's ruminations were interrupted as a flight attendant announced over the PA system it was time to put seats in their upright position, and buckle seat belts for landing.

I don't know whether it was my reminding her about that conversation, or Chris' well-stated apologia for what we had done and might be asked to do again. Or maybe what he and I both said. Anyway, by the time we ended the conversation, Elaine was back on board.

CHAPTER 104

Just as they had done years ago when Francis Xavier I summoned them to the Vatican, they checked into the Parco dei Principi Grand Hotel, bordering the Villa Borghese Park. Rome has a multitude of fine hotels to choose from, but they knew this one and liked it. They especially enjoyed the hotel's elegant Pauline Borghese Restaurant last time, and looked forward to having dinner there again.

The next morning they took a taxi to the Apostolic Palace for their meeting with the pope. The porter, Gino Cogliano, greeted them when they arrived.

"Mr. Whitaker, it's good to have you and your wife here! I had no idea I would see you again, especially so soon." He escorted them to the pope's sitting room where Cardinal Paganelli was waiting.

"Mr. Whitaker, welcome back to Rome! The pope has asked me to sit in on this meeting – I hope you don't mind."

"Not at all, Your Eminence. It's good to see you!" Fred introduced Elaine, and the three of them chatted for a few minutes until the pope arrived.

The visage of Pope Francis Xavier II, as he came through the door, was exceptionally striking. This tall, trim, good-looking man, with a walnut-colored complexion and silver grey hair, clothed in a white cassock and a white zucchetto on his head, exuded the dignity and authority of the pope.

Fred and Scotty had observed how thin and drawn Cardinal Patel had appeared when they had met him in Chicago to plan the mission of the Working Group. He was still thin, but no longer appeared haggard. His countenance radiated purpose and self-confidence, the image of a well-integrated individual who knows who he is, and where he is going.

"It is indeed a pleasure to see you again and meet your wife, Mr. Whitaker. Please be seated and bring me up-to-date on what's happening in Chicago."

After discussing the upcoming Chicago trial for Albert Rooney's murder, and engaging in small-talk, the pope changed the focus to the purpose of the meeting.

"What I have in mind will be of no surprise to you, Mr. Whitaker. As you know, I had the pleasure of serving as Francis Xavier I's secretary of state during his tragically short pontificate.

"He dreamed of revitalizing the Catholic Church in several ways. You were intimately involved in the mission at the top of his priority list – giving an effective voice to the laity and getting them actively involved in forging policies and procedures affecting the way they practice their faith. You are all too familiar with the extreme reactions of the ultraconservative forces determined to make this initiative fail, by any means possible.

"Many of the hierarchy were not enthusiastic about Francis Xavier I's objectives. However, much has changed: the murders of this pope and of Albert Rooney, the indictments of Lusardi and Kaufmann, and the unquestionable guilt of Antonio Ruggieri who then became pope. This sequence of events has had a profound affect on many prominent churchmen who didn't believe change was good for the church, but now have reevaluated that position. It's because of this reconsideration I have been elected pope.

"I want to take advantage of this epiphany while it is still strong, while the expectations for my pontificate are still elevated. That's where you come in. I need you to take up where you left off three years ago."

"When you phoned me and asked me to see you at the Vatican," Fred commented, "I had no doubt about what was on your mind – re-launching the Voice of the Laity initiative. Your Holiness, I don't think you can possibly realize the toll Francis Xavier I's mission took on me and my family. And not just that mission – the stress involved in our Working Group's assignment. Elaine and my younger son Chris were a vital part of that. And Chris was shot, severely wounded. He could have died.

"Francis Xavier I tried to initiate a transformation, and now you're also attempting to change the culture of the Catholic Church – a culture dating back almost two millennia. I fully endorse these goals. I think you know that. Otherwise, I wouldn't have taken the assignment from the first Francis Xavier. I also think a large number – maybe even the majority – of the faithful throughout the world welcome these changes. But probably not most of the hierarchy.

"I don't know what metaphor I can use – poured in concrete, moving mountains, carved in stone, maybe something else – to characterize the near-impossible task you and Cardinal Paganelli have undertaken. The church seems impervious to evolution, and yet you are proposing revolution."

"I think you just said 'near-impossible,' Mr. Whitaker, not 'impossible,'" the pope noted. "There's a world of difference. You probably recall from your study of Catholic history, the church in the Middle Ages was characterized by corruption, scandal, immorality at the highest levels, and ungodly practices, such as the unbridled selling of indulgences. These activities culminated in the Protestant Reformation. Many felt Catholicism's death was long overdue, and the Church should be buried for good.

"But that was not to be. New leadership evolved, the Council of Trent initiated reforms, and the Catholic Church pulled itself up by its own bootstraps. Barely on life support, the Counter Reformation revitalized the patient and gave it a new lease on life.

"The Holy Spirit was alive in the church, and still is. Change is possible. With God, all things are possible. Francis Xavier I was martyred for trying to make this happen. It's not hyperbole to say, like the saints of old, his blood has become the seed for a new flowering in the church. You and I have the privilege and obligation to bring it into being."

Fred and Elaine were stunned, mesmerized. So was Cardinal Paganelli. The pope's words, his rich baritone voice, his oratorical style with effective pauses and emphases, captivated those listening to him and made him an eloquent spokesman for his point of view. Stefano Paganelli was the first to react.

"Mr. Whitaker, you and I have a lot in common. We're both trained in the law. We're both litigators – we know good preparation is more than half the battle, and good timing is probably the other half. We don't always have control over timing – we take what we get.

"Time is plainly on our side. Catholics at all levels – bishops, priests, people in the pews – are chagrinned, angry, and ashamed the church leadership has brought such disgrace to Catholicism. Even non-Catholics are sympathetic with the faithful and the dishonor visited upon them. Everyone would like to see Antonio Ruggieri – if he's still alive – brought to justice. And as far as Kaufmann and Lusardi are concerned, everyone would like to lock them up and throw away the keys. People want change now, as much if not more than at any other time in memory.

"What better time is there to 'reform' the church? Conditions are not as bleak as they were in medieval times, but they cry out for action. Even the most conservative will now be more tolerant of innovations if they have the potential of strengthening the church's ability to meet the needs of the faithful and toughen the moral fiber of those who seek to do God's will. The tide is in, and we need to take advantage of it."

"I'm a good enough lawyer to recognize winning arguments, and smart enough not to take on a losing battle," Fred stated as he smiled at Paganelli.

"We agreed to come here today, almost certain of what the agenda would be," Fred began. "Elaine and I have weighed this reality against all that has transpired to date: murders, pandemonium, disruption of our lives, postponement – perhaps permanently – of our retirement plans – everything! Both of us believe in the Holy Spirit as well. And we know our plans may not be what God has in store for us. Sometimes the only reasonable choice is to roll with the punches.

"This involvement of the laity in the church must be pursued by someone. And I'm egotistical enough to think I can do it as well if not better than anyone else on the horizon. I've got the background – I wouldn't be starting from point zero. I even have a family who've already been involved and can help me when I need it. Given the urgency – as Cardinal Paganelli said, we're at high tide now – I don't see how I could enjoy retirement when I know this has got to be done, and I'm the guy to do it."

"That sounds like a 'yes' to me," Francis Xavier II enthusiastically observed.

"I'm assuming I would have your unqualified support, Your Holiness."

"More than that, Mr. Whitaker," the pope responded, getting up and going over to shake Fred's hand. "First of all, I will make you a cardinal."

"Again?" Fred facetiously asked as he rolled his eyes. The pope laughed.

"Of course! This time, however it will be a permanent appointment – it won't expire if I die or resign the papacy. Moreover, just like other new cardinals, you will be named at the Consistory that I will hold in two months. Very public, and symbolic.

"Further, the scope of your responsibilities will be, not just for Chicago, but worldwide, starting with the United States. Ultimately you'll need a staff."

"I can provide that for Fred, at least initially," Elaine informed the pope.

"I know that, Mrs. Whitaker. This time, however, you'll get paid a salary. More than that – I'm hoping the new cardinal-elect will take responsibility for focusing on the role of women in the church. We keep talking about doing this, but very little gets done. That might be an area of interest to you."

Elaine beamed! She could hardly believe what she was hearing.

"I have a long-standing interest in the role of women in the church, Your Holiness. There is much to be done! Yes, I would welcome the opportunity to contribute what I can."

"Splendid! A final thought, Mr. Whitaker. Pope Francis Xavier I, when he gave you your assignment, recommended you take certain precautions regarding your personal security. Even though the atmosphere is healthier now than then, such safety measures are still prudent. There are always crazy people and ideologues running around, and you don't want to present an easy target. You will still need the services of security agents, and the Holy See will underwrite the expenses."

***

After receiving the pope's blessing and congratulations from Stefano Paganelli, Fred and Elaine returned to their hotel to relax and pack their suitcases for the next day's trip home.

"What's Scotty going to say about this?" Elaine asked Fred.

"He's going to think it's great," Fred guessed. Actually, he was sure of that. "He'll probably want a role for himself when all is said and done. He certainly was involved when we were working on the opinion survey, partly, I think, because of the excitement that came with all the danger we faced. Hopefully, that incentive won't exist this time."

"I wouldn't bet on it," Elaine cautioned him. "There are still folks whose mind-set is about 200 years out of sync, and they think they're on a mission from God.

"My concern is my job with the Muscular Dystrophy Association. Our executive director, Ralph Morrison, has been very understanding of my long leaves of absence, but his patience can't last forever. Depending on how things unfold, I may have to resign my position."

"In general, I'm pretty optimistic, Elaine. The wind is at our back this time. The second Francis Xavier has more support from church leadership than the first Francis Xavier. And we have his support. I know there will be obstacles, but I'm confident we can overcome them."

EPILOGUE

May, 2049
Region of Calabria

Nxhiku "Francesco" Schiro was angry. It had been a difficult week. The truck that always brought him fresh fruit and vegetables from Aquaformosa's surrounding farms had broken down, and he didn't get his usual supplies on Friday morning for the weekend shoppers. He was running out of several things. Not only that – many farm products he carried had a short shelf life, and a number of "farm-fresh" items still in stock weren't so fresh any more.

Francesco felt a special affinity with his customers in Aquaformosa. Most of this community of less than 2,000 people were, like Francesco, descendents of the Arbëreshë people, refugees who fled Albania from the 15th to 18th centuries to escape persecution from the Ottoman Turks. They continued to attend the Eastern Rite Italo-Albanian Church and speak the Artbërech language. They were one of the major linguistic minorities in Southern Italy and Sicily.

By Saturday afternoon, Francesco was exhausted from having to explain to customers – over and over again – why he couldn't provide them with the ingredients they were counting on for their weekend meals.

To top it off, Gaetano Biamonte from Cosenza, 64 kilometers south of Aquaformosa, phoned him that morning, asking him a favor. Not a favor, really. It was more like a command. Francesco was instructed to drive two men from his grocery store to the coastal town of Cirella, where a small motor launch would be waiting to transport them to Messina, Sicily.

Francesco always closed his store at 5:00 p.m. on Saturdays, but these men would not arrive until 5:30. This Saturday of all Saturdays! His wife Angela had invited friends over to celebrate Francesco's 59th birthday. The round-trip by car from Aquaformosa to Cirella would take all evening, and Francesco wouldn't be returning until after midnight. What was he to tell his wife and friends? He couldn't say "no" to Gaetano.

Francesco considered Gaetano a business associate, but, in reality, he was much more. Francesco operated a pharmacy attached to his grocery store, and Gaetano made sure his pharmacy was supplied with the narcotics he needed for certain customers who were not able, or not willing, to get a physician's prescription for them. Since Francesco was not receiving the drugs from a licensed supplier, he could accommodate users without filling out forms or accounting for the amounts he was selling.

In turn, he assisted Gaetano by storing fairly large amounts of narcotics that were in transit to Gaetano's drug dealers. Francesco served as a "middleman" without getting involved in Gaetano's business – a low profile middleman since, after all, he operated a pharmacy. He didn't know where the drugs came from, or where they went. And he didn't want to know. This arrangement worked for both of them.

Between 5:30 and 6:00 p.m., an SUV with four passengers appeared in front of Francesco's grocery store. Two men in the front seat got out, walked to the back of the vehicle and removed two large suitcases from the baggage area. They placed these bags in Francesco's minivan which was also parked in front, just as Gaetano had requested. Then they returned to the SUV, and led the two men sitting in back to the rear seats in the minivan. Francesco observed all of this through the store's front window.

"Your passengers are ready to go," the driver of the SUV told Francesco when he came into the store to get him. "As Gaetano instructed you on the phone, you are not to engage them in conversation. You know where the boat will be waiting in Cirella."

"I understand," Francesco replied. The SUV drove away, and Francesco locked the store door as he left.

***

The 64 kilometer drive from Aquaformosa to Cirella, through the hills on Route SP163, usually takes about one hour, forty minutes. But with the late afternoon sun in his eyes, and more traffic than expected, it was over two hours before he reached the pier where the motor launch was waiting.

Without a word, Francesco's two passengers got out, retrieved their suitcases, and climbed aboard the launch. The boat immediately started its engine, and pulled away. The skipper waved to Francesco. No words were exchanged by anyone.

After a few minutes, when the boat was well on its way down the coast towards Sicily, Paolo Andreano breathed a sigh of relief, and addressed Antonio:

"I can hardly believe the luck we've had! The Carabinieri and every other law enforcement organization in Italy have been looking for us, but we've evaded them all! In Sicily, my contacts will see to it that we disappear from sight. Our worries will be over!"

"Our worries will be over?" bellowed Ruggieri. "You can't be serious! Patel and his cabal have turned us into fugitives! My life's work has been devastated by an unholy alliance that doesn't understand what the church's task in this world needs to be.

"I'll tell you this, Paolo. This gang of misguided reformers thinks they've prevailed. They are deluding themselves! They haven't heard the last of Antonio Ruggieri – not by a long-shot!"

About the Author

Harry L. Sheehy graduated from Stanford University with a BA and an MBA before going on to earn a DDS from Northwestern University.

Over the years, he has worked as an industrial engineer, business executive, management consultant, health care provider, university professor, arbitrator, and liturgical director. Sheehy now serves as a volunteer career coach at the Career Transitions Center of Chicago.

A former Jesuit with an interest in the Catholic Church's role in modern society, he is the author of multiple nonfiction works, as well as the novel *The People's Cardinal* and its sequel, *The People's Church in Crisis.*

Sheehy lives with his wife Carolyn in Chicago, Illinois.

www.ingramcontent.com/pod-product-compliance
Lightning Source LLC
Chambersburg PA
CBHW060523180626
46817CB00002B/472
* 9 7 8 0 6 9 2 5 7 6 2 7 4 *